The Cosy Little Cupcake Van

Annette Hannah is a Liver Bird who relocated to leafy Hertfordshire in the 80s and now lives near a river with her husband, two of their three grown up children and a crazy black cocker spaniel. She writes romantic comedies in settings inspired by the beautiful countryside around her and always with a nod to her hometown.

She worked in marketing for many years as a qualified marketeer which she loved as it tapped into her creative side.

As an avid reader, she began to review the books she read, became a book blogger and eventually plucked up the courage to fulfil her life-long dream of writing a book.

For four years she was a member of the Romantic Novelists' Association's new writers' scheme, during which time she wrote a book a year. After signing a two book deal with Orion Dash in 2020 she graduated to full member of the organisation and is also their Press Officer.

She loves long walks along the river, travelling to far flung places and spending time with her friends and family.

You can follow her on
twitter @annettehannah
www.sincerelybookangels.blogspot.com
www.annettehannah.com

Also by Annette Hannah

Wedding Bells at the Signal Box Café

The Cosy Little Cupcake Van

Annette Hannah

This edition first published in Great Britain in 2021 by Orion Dash,
an imprint of The Orion Publishing Group Ltd.,
Carmelite House, 50 Victoria Embankment
London EC4Y 0DZ

An Hachette UK Company

A CIP catalogue record for this book is
available from the British Library.

ISBN (Paperback) 978 1 3987 0811 2
ISBN (eBook) 978 1 3987 0088 8

www.orionbooks.co.uk

To the Young sisters, my beloved mum Irene who will be forever in my heart, I still can't find the words I need to describe how much I love you and my wonderful Auntie Margie. Thank you for being 'always by my side.'

Prologue

'Make everything you do a happy future memory to look back on and be proud of.' Camilla Lockley embraced her mum's wise words, which had convinced her to enter the competition, despite her lack of confidence. Now, though, she was halfway through the final challenge of 'The Wedding Cakeathon' – *The Great British Bake Off*'s closest rival – which was being filmed by a new streaming network.

The competition had been fierce, and Camilla had fought off incredibly strong rivals. Previous rounds had included musical instruments, for which the judges had declared her Fender Ukulele tribute world class. They especially loved the sound effects from the music box she'd hidden inside which played a rock version of 'Here comes the Bride'.

The animals round had been an easy choice for her; she had always been fascinated with sloths ever since she was a child and found out that the two-toed sloth actually had three toes, well on their back feet anyway. Her masterpiece had consisted of a thick tree trunk with a whole sloth family on it. The mummy sloth hanging upside down with a baby on her chest and the proud daddy hanging off the side of the trunk, the right way up. This one was awarded with gasps from the judges. The baby sloth had really stolen the show.

Some rounds had been quite hair-raising as she hadn't done so well in them. She'd chosen to make a tractor in the unusual wedding vehicles round and the judges said the wheels were as rubbery as real tyres. She scraped through by the skin of a rice pudding only because another opponent's aeroplane somehow tasted like feet. She thought she was going to be saying au revoir that week, but she'd survived another day.

Filming of the main group had stopped for lunch and Camilla was called for her piece to camera in the beautiful gardens of the French chateau where the competition was being held.

The make-up girl patted her face with some powder whilst one of the crew spoke to her.

'Okay, Camilla, once we start rolling we just want you to tell us how you came to be in the competition, your hopes and dreams and what you would do with the prize money if you win. Is that all right?'

'Err, yes that's fine,' she replied trying to fight off the sudden need for a nervous wee and an incredible urge to giggle uncontrollably.

'Hi, my name is Camilla and the reason I'm here is because my mum nominated me to enter. I suppose she was bound to believe in me though, seeing as she was the one who taught me how to bake before I could even talk. She has a recipe book at home, which is covered in eggs, flour and cake mix from years gone by, which I still follow to this day. I think the thing I love most about baking is that it's so emotive isn't it? The rolling up of the sleeves and washing of hands, using ancient wooden spoons that hold a thousand memories. Traditions and methods are passed down from generation to generation. Baking together is a perfect way to bond. My mum could ease any problems I may have had at school out of me just by saying the words: "Let's bake a cake."

'My mum always talks about me with a mother's pride, but I want her to know how proud I am of her. She's an amazing woman who has gone through so much. She brought me up single-handedly and made so many sacrifices through her life. We're so close that people often mistake us for sisters and she is undoubtedly my best friend. If I win the ten-thousand-pound prize money I would like to fulfil her lifelong wish by taking her on holiday to Hawaii and I would use the rest to set myself up with some proper business premises so I can make even more sweet creations.'

'And cut. That's great thank you, Camilla. We'll see you back in the chateau after lunch,' said Suzy the camera operator.

'Was that okay? I was so nervous I felt like I was stumbling over my speech.'

'No, you were brilliant. Good luck for tomorrow.'

'Thank you so much.'

After lunch Camilla joined the other two finalists as they continued to work on their masterpieces. They still had all day tomorrow to work on them and the judging would be at the end. The final theme was dream wedding venues and Camilla had chosen a Hawaiian wedding scene, complete with a beach hut, beach scene and the ocean and topped with a hula bride, which would spin around to the sound of a ukulele playing 'Somewhere over the Rainbow.' She knew her mum would love it as it was her favourite song. As she worked on trying to stop her hands from shaking after cutting out pieces of coloured fondant to decorate the five-tier structure, she thought about how far she'd come.

She'd been baking for family and friends forever and had just about worked on every theme known to man, starting with Teletubbies that looked like they'd been murdered and a wonky Thomas the Tank Engine that looked like he was on acid. She was amazed that the children who received these cakes hadn't burst into tears and run off screaming in terror, but they'd seemed to love them. She had worked her way through various themes, improving tremendously as she did so, and was now really well known for her cakes in her local area. Thanks to collaborating with a wedding planner who was now her good friend, she had become hugely popular on the wedding cake scene, but there was only so much she could do on her own. She was ready to expand the business.

The atmosphere in the chateau was now fraught with anxiety as the three remaining contestants raced around trying to do too many things at once. The time seemed to go ten times quicker in there than it did anywhere else.

With two hours still to go, one of the judges appeared in the kitchen and made her way over to Camilla. The judge, a comedienne who had starred in many hilarious sitcoms, normally joked with the contestants, but her face looked serious.

'Camilla, could you come with me a minute please.'

'Oh, it's okay,' she replied, smiling. 'I've done my piece to camera.'

'You probably should wash your hands, my love,' she said. Camilla looked down at the vivid stains on her fingers from the food colouring then up to see sympathy shining in the tears that welled up in the other lady's eyes.

'What's happened?'

Chapter 1

'Camilla Lockley?' asked the heavyset man who towered over her, blocking out the light as she placed the second of the boxes in the back of the car.

'Yes, that's me. Can I help you?' She slammed the boot shut and made her way to the driver's seat.

'I'm from Bingley and Dobbs and I'm afraid we are repossessing this vehicle due to non-payment. The details are all here.' He shoved a couple of scary-looking legal documents into her hand.

She tried to make sense of them, but the words seemed to dart around the page like ants on a pavement as her nerves got the better of her. The red stamp saying 'Repossession' across it though made it quite clear.

'Can I have the keys please?'

'Look, there must be some misunderstanding. I'll be getting paid for this wedding cake in a couple of hours, so I'll be able to pay this month's instalment.'

'I'm afraid it's gone beyond that, miss, so can I just have the keys and I'll be on my way?'

Resigned to the fact that this was a fight she couldn't possibly win she lifted the two square white boxes from the boot, one by one, and carefully rested the heavier one on a sturdy hedge with the smaller one next to it.

'I don't suppose there's any chance you could give me a lift is there?' She gave him an exaggerated smile that she imagined made her look more delirious than friendly. He didn't bother to respond and closed the boot with a slam. 'Would you consider a cake in lieu of payment?' she shouted to what used to be her little pink Fiat 500 as it sped off.

Trying not to panic she checked her watch, pulled out her phone and dialled her friend Lucy's number. 'Oh come on please answer, Lucy.' Her foot tapped on the floor as she waited for her to pick up. She hung up when Lucy's answerphone came on. 'Shit, shit, shit.' She desperately needed to get this cake to its destination pronto and had no money for a taxi.

As she racked her brains for an answer, the solution came heaving round the corner in the form of a double decker bus. She grabbed the top tier of the cake and ran to the nearby bus stop, hoisted one leg up to rest the cake on it and thrust her arm out, the overall effect resembling the crane kick that the karate kid had spent a whole movie trying to achieve. Mr Miyagi would be so proud, she thought as she jumped on the bus and placed the cake box on the luggage rack.

'I won't be a minute,' she called as she fought her way through a few more passengers. She ran to the hedge to rescue the heavier of the cakes, and with sweat dripping down her back she made her way back to the bus.

'Noooo!' she cried as the door closed in her face with a loud hiss. She couldn't even knock at the door as her hands were full. 'What the hell?' she shouted.

'Don't worry, love, another will be along in a minute,' said an old man behind her. 'That one is usually late because it gets too full but the other one flies along and soon catches up.'

Camilla could feel herself burning up. She looked up to the sky and prayed to her mum that the other bus would hurry. Having not been able to face making cakes – especially wedding cakes – since losing her mum so suddenly, she'd finally taken the plunge as her friend Lucy was desperate after another baker had let her down. Now she seriously wished she'd stuck to her guns. Who needed all this stress? Not her that's for sure. If she hadn't been faffing around baking cakes in France, she wouldn't have missed saying that final goodbye to her beloved mum and she would never forgive herself for that. The producers of the competition had been amazing and paid for her to get back home but she was too late. The show had aired a couple of months ago and she and her Auntie Edie had watched every episode together raising a glass or two of bubbly for her mum. They had shed many a tear on that last episode. Even though she'd had to drop out of the show the producers had awarded her third prize and a mini break which her Auntie Edie said she should think of as a present from her mum.

She shuffled from one foot to the other, trying to evenly distribute the weight of the cake, and now to top it all she needed a wee. Within a couple of minutes, the virtually empty bus rolled up. Camilla jumped on and placed the cake on the luggage rack.

'Follow that bus,' she said to the driver in a tone quite a few octaves higher than usual.

'What bus?' he asked confusion etched on his face.

'Sorry I was joking; you know how they always say, "Follow that cab!" on the films. I've always wanted to do that.'

The driver chuckled.

'But seriously do you think you can catch it up because I've left something on it?'

'Oh no, what was it?'

She gestured to the box on the luggage rack. 'It's like that box but smaller.'

He looked in the rear-view mirror. 'A cake?'

She put her face in her hands. 'Yes. It's someone's wedding cake and I've left the top layer on the other bus. Can you speed up please?'

'I can't speed up, but I can go one better than that.'

She peeped through her fingers and saw he was waggling a radio at her. Her mouth opened wide into a hopeful smile.

'What stop are you getting off,' he asked.

'Bramblewood.' She held her hands as if in prayer as he spoke to the bus depot and asked them to pass a message to leave the cake at the stop.

'Thank you so much,' she gushed. 'I owe you a cake, a really big one, shaped like a bus.'

He laughed and saluted her.

After what seemed like the longest journey ever but what was probably only five minutes, her heart leapt for joy on turning the corner and seeing the cumbersome vehicle still at the stop. She waited until her bus came to a standstill and carefully lifted the heavy box.

'Good luck,' said the driver.

'Thank you so much.' She walked as quickly as possible bearing in mind she was carrying a ton of what used to be sugar, eggs, flour and butter.

A passenger stepped off the bus holding the cake like Rafiki with a new-born Simba in both hands. Camilla breathed a sigh of relief; maybe good things do happen to people sometimes. Then as though in slow motion the woman caught her shoe on the step, the box flew through the air and landed with a splodge upside down on the bus stop seat. The woman righted herself, an apologetic look on her face.

Camilla stood open-mouthed. She could see her driver facepalming with his head in his hands and the passengers on both buses wore horrified expressions.

'Don't worry,' she said. 'We did our best. We really did.' Then whispered quietly to herself, 'What actually is the point?'

The buses pulled away with heavy groans and puffs of black smoke when a little red Mini appeared as if by magic as the smoggy cloud dispersed.

'Are you okay, Camilla?' asked her friend Lucy, her blonde curls bouncing round her shoulders as she got out of the car. 'Ah good you've got the cake. Let me help you. Where's the other one?'

Camilla couldn't quite find the words to answer her as she placed the heavy box in the boot. She gestured her head to the squashed box still lying upside down on the seat and watched as Lucy's jaw dropped and eyes widened in horror.

'There was a bit of a bus-tastrophe I'm afraid,' said Camilla thinking she'd found the perfect word to describe what had happened. Together they rescued the box, turned it the right way up and lifted the lid to survey the damage.

'It's not too bad,' said Lucy, biting her lip as she peered at the mixture of smashed-up sponge and cracked pieces of delicately piped icing. A pigeon swooped down and pecked at the groom's head, which had rolled onto the ground. 'I've heard of Eton mess so do you think they'll go for Beaten mess?'

Camilla's eyes filled up. 'I'm so sorry. Lucy, I feel like a disaster area lately.' She sniffed.

'Don't worry we'll work it out. Come on let's go.'

Five minutes later they were in the Signal Box Café and the destroyed cake was safely in the bin.

'Right, at least we've got one layer and we've got two hours before the bride and groom get here. Tell me what you need, and I'll pop to the shop and get it,' said Lucy.

'It's impossible, Lucy. There's no way I can do that intricate icing in such a small space of time.'

'Don't worry, we'll manage something. You make us some coffees and I'll grab the ingredients. Just text me what you think you'll need.'

Camilla put the kettle on, typed a shopping list into her phone and sent it to Lucy. Her heart was pounding. This was meant to be the cake that would get her business started again. She hadn't felt like baking since losing her mum; her heart just wasn't in it anymore and she'd let Lucy down a lot. She'd forced herself to make this one as she didn't want to disappoint her again and she desperately needed the money – but now look what had happened. This was surely a sign that she should give up, move on and find something else with less responsibility.

She could hear the hustle and bustle of the staff in the café as they decorated it with flowers and bunting ready for the wedding. Normally she would be a part of it, setting up her fabulous creations with huge pride. But she was at a loss as to how to get out of this mess. She would have to put her thinking cap on and come up with a suitable plan. Lucy was back in a flash with the ingredients and cake tins, they quickly whipped up a fresh lemon sponge and Camilla – despite shaking hands – managed to create a replica fondant bride and groom.

'Now I know you can't possibly ice it as intricately as before, so I thought what about a quilted effect with this rolling pin and these little edible pearls? And look at this.' She opened a tiny pot of powder, which when brushed onto the icing gave a pearlised shimmer. She rubbed some on the back of her hand and turned it from side to side to admire the lustre of it.

'That will look amazing. Okay we can give it a go and see what it looks like. I was wondering whether it would be worth asking Flossie out there whether she has any leftover flowers we could use too. To make it a little more dramatic.'

'I think that's a great idea, and then I'll put the kettle on whilst you get rolling.'

Camilla was relieved to hear that, as her throat was so dry from panicking. She sprinkled icing sugar on the worktop and set to work.

'So now we've got a chance to breathe what happened to your car?' asked Lucy as she plonked the coffee cups down.

'Well it's embarrassing really but it's been repossessed for non-payment. They had emailed me a few times, but I was kind of turning a blind eye to it.'

'Oh, I wish you'd said. I could have helped you out.'

'That's really kind of you but it's my problem and I need to deal with it. I've been fighting to get my mum's house back but the legal fees are crippling, I had to use all my savings to pay them a lump sum up front after them saying I stood a good chance of winning. But after so many letters, various searches and a few meetings with them the money has dwindled away. It's cost thousands and I've got nowhere. I really don't know what to do.' She swiped away an errant tear, determined not to shed any more than she had already. 'The other thing is I've only got a couple of days left on the lease of the flat, as I thought I would have been moving back home to Mum's by now.'

'But how can her husband have the house when your mum left it all to you?'

'Because he's underhanded. He tricked me into thinking he was sorting everything out for me, but he actually destroyed my mum's will and I've since found out he transferred the house into his own name. I wish she'd never met him.' Camilla went quiet as she expertly wrapped the icing around the cake.

'He sounds like a right scumbag,' said Lucy, her face curled in disgust. 'Excuse me, I won't be a minute.' She grabbed her bag and left the kitchen.

Camilla hardly noticed she'd gone as she concentrated on placing the tiny pearls in the crosses of the quilted icing.

'Right that's sorted, then.' Lucy burst back into the kitchen and tore a sheet of paper from her notebook. 'Dom has made an appointment for you with a solicitor tomorrow.'

Camilla went to object, but Lucy held her hand up.

'Don't worry, it's free of charge. He said to email any documentation you have to him and that this guy is the best in the business. I'm not going to lie; he doesn't think there's anything you can do without a will, but at least he will tell you the truth and you won't get ripped off anymore.'

Camilla managed a weak smile; maybe tomorrow would be a better day. Lucy joined her and they worked together on the cake.

In less than an hour their creation stood resplendent on the cake stand surrounded by a colour burst of fresh flowers. Camilla's heart had stopped pounding.

'Oh, Lucy, dare I say that looks even better than before. Thank you so much for your help. I've never made a cake so quickly. My hands are still shaking. I'm finished though – I really can't take the stress at the moment. I'm looking for a new job.'

'I think it will be such a shame to lose you from our little wedding business family but ultimately you have to do what's right for you, and we are always here waiting for you if you ever change your mind.'

'That looks just like a photo from a wedding magazine,' said one of the caterers as they walked past it.

Camilla smiled as her eyes met Lucy's. Her mind was made up though.

Chapter 2

Just when Camilla thought things couldn't get any worse, fate threw another rotten egg into the mixing bowl of her life.

'I'm sorry, Miss Lockley, I only wish we could give you better news. But without your mother's will then I'm afraid legally the house belongs to her surviving husband – whilst morally wrong, from what you've told me. Without any proof that he destroyed the will, he's well within his legal rights to have sold it.'

She looked at the portly solicitor. Camilla's mouth was moving but no words were coming out. She cleared her throat and slowly shook her head from side to side. His grey eyes alternated between peeking at her over the top of his round, wire-rimmed glasses and looking through the lenses to read the paper he held at arm's length. He continued, 'Mr Twuncatt has already arranged for the contents of your bedroom to be boxed up and delivered to your neighbour—' he checked his notes again, chewing on his bristly grey moustache as he did so '—a Mrs Edith Kelly?' He looked over his glasses at Camilla who gave a nod of confirmation.

'Yes, Auntie Edie, she is . . . *was* my mum's dearest friend.' She bowed her head and looked down at the shreds of a tissue in her hands; she would never get used to talking about her mum in the past tense.

With eyes full of sympathy, he continued in as gentle a tone as he could muster, 'But as for other items in the house, he has claimed they belonged to his wife and therefore now belong to him.' He shook his head and tutted as he uttered the final words: 'Unless you can provide a receipt.' He shuffled his papers together noisily and Camilla could sense the distaste he had for this unpleasant-sounding man.

'But I don't understand how this could have happened.' Camilla's brow furrowed. 'Roger, I mean Mr Twuncatt, had promised me he was sorting everything out. He told me he had her will and he would arrange to find somewhere else to live as soon as possible so that I could move back in; his plan was to move back to Scotland. He knew my mum wanted me to have the house. She bought it, on her own as a single parent. He was just the lodger, until she married him that is.' She reached into her bag for a folder. 'What about the evidence I showed you, the deeds of the house in my mum's name when she first bought it all those years ago. Surely that's proof enough that it was never his?' Her throat ached as angry tears threatened to spill from her eyes. She gratefully accepted the tissue he offered and dabbed underneath her eyelashes.

'I'm afraid in that time he transferred the deeds of the house into his own name and without a physical will he can just say it's your word against his. I take it you've tried all the local solicitors to check whether she stored her will anywhere.' Camilla nodded. He spoke kindly: 'To be honest even if you found your mum's will now, it would cost you at least ten thousand pounds to even begin a court case at this stage. In the absence of a will your mum's estate goes to probate and unfortunately because she married him, it's legally his. Had the house been worth more you would have been entitled to half of anything over 270,000 pounds.'

'Is there absolutely nothing else I can do to stop the sale?' she pleaded.

'I'm sorry but no. The house is sold and as there is no proof that there ever was a will there's nothing we can do. This isn't the worst case I've come across unfortunately. I've seen young children be made homeless in these circumstances. The law does not favour stepchildren at all.'

The words of the solicitor were still ringing in her ears as she stepped out of the offices into the busy high street. She exhaled slowly as if by doing so she could release all the negativity she'd just heard. Her chest ached from holding her breath for most of the appointment. She breathed in deeply; the cool air filled her lungs. Her head felt woozy as though she were about to faint. She leant her forehead against the cold glass of the door until the burning subsided. Her phone buzzed with a text. She fished it out of her bag to see a message from Auntie Edie.,

'Have you finished yet? I've got us a table in the Signal Box Café like you asked. It's lovely in here isn't it? Your friend Lucy is looking after me well. Come on, I'm dying to know what he said. What do you want to drink? When do you get to move back home?'

'I'm on my way. Can I have a cappuccino please with loads of chocolate on the top – and when I say loads, I literally mean whole bars of chocolate on the top.'

'Roger that,' replied Edie, who still treated phones like walkie-talkies.

'That word is banned from our vocabulary forever now,' Camilla responded as she made her way to the other end of the high street.

'Rog— oops, I mean okay see you soon.'

Camilla signed off with a kiss and was about to put the phone in her bag when it bleeped again.

'*ffffnnnnnzzznzn,*' replied Edie as she so often did without realising, usually when shoving her phone back in her bag. Camilla smiled at the familiarity of the regular occurrence. She braced herself to let her friend know that as of tomorrow not only was she motherless and carless, but she would also be homeless. Her mum always did say that things came in threes.

Grey clouds accompanied her to the Signal Box Café. Even the river looked dreary as she walked across the bridge. Canada geese honked and chased ducks away from the scraps of bread thrown by parents and children.

'Typical,' she muttered, as she approached the railway station just as the barriers were coming down, blocking her way with a fanfare of red flashing lights and a noisy siren. The café was just across the track and looked as pretty as ever with colourful flowers in the window boxes. Her friend Lucy had converted it from a dilapidated old signal box to the most unique little café and private wedding venue around. Auntie Edie was sitting at one of the window tables and waved at her. Camilla could practically hear the jingle of the solid silver charm bracelet that she always wore at her wrist. She waved back; the corners of her mouth lifted slightly trying to return the smile.

She looked at the staircase up to the bridge, which traversed the track, and contemplated whether to be lazy and stand and wait for the train to pass so she could walk across, or shake herself up by trying to shift some of the excess pounds she'd put on in the last few months. She couldn't help it; food was her thing. If she was happy, she ate; sad, she ate; every emotion under the sun she could find a reason to eat. But right now, she was eating for pure comfort and she excused herself for it. Her guilty conscience got the better of her and she climbed the steps. She felt a little queasy when walking across the bridge as she could feel the vibrations of the train rumbling through below.

She walked down the staircase, round the side to the entrance of the café and pressed the button for the door.

The whooshing noise sounded just like a real train door as it slid open automatically, which was no surprise, considering it was a real train door that Lucy's grandad had reclaimed.

Once inside, the warm air, ambient chatter and delicious cooking smells swirled round her like a cosy hug and pulled her inside. Auntie Edie waved again from her window seat; steam spiralled from the spout of the teapot on the table in front of her. The kitchen door burst open and her friend Lucy glided through balancing a tray with plates of food on it. She weaved her way to the other end of the café, whispered, 'I'll be back in a minute,' and blew a kiss to Camilla as she passed.

Camilla kissed Auntie Edie on her soft, crinkled cheek and slid into the seat across the table from her, where a huge bowl of cappuccino was waiting.

'Do you want the bad news or the worse news?' she asked Edie as she slipped her arms out of her jacket and placed her hands around the mug. 'Ouch,' she uttered, before quickly pulling them away again and blowing on the drink, shifting the frothy topping and distorting the cocoa powder love heart on the top.

'There's no such thing as bad news, apart from when someone dies of course, but as you know there's absolutely ,nothing we can do about that as it will come to us all one day.' Edie topped up the tea in her cup as she continued, 'There's just news that we maybe need to adjust our expectations for. But there's nothing given to us in this world that we can't handle. That's what I've always told your mum and that's what I'm telling you now.' She added two heaped teaspoons of sugar to her cup and stirred it loudly. 'So come on, what's happened?'

Camilla opened her mouth to answer but was interrupted by Lucy who placed a toasted teacake in front of each of them. Tantalising swirls of butter drifted across the top before melting deliciously into the fruity bread. She added another bowl of cappuccino to the table for herself and a pot of hot water for Edie. She hugged and kissed her friend and scooted into the seat next to her. Camilla could see the hope of a positive outcome in Lucy's eyes and as both women looked at her, rooting for her as they always had done. She almost didn't want to burden them with her troubles. However, she knew she would have to get it over with at some point, so she blurted it out.

'Basically, the sneaky – forgive my French – bastard has definitely sold the house. He requested no estate agent's boards or anything and he'd already transferred the house into his name. It's all done and there's nothing I can do about it and even if I could it wouldn't matter as although he told me he was going on holiday he's obviously done a moonlight flit.'

'What an absolute fucker. I never did like that idiot,' replied Edie.

Lucy spluttered on her coffee and had to grab a napkin to mop the spray up from the table. Camilla choked on the piece of teacake she'd just popped in her mouth; she took a sip of coffee to wash it down. 'Auntie Edie!' she shrieked. 'I've never heard you use the F word.'

'I've never had cause to until that absolute F word stole your mum's house.'

'There must be something you can do.' Lucy put her arm round her and gave her a reassuring squeeze. 'What about a different lawyer? I'm sure Dom could recommend another one. I can call him now if you like?'

'No, thank you, it's fine. Dom has helped so much already by introducing me to this one. He told me the other ones I was dealing with were a bunch of ambulance chasers. I've already lost my car thanks to them raising my hopes into thinking I could win this. I had to pay up front and the money quickly ran out after a couple of meetings with them and a few letters they sent. I mean each letter cost three hundred pounds. I should have gone to this solicitor in the beginning. His office wasn't as high tech as the others, and he doesn't come across as dynamic, but he was real old-school and really knows his stuff. My other problem is that I have to be out of the flat tomorrow and now I've got nowhere to live.'

'Don't you worry about that, my dear; my couch is always there for you if you need it.' The old lady pinched Camilla's cheek gently as she had done ever since she had known her.

Camilla didn't want to seem ungrateful, but she had a vague recollection of sleeping on Edie's tiny two-seater many years before when she had locked herself out of the house and it wasn't something she wanted to repeat. She could almost hear her bones creaking in protest at the thought of it.

'Oh, Auntie Edie, thank you. That's so kind of you but you're already doing me a huge favour by storing my bits and pieces from Mum's house in your garage, and I'll have a few more things from the flat to add to that if that's okay?'

'Of course, it is, chick – anything you want.' She took a slurp of her tea.

'I'm so sorry, Camilla. You're absolutely welcome to stay at mine too. Please let me know if there's anything I can do to help. This is all so grossly unfair.'

Touched at seeing her friend's brow furrowed with concern, Camilla squeezed her hand.

'I'll be fine, don't worry. In hindsight I probably shouldn't have kicked Freddy out of the flat before the lease was up as I could have done with his half of the rent for these last few months, but what's done is done I suppose.' She shrugged.

Lucy replied, 'You did the right thing, Camilla. I guess you've had to rethink a lot of things in your life since losing your mum and life's far too short to spend it with the wrong person.'

'That's very true.' Camilla looked thoughtfully into her empty cup as she swirled the remnants of the chocolatey froth around. 'My mum liked him, but I just knew he wasn't the one. I felt terrible because he thought he'd done something wrong. I just need time to be on my own and work out what my next step is.' She lifted her eyes to look out the window. 'Anyway it's all going to be fine from now on. It's a chance for a new start and I've seen a job I'm going to apply for: a live-in housekeeping job in a hotel in Wales, so I'll possibly be moving away.' She saw Lucy and Auntie Edie exchange glances.

'Don't look so worried, you two. I'll be fine. I won't have to worry about bills or anything. It will be good for me to get away.'

Lucy jumped up. 'Well you're not moving anywhere until we've had more drinks.' She cleared away the cups and saucers and made her way to the kitchen. 'I'll be right back,' she called over her shoulder.

'Housekeeping? But what about your cake business,' asked a squinting Edie who had taken off her glasses and was rummaging in her bag for her lens cleaning cloth. She located it quickly, breathed on the lenses and rubbed them vigorously.

'I haven't been able to face cake making since I lost my mum,' Camilla admitted. 'You know I told you that Lucy's a wedding planner as well as owning this place?'

Edie nodded and replaced her clean glasses firmly on her nose, checking that she was satisfied with the job she had done by closing one eye at a time so she could inspect each lens. Camilla smiled. She loved Edie's eccentric ways. She continued, 'Well I felt terrible because I'd had to let Lucy down on a couple of wedding cakes at the last minute. I mean she managed to find someone else to do them, luckily. But then yesterday after breaking through my anxiety and baking a cake I had a complete disaster. The bride was okay, but her mum rounded up some people to leave complaints on my Facebook page. The cake wasn't quite how she'd visualised it because the original one met with a disaster,'

'What sort of disaster?' asked Edie before slurping her tea loudly.

'I accidentally left it on the bus and I was so close to getting it back in one piece when the lady on the bus tripped and it literally went flying through the air in slow motion and landed with a splat on the bus stop seat.'

'Oh bloody hell.'

'We did our best to salvage a new one, which was perfectly acceptable and we didn't even charge her in the end but there's just no pleasing some people.'

'But the people who know you wouldn't take any notice of that would they?'

'I don't know. Maybe not, but my anxiety has been going through the roof over even the smallest of things

– something like choosing whether I want coffee or tea can set me off with palpitations. I've lost my confidence and I'm now in, as you would say, "a bit of a pickle" and I really don't think I can bake myself out of it.'

Edie grabbed her hand and squeezed tightly. 'One day at a time, my lovely,' she said, then jumped. Her hand rushed to her chest as she heard a choo-chooing sound behind her. 'What's that?' she asked, as a miniature electric train appeared at the tracks at the side of the table. The carriages of the train contained a portion of halloumi fries and a portion of thick-cut chips with a couple of dips. 'Oh, how adorable, I wondered what those tracks were for, I thought they must have just been part of the decoration. I really must bring my bingo ladies here – it's amazing.' She laughed. 'It frightened the bleeding life out of me at first, though.'

Camilla helped her lift out the snacks and pressed the top of the train – the signal for it to go back to the kitchen. 'I'll never tire of this place,' she said as she dipped a halloumi fry in the mango dip and took a bite of it.

'That's good because it's all sorted.' Lucy appeared with another tray and placed fresh hot drinks on the table. 'Ah good, the snacks have arrived. Now come on, scooch over,' she said to Camilla, 'and I'll explain everything.'

Chapter 3

'I'll be forever in your debt,' said Camilla to Lucy the next day when she picked her up from her flat in her clapped-out old red Mini. It took them two trips – the first to Auntie Edie's to store a couple of boxes of belongings along with the others from her old bedroom and the second to the place she would be staying for as long as she needed. 'Kitty's Abode', a cosy B&B in Market Square, slap bang in the middle of the bustling market town of Bramblewood and just around the corner from the Signal Box Café.

'Nonsense, I only made a phone call and it was absolutely no trouble at all. Carrie was delighted to have you to stay in the B&B and she always needs help in the cattery, so it's worked out perfectly.'

'I really appreciate it; maybe I can help out in the B&B as well, as I hate the thought of taking charity.'

'Don't be daft. I've seen how hard they work in that cattery. You will definitely be earning your keep.' Lucy parked the car round the back of the B&B. Carrie greeted them at the back door and helped them up to a room on the first floor. Her cats purred and didn't take much notice of their new guest, having not long been fed.

The room felt comforting and welcoming to Camilla but as much as she was grateful for the help, her body felt weary and she needed to be alone.

'Are you sure you don't want us to help you unpack?' asked Lucy.

'I'm positive but thank you both so much. You will never know how much this means to me.' She hugged Lucy and assured her she was fine.

'Okay, I'll call you in a couple of days. Make the most of the rest because between working with me at the Signal Box and at the cattery, your feet won't touch the ground.'

Camilla smiled at the memory of the day before when Lucy had told her the plan. One of her staff was going on a sabbatical the following week and she offered the job to Camilla who despite her nervousness had jumped at the chance to help out. She appreciated it was a lifeline being thrown at her.

As soon as they left, Camilla gave in to the flu-like muscle ache she was feeling, climbed into the inviting bed and didn't wake up until the next morning.

After a couple of days spent secluded in her room, Camilla had allowed Carrie, the landlady, to persuade her to sit under the old sycamore tree in the small garden at the back of the guest house. The late September air was crisp and fresh and she drew it into her lungs hungrily. The oxygen replenished her brain and she felt light-headed. Her eyes were closed, her face lifted towards the sun. Its warming glow felt comforting.

'Just let me know if you need anything, love.' Carrie placed a cellophane-wrapped package on the table next to her. 'Here's some of my home-made choc chunk short-bread. Do try and eat something as you need to build your strength up.'

She flinched as something hit her hand. It was a syca-more leaf. She noticed others scattering around the garden amongst the leaves, which covered the grass with a crunchy carpet of amazing autumnal colours. She gazed at the tree in wonder at the myriad hues. Patches of leaves were still green, others saffron, some shades of burnt umber and all held a majestic beauty. The end of a chapter. Their purpose had been fulfilled and yet they would still provide fun for children kicking through the thick covering as they waited for winter to approach with its promise of sledges sliding down snowy hills.

For the last few months she had been trying to come to terms with the loss of her mother, the untimely end of an important chapter in her life, and although she knew she would never ever get over her loss she would gradually need to learn to live with it.

Her cake-making business had been going from strength to strength and she was quite well known in the area for her amazing masterpieces. But right now, she was crushed; she had lost faith in most things and her creative edge seemed to have abandoned her. The house that her mum had worked so hard to buy, the final link to the most important woman in her life, had been cruelly snatched from her. It felt like losing her all over again.

She turned as she heard footsteps behind her.

'Camilla. How are you? I tried to ring but got no answer.'

Tears sprung to Camilla's eyes as Lucy gathered her in her arms, her piercing blue eyes filled with concern and teardrops. She tried to speak but the words got stuck in her throat so she did the only thing she could do; she wept.

'Don't worry,' said Lucy as she stroked her soft platinum hair and held her tightly whilst her body racked with sobs. 'Just let it all out.'

When the sobs had subsided Camilla squeezed Lucy's hand to reassure her that she was okay and only then noticed that a tray had been put on the table with two steaming mugs of hot chocolate. Tiny pink and white marshmallows floated gaily on the top.

'Sorry, I think with the house and the moving out everything just got too much for me. My body just seemed to shut down and I've done nothing but sleep since I got here.'

'I'm not surprised. It's been another huge shock to your system. I'm sure you're both physically and emotionally exhausted after what you've been through. I imagine you've been running on pure adrenaline lately. Please don't take this the wrong way but have you considered therapy?'

'Yes, I started a couple of months ago. When my mum first . . . you know.' Her eyes searched out Lucy's imploringly so she wouldn't have to say the awful word.

Lucy nodded in acknowledgement and Camilla continued.

'At first I felt as though the ground beneath me had disappeared. In my head I imagined myself teetering around the top of a massive volcano and I knew if I went down into the blackness, I would struggle to pull myself back out of it. I went to the doctor and he gave me details of a therapist who has been brilliant. Also, Auntie Edie never tires of talking about my mum with me and she's a real tonic. She has so many amazing memories of her and helps me keep her alive in my mind. I also do meditation now, which really helps. I basically have to listen to my body and do what it needs. If it needs rest then I rest.' She shifted in her seat to get more comfortable.

'I feel happiest when the sun is on my face and I know it might sound crazy but most of the time I imagine that my mum is away on holiday. She always wanted to go to Hawaii, so I think of her with beautiful exotic flowers in her hair doing the hula and it makes me smile. Maybe one day I'll get to go there. I hate the thought of parting with her ashes but that is the one place I would consider scattering them. Anyway . . .' She patted Lucy's hand. 'I'm looking forward to working with you at the Signal Box and helping out at the cattery. Carrie's cats have been such a pick-me-up. There's always one that needs a cuddle and there's a lot to be said for fur therapy.'

'You're stronger than you know, and you will get there,' Lucy replied.

A gust of wind swept through the trees, scattering more golden leaves around them. Camilla nodded to the tree.

'There's something quite magical about autumn isn't there. I remember making a wedding cake and they wanted an autumnal scene. I had such fun cutting out all of the different leaf shapes and in such amazing colours. I've always thought of it as a sad season because the leaves are dying and some of the trees will be bare but actually it's a real season for change.'

'And new beginnings,' added Lucy. 'I promise you will get through this and we're all here for you, for whatever you need.' She handed her the hot chocolate.

Camilla blew her nose on another of an endless number of tissues she was getting through lately and gratefully accepted the drink. Lucy opened the pack of shortbread. 'Come on, I'll have one if you will.' She winked. Camilla managed a weak smile and took one of the thick pieces from the proffered pack. Her stomach rumbled loudly in anticipation of having some food in there to soak up the delicious drink. Things did seem better when you had the support of a friend.

Making the most of the last of the sun before it disappeared completely behind the building at the back of them, they sat in amicable silence whilst they demolished the delicious shortbread. A sycamore seed twirled past joyfully, catching their attention. Lucy picked it up and threw it again.

'Jackson loves these. We call them helicopters.'

Camilla smiled at the thought of Lucy's son. She was hugely fond of him.

'How is Jackson?'

Lucy's face broke into a huge grin as it did every time she thought of her boy. 'He's doing really well, thank you. He has lots of friends now and is the happiest I've ever seen him.'

'I'm not surprised. He's got fab parents in you and Dom.' Camilla opened the other pack of shortbread that was on the tray. She suddenly felt starving.

'I still get a little flutter every time I hear him call Dom Dad, because for nine years I'd never heard him call anyone that and now he's got two dads he couldn't be happier. I wish I'd let him see his biological dad earlier now, but never mind – what's done is done.'

'You should never have regrets in life especially for things you can't change,' Camilla added, quoting her mum and relieved at not having to focus on her own woes for a while. 'How's the Signal Box Café?'

'It's going from strength to strength. I really can't believe how successful it's been. Are you looking forward to starting next week? I can't wait.'

Camilla's stomach lurched at the thought of it – facing people again. 'I am but I still feel bad about letting you down on the wedding cakes.'

'You really shouldn't worry about it. You know how supportive our little wedding planning world is. Some of the other cake ladies picked up the orders you couldn't manage without a problem.'

'But I felt terrible leaving you in the lurch with no notice.' Camilla could feel the familiar lump in her throat. 'And as for bus-gate, that's just finished me off.

'Don't be daft,' Lucy replied. 'We'll have you back on the circuit before long. Everyone misses Camilla Cupcake; it simply hasn't been the same without you around.'

Camilla sniffed.

'The thing is, Lucy, I'm not sure I can do it all again. I've lost absolutely everything and now thanks to the legal fees I'm completely broke.' She tried not to fall apart again as Lucy hugged her and nodded her head towards the sycamore.

'I'm sure that tree thinks it's lost everything when winter comes along but by spring those branches will be laden once more. I promise you, my lovely friend, however bad you're feeling right now, it will pass. So you keep searching for that blue sky of spring and never ever give up hope. You are stronger than you think.'

The sun had left the sky with streaks of bluey grey, pinks and peach, taking with it the last of the warmth. The bitter chill pinched Camilla's cheeks.

'Come on,' said Lucy gently as she gathered up the cups on the tray. 'Let's get into the warmth. Carrie has invited me to have dinner with you tonight.'

'Oh no, I'm not really . . .' Camilla protested. 'I've just been eating in my room.'

'You can't live on cuppa soups for ever. Now I don't know about you, but I can smell that carrot and coriander soup and I can't resist it so I'm staying.' Lucy gave her a reassuring squeeze.

Chapter 4

Rudely awoken by persistent hail tapping on the window, Camilla emerged from her duvet cocoon and rubbed her eyes. As with every morning she was dragged out of blissful dreams to the harsh reality that was her life at the moment. Something gnawed in the pit of her stomach, a constant reminder of how unjustly she'd been treated.

Feelings of anger, hurt and quite frankly embarrassment at her own stupidity wrestled in her mind, each one thinking themselves the worthy winner, but each day a different one would emerge stronger. Today's winner was anger but that was fruitless. Her anger had nowhere to go. The solicitor, although very sympathetic, had made that quite clear. She asked herself how she could have been so stupid as to believe Roger Twuncatt, when he said he would sort everything out. She knew the truth was that she had been so fragile at the time. The disbelief at her mum not being there anymore had overwhelmed her completely. She was torn between wanting to run away and not wanting to leave behind her memories and her special friends.

After speaking with Lucy last night, she fully realised the value of friendship and when Carrie had joined them later on for a nightcap, she had been amazing too and offered for her to stay as long as she wanted.

As she opened the curtains she was greeted by a grey and dull sky. This was a perfect pyjama and duvet day. She held her mug of coffee in her hands as she stood by the window, which overlooked market square, and watched people scurrying in and out of the quaint little shops. She smiled as a mum ran after her daughter's battered pink umbrella. The little girl wore pink wellies and a matching raincoat. It reminded Camilla of a photo she had of herself wearing a little red shiny hat and coat when she was about three, standing next to her mum holding hands. Her mum had kept it in her purse for all those years. The memory twanged on her heartstrings; the pain still raw.

No one was sitting around or admiring the fountain today, which stood in the centre of the square. The weather was far too horrid. She looked up to see a particularly dark cloud that came sweeping across the gloomy sky and noticed the silver lining curling its way around the edge of it. It wasn't much and it was soon eclipsed by an even darker cloud but just that tiny chink of light had provided some hope and she knew she needed to cling on to that to get through this dark time.

Lucy and Carrie had offered her a chink of light and she'd be a fool to turn them down, but she would repay them however she could one day. She drained the dregs of her cup, put the kettle on again and got showered and dressed. Today was the first day of the rest of her life and the day she began working at her favourite café.

She stared at herself in the mirror. Her heart began to race; her anxiety levels were hitting the roof. She wasn't sure whether she was ready. Her bravado was abandoning her. She'd considered asking Lucy for a couple more days to adjust to the idea of restarting her life. But then her mum's voice echoed in her mind: 'Don't delay, do it today.' It was advice she had heard so many times from her mum whenever she tried to put something off that she wasn't looking forward to and she knew that now the time was right to begin her journey. She'd had enough pyjama and duvet days.

The fear was overwhelming, but she knew if she didn't do it now then she quite possibly never would. She felt something shift slightly inside her. It was only a small step, but she was beginning to take control again. She had a good few hours to get ready and her nose began to twitch as the tantalising wafts of sizzling bacon crept under her door. She had felt much too ill to even contemplate eating breakfast on previous mornings, but this morning she felt ravenous.

She skipped down the stairs to the dining room where Carrie and two of her five cats greeted her warmly. The full breakfast chased away the light-headed feeling that came from being upright for a change and not curled up in her bed. She helped Carrie with the dishes and to chop some vegetables for dinner later on. After a few hours helping out in Kitty's Kattery, she came home, showered and changed, and then left for the short walk to her next job of the day.

Pressing the button to the door of the Signal Box Café was a novelty that would never wear off as far as Camilla – and she guessed most of the other customers – were concerned.

The worry she had felt at coming today dissipated as soon as she set foot in the familiar building. Lucy and her grandad had carefully designed and reconstructed the café to look exactly like the inside of a train carriage. The ambience was friendly and welcoming. She could hear snippets of conversations that were ongoing in each of the little booths. Lucy's eyes met hers over the head of a customer she was serving. She smiled and rolled her eyes

33

in a mock-exasperated look. She greeted her with a hug and a smile and led her into the kitchen.

'I'm so pleased you're here, as it's gone crazy busy ever since the weather turned.' She shouted the order to the chef and went to a large cupboard to find a new apron for Camilla.

As she tied the strings around her waist Camilla felt a burst of warmth inside her. She smoothed down the granite-grey apron, her fingers stroking the silver embroidered logo at the top. A sense of belonging washed over her; she was part of a team here, not on her own. She had a feeling that she wasn't going to get a minute to herself in this place and that's exactly what she needed.

Baking and cake decorating had been her life. But the trouble with that was all that folding and creaming and moulding exquisite shapes out of icing gave her far too much time to think and she was still feeling much too bitter to want to remain in her own head.

She had also lost confidence in running her own business and the thought of someone relying on her for their wedding cake made her feel sick to her stomach. Especially after she had been trolled on her business social media pages. Pictures of the smashed cake after the unfortunate bus incident had appeared online and the mother of the bride had not forgiven her. Other nasty comments that simply weren't true had followed. She hated the thought of letting anyone down but she had had to for her own sanity lately. This was better: hugely busy and ultimately not her responsibility. She could cope with that.

In the kitchen they could hear the siren for the level crossing and that meant that a train was imminent. Lucy had shown her where all the named pre-ordered meals were for the commuters who would soon start arriving home from London. They were served in one of the windows that made up the serving hatch directly onto the station platform. The other window was for new orders being taken. Lucy continued to look after the seated customers.

A few hours later Camilla felt exhausted yet revitalised at the same time. She was sharing a coffee with Lucy.

'That was amazing,' she said as she dipped a chocolate hobnob into her cappuccino. 'I hadn't realised how busy this place had got. I love it and it's just so cosy in here.'

Lucy snapped her biscuit in half before dunking. 'It is cosy and I love nothing more than sitting here on my own and doing my paperwork, especially upstairs where I can people-watch but they can't see me.' She kicked her shoes off and put her feet up on the seat opposite her and snuggled down into her reclaimed train seat.

'I was scared to start work here because I wasn't sure if I could face people. I feel humiliated in some ways, but thankfully I didn't see anyone I knew today.'

Lucy squeezed her hand gently. 'You've got nothing to be ashamed of. You can always hold your head up high. It's that despicable swear word who should feel ashamed.'

Camilla was grateful for the support and for the first time she didn't cry when thinking about the situation she was in. She picked another biscuit up from the plate and joined Lucy by putting her feet up and having a well-earned rest.

Chapter 5

The long autumn evenings flew by as Camilla adjusted to her new life. The hours she worked at the Signal Box Café provided her with enough money to stay at Kitty's Abode and to start putting a little bit away to save for more long-term living arrangements. Volunteering two days a week at the cattery had also given her a real sense of purpose and she couldn't believe how therapeutic it was. She had laughed with Carrie over a Baileys hot chocolate after a particularly long but completely satisfactory day.

'I love the fact that I can go into the cattery with not a scrap of make-up on, some scruffy old leggings and an old jumper and those cats just love me anyway.'

Carrie agreed. 'Give me cats over humans any day, apart from my Jim of course.' She chuckled as he'd just walked in and mocked offence at what he'd heard.

'I love the fact that we get to spend at least half an hour with them in their run just to cuddle and stroke them.'

'That's why we're so popular; we're an award-winning cattery.'

'Well deserved too,' added Camilla, yawning and stretching her arms. 'I'm off to bed then. I'm exhausted.'

The next day at the Signal Box Café, Camilla came to realise just how well thought of she was. One man in particular called Ron had recognised Camilla straight away.

'Hello, love, how are you?' he asked as she came to take his order.

'Hi, Ron, I'm good thanks. How are you? Is this your grandson?' She nodded and smiled at the boy who looked about ten years old.

'Yes.' He ruffled the boy's hair good-naturedly. 'And we've got another on the way. You know my Becky got married last year? Well, she's due next month.'

'Oh that's lovely news. Congratulations, Ron.'

He smiled, shook his head and scratched his beard. 'I always felt so bad that I couldn't pay you for her cake that time. D'you remember the dealership was going under? I tried to cancel it, but you made it for us anyway. You were so kind to us.' He nudged his grandson. 'See this lady – she's got a heart of gold.' 'Oh, that was nothing, honestly. I enjoyed making it.' She blushed.

'It was very much appreciated, I can tell you.' He held up the menu. 'We'll both have the moussaka, please. It smells delicious. I'll have a beer and me-laddo will have a glass of home-made lemonade, thanks.'

Camilla jotted down the order and made her way to the kitchen. She felt a warm glow inside. It was nice to feel appreciated like that. She remembered how upset Ron had been at having to cancel many of the special extras for his daughter's wedding and it had tugged at her heartstrings to see how broken he was.

When she returned to the table with their meals she smiled as Ron's grandson was excitedly retrieving their drinks from the little train that had delivered them.

She placed the steaming plates in front of them; Ron tucked his napkin in the top of his jumper and gestured for his grandson to do the same. Camilla was about to walk away when Ron spoke.

'Are you still driving that little pink Fiat 500 around, Camilla? I used to always see you delivering your cakes here, there and everywhere but it's just occurred to me I haven't seen it, nor you, for ages.' He blew on his moussaka before putting the fork in his mouth. He nodded approvingly.

Her cheeks flushed again. 'Erm no, I haven't got it anymore.'

'Oh what are you driving now then?' He was too busy looking down at his next forkful to notice her discomfort.

'I'm not driving anything at the moment; I suppose you could say I'm between cars.' She could hardly tell him that she'd lost the car because she couldn't manage the repayments.

'Oh that's a shame,' said Ron still completely oblivious to her embarrassment. 'So how do you deliver your lovely cakes now then?'

'Well that's not a problem because I'm no longer making them.'

'Oh no, the world will be a sadder place without your baking skills; in fact I was going to ask you to make the christening cake, which I will pay double for to make up for last time.'

'No sorry, that will be impossible for me because . . .' She considered whether to tell him she was between homes as well but thought better of it. 'Let's just say I haven't got any premises.'

She scuttled off to the kitchen with burning cheeks. The look of concern and pity was too much to bear. She shouldn't have blurted her private business out to all and sundry but she'd felt as though she'd been put on the spot and couldn't help it. The part that upset her the most is that she had almost called herself homeless and in a nutshell that's what she was. She was homeless and carless and motherless and broke.

Lucy had seen her rush past so had followed her into the kitchen.

'Are you okay, Camilla? What's happened?'

Camilla had splashed cold water on her face and was drying it with a napkin.

She sniffed and put her hand on her friend's arm. 'I'm fine, sorry – just had to face up to a home truth or should I say *homeless* truth and now that I've said it out loud I need to learn to accept it. But don't you worry; I'm still looking for that beautiful blue sky you promised me. I've just got to fight my way through a little bit more of this nasty grey cloud.'

Lucy hugged her. 'You're so much stronger now than you were a month ago and next month you'll be stronger still. Let's just take this one step at a time. You can stay in the kitchen if you like as there's a train due in a couple of minutes so lots of hungry customers who don't have much time for chit-chat.' She gave her a quick squeeze and picked up the next order to be taken back into the dining room. Camilla nodded to her, her eyes shiny with unshed tears; she was getting better now at not crying at every little thing. As the door swished open, she could see Ron waving her over.

'I've got this, don't worry,' said Lucy, heading over to him.

The train whizzed past the window and she knew the next couple of hours would also thankfully pass in a blur.

Chapter 6

Camilla's face lit up the next day when she read a text from Lucy asking if she would mind looking after Jackson that afternoon as he had an inset day and she had to go to meet a couple whose wedding she was planning.

Camilla loved the idea and picked up some comics and sweets for him on the way round to Railway Cottage, which was just opposite the café. She lifted the knocker up and before she could bang it back down on the shiny black door, it swung open and a harassed-looking Lucy barged out of the house, the phone jammed between her ear and shoulder as she tried to reassure a nervous bride that everything would be all right. She opened the door to her little battered red Mini, made an apologetic face to Camilla and handed her a note and a bunch of keys. Just before driving off she wound her window down.

'Thank you so much, Camilla. You're a life saver. I hope you don't mind helping but if it's too much then don't worry. I'll do it when I get back.'

Camilla watched the little car drive off and went inside Railway Cottage. Jackson was lying on the floor watching telly with his dog Baxter.

'Hi, Jackson,' she said lightly. He didn't hear her as the telly was too loud. 'Hi, Jackson, I'm here.' Jackson jumped up to hug her and Baxter excitedly pounced around her, his tail smacking against the sofa.

'Mum said that's for you,' said Jackson pointing to the side table where Lucy had placed a cup of coffee and a plate with assorted biscuits on. 'I think she said that I could have some of them too.'

'Well I couldn't possibly eat all of them myself, could I?' She laughed and handed him the comics and sweets.

'Oh wow, thank you,' he said and sat next to her on the settee.

'You're very welcome. Now do you think we are allowed to give Baxter a biscuit?' She found it hard to nibble on hers whilst Baxter sat to attention at her feet, his brown eyes gazing lovingly and hopefully at her.

'Just one and that's all, Baxter,' said Jackson, shaking his finger at the dog in a very grown-up way, obviously mimicking his mum. Camilla gave the dog a biscuit, which he gobbled up in no time, scattering crumbs all over the carpet, and then nudging her feet out of the way so he could get at every last one. Camilla sat back in comfort to enjoy her coffee and opened the note from Lucy; her heart fluttered nervously as she read it.

'It says here that you have a cake bake sale tomorrow in school, Jackson.'

He looked up from his comic. 'Yes and everyone will be so jealous because I've got Camilla Cupcake to help me make mine. I mean Mum makes nice cakes; well what I mean is they taste nice but they sometimes just look a bit funny. She tried to do Union Jack ones for me once but they just looked like red and blue blobs on white icing. They were good if you closed your eyes though.' He demonstrated by eating a biscuit with his eyes tightly shut whilst saying 'mmmmm.'

Camilla reasoned with herself and tried to calm down the sickly feeling in her stomach that suffering with anxiety

41

had left her with. Sometimes even the most trivial of things seemed overwhelming and massive but this was just teaching a ten-year-old boy how to bake a few cupcakes. She wasn't going to be judged on them. She took a deep breath.

'Okay, come on then, let's do this. Apparently your mum has put all the ingredients in the Signal Box Café's kitchen as she said there'll be more room for us to work there. They put Baxter in his bed with his cuddly toy kitten and headed the few yards to the café.

The Signal Box Café door whooshed open and they headed straight for the kitchen. Jackson had brought a speaker and put some music on whilst they worked. Lucy had pretty much filled up half of the counter with the packets of ingredients and just seeing the familiar branding made Camilla's heart flutter. This was the perfect place to whip up some cakes.

'Right first things first, Jackson, let's wash our hands.' She got the water to a pleasant temperature and they both washed their hands under the stream as it poured from the tap. Camilla dabbed a few of the soapy suds onto Jackson's nose and made him giggle, then it was her turn to giggle as he pulled a funny face, crossing his eyes so he could see the end of his nose.

They put on aprons and she rolled up Jackson's sleeves for him. The simple action brought her mind swiftly back to the past and memories of her mum rolling Camilla's sleeves up for her as they prepared to do their favourite thing together: baking cakes.

Soon the air was filled with clouds of flour, icing sugar and the sweet smells of vanilla and cocoa. Camilla had found a huge bowl and a smaller one for Jackson and she worked slowly at first, allowing him to follow every step she made. As they came to the flour she could hear her mum's voice in her mind and she repeated her words to Jackson.

'Now when you add the flour we must be very gentle and we swap our wooden spoon for a metal spoon.' She waited whilst Jackson got the metal spoons from the drawer and then continued as his eyes looked up to her eagerly, through flour-coated glasses, awaiting her next instruction. 'And now we have to fold the mixture in gently so if you do it like this in a figure-of-eight motion then we can make sure all of the flour is mixed in evenly.' Slowly but surely Jackson followed her instructions, his tongue poking out as he concentrated.

'Why do we have to fold it like this?' he asked, ever inquisitive.

'That's a very good question and I have a very good answer. You see when we beat the other mixture furiously that was ensuring that lots of air goes into the cake and that helps it rise but if we beat the flour in too then it would get heavier, release all of the air and we'd be left with a very sunken cake. Oh my goodness, Jackson, I think I got a bit carried away here and I don't think we have enough cupcake cases for all this mixture.'

Jackson's eyes lit up. He stopped spooning his mixture into the cases and looked at her hopefully. 'Does that mean we can lick the bowl?'

She laughed. 'As yummy as that seems I think you would have a sickly tummy if you ate that much cake mixture. Now how many have we got?' Jackson counted them using his cake-mix-laden spoon to point at each one.

'Thirty-six,' he replied.

'Oh, I did get carried away; let's have a look in here.' She searched through the cupboards until she located some round cake tins. 'Ah this should do it. Jackson, can you grease these for me?' She smiled at his puzzled face and tore off a strip of greaseproof paper, smothered it in the margarine and rubbed it on the inside of the tin. 'There you go. It's as easy as that.' Jackson took over the important job and Camilla put the first three sheets of cupcakes into the oven and set the timer. Right then let's make a couple of sandwich cakes too. Have you ever had chocolate marble cake?'

He shook his head. 'No but I have got marbles back at home.'

She laughed as his willpower finally gave in and he licked his chocolatey spoon.

'Well now we need a clean spoon but it's okay – here you can use this, and we are going to stir all my vanilla cake mix into your chocolate one and it will be so yummy.' She held the bowl for him whilst he used the spatula to scrape out the mixture, ensuring he left enough in the bowl for him to eat. 'That's it. Now fold it in again using the figure of eight and you'll see the chocolate will make a lovely pattern.' They filled the tins and placed them in the other oven and whilst Camilla began to fill the washing-up bowl with dishes, Jackson got on with his favourite part of cake making: licking the bowl. Camilla couldn't resist having a spoonful herself. It was delicious, first vanilla and then a burst of chocolatey heaven. It tasted like childhood, happiness and feeling safe in her mother's arms, just the two of them against the world. That's how it had always been. She could still feel her mum's love around her, as strange as that may seem, but that devastating feeling of loss still left her hollow inside.

Before long the kitchen was filled with the smell of fresh baking, she'd cleaned up the pots and they'd taken the cupcakes out. Then her mum's voice echoed in her words to Jackson.

'So you just press very gently and if the sponge bounces back then you'll know that they're done, you see.' Jackson prodded a little too hard and his sponge had no chance of bouncing back.

He giggled through a cloud of icing sugar as they made the buttercream. He was licking the air. 'I can taste it. Why can't the air always taste like this?' he joked.

'It used to for me,' she said dolefully. The timer went for the sandwich cakes.

'I'll get it.' Jackson ran to the oven and put on the oven gloves, then as carefully as he'd been shown he retrieved the cakes. 'I've got a good idea,' he shouted, his glasses steamed up from the heat of the oven. 'They're always asking for cakes for the raffle so maybe we could raffle this one.'

'That's a great idea, Jackson. Now let's get piping.' She showed Jackson how to pipe roses on the top of each cake and they added some sprinkles on top. Then she piped the sandwich cake, starting with chocolate buttercream roses at the top and gradually blending into vanilla.

Jackson clapped as he saw the cakes all laid out in little rows. 'These are the best cakes I've ever seen. Normally I only take twelve in and this time there are so many. I think these will raise lots of money for the school.'

'I hope so because you've worked really hard on these cakes and you've done a brilliant job. Now how about we finish the washing up and then do the most important job that's involved in cake making.'

'What's that?' he asked as he carried the dirty bowls to the sink, scraping the last of the icing out with his finger and licking it.

'The taste test of course. I already know which one I'm having – that great big chocolatey one over there.'

As they sat sharing cupcakes, biting into the soft melt-in-the-mouth buttercream and then the light moist chocolate sponge, they drifted into a blissful cake-eating heaven.

'Camilla,' said Jackson, chocolate buttercream almost up his nose, 'next time would you show me how to make little men out of icing like you did on Mum's wedding cake? I don't mean wedding people; I mean like Spider-Man?'

The thought of next time made her heart flutter a little but then she realised she didn't have to put any pressure on herself. She wasn't creating elaborate masterpieces like she used to; she was just taking it one cupcake at a time.

'Yes of course I will.'

She and Jackson took photos of their creations and some fun ones posing with them. It had been enjoyable and she'd coped; maybe things were going to be okay after all.

Chapter 7

The first few seconds of wakefulness each morning were like a blank new page for Camilla, full of hope and joy of what the day would bring. But then that was quickly overshadowed by reality, the stab of pain in her heart from losing her mum followed by the stomach churning caused by the completely unjust situation that tormented her.

The darkness would start in her mind and cloud her judgement, then gradually seep into the rest of her body until her limbs felt heavy, as though swimming through thick, sticky mud that tainted everything around her. But then these last few weeks she had been taking yoga classes and learning about meditation. She now knew that the best thing she could do was to relax and clear her mind, and a healthy mind meant a healthy body.

She had found an online guide to meditation that she was really happy with. The lady called Orla had such a relaxing voice; it was like the aural equivalent of melted chocolate and it appeared to be working. After the ten-minute session, her body had relaxed so much she almost felt like she was part of the mattress. She was cosy but thinking happy thoughts helped her to jump out of bed with renewed vigour. The last few months had made it so hard to tear herself away from sleep and back into the real world; it had been too painful. Now she had come to accept that there are some things in life that we have no control over and we need to know when is the right time to walk away from it before it consumes us entirely. The loss of her mum would obviously stay with her forever, but she needed to distance herself from the loss of the house.

'It's only bricks and mortar at the end of the day,' Auntie Edie had said many a time. 'If you get those thoughts about that obnoxious bastard popping into your head then I want you to imagine yourself with my old broom sweeping them back out again. Shooing him out until he falls on his arse – because I promise you that's what's going to happen.'

With a smile on her face she attended to the offending thoughts as per Auntie Edie's advice, put the kettle on for her morning coffee, switched on the radio and began to dance around to some eighties tunes, which always cheered her up. She only had one more week left working at the Signal Box Café as the staff member she was covering for was back from leave. She had loved her time there. The difficulty she faced now would be finding another job, but she felt able to do that; she didn't feel she was at rock bottom anymore. The old Camilla was back. She'd taken several hard knocks, but she'd survived and was getting stronger every day, thanks to her close friends to whom she would always be grateful.

The other thing she was looking forward to was Jackson coming home from school as she had promised to show him how to make figures out of icing, which she could do before her shift started. She headed over to work a couple of hours earlier as Lucy had invited her for coffee, so she had plenty of time to get ready leisurely and then do a little shopping for some essentials. She bought red and black food colouring for Spider-Man and blue and green for Batman and the Hulk respectively. She would need to take her special toolkit, which had all of her cake-decorating tools in.

She arrived at the Signal Box Café at the same time as Lucy and as the door whooshed open they were greeted by the delicious aroma of Signal Box Scouse, which was a speciality of the house made by Lucy using her beloved nana's secret recipe.

'Ah that smell is making my stomach growl at me. It's delicious,' said Camilla. 'By the way, Auntie Edie was thrilled to see scouse on the menu. Her husband Albert was from Liverpool and loved a bit of scouse.'

'Oh yes, she told me when we were waiting for you. She took some home with her. What a lovely funny lady she is. Have you had lunch? Because you can have some if not,' replied Lucy pushing through the door to the kitchen and putting the kettle on.

'Oh no really I couldn't. I've started filling out again since I've been working here, what with Carrie's cooked breakfasts and the delicious meals you send me home with. I'll soon be the size of a house. Besides it might put us off eating these.' She extracted two large chocolate eclairs from a white box and went to the cupboard to put them on Signal Box Café plates.

Lucy's eyes widened and she licked her lips as she stirred the coffees. 'Ooh I can resist anything but cake – especially one of your cakes. I really miss your cupcake kisses, you know.'

Camilla followed Lucy into the dining room and they sat at their favourite booth with their coffees and cream cakes.

'Yes, the cupcake kisses were very popular and because they were half the size of the traditional cupcakes, I could market them as half the calories.' She laughed and bit into her eclair. 'You know no matter how long I've been baking for I could never ever get the hang of this choux pastry. That's why it's always a treat for me to buy an eclair.'

'The thing is, Camilla, I'm not the only one who's been missing your cakes. Everybody has and I'm getting so many requests for you from people who are getting married.'

Camilla's tummy flipped over and back again and the eclair almost got stuck in her throat. She took a sip of coffee to help it on its way.

Lucy looked concerned and tried to reassure her.

'I'm not talking about immediately and there would be nothing you couldn't handle. If I'm honest the other cake makers are fantastic but you are the best. Your cakes are outstanding.'

Camilla wiped her mouth and hands on a napkin and picked up her coffee. 'I don't know, Lucy. I think I need a bit more time.'

'That's fine – you can take all the time in the world but in the meantime, I have a proposition for you. I would like you to supply the Signal Box Café with cupcakes. We are constantly being asked whether we have something sweet for after the meals we serve and they would be simple and lovely.'

'It's a great idea, Lucy, and I could probably cope with doing them, but the thing is I have nowhere to bake them. I couldn't ask Carrie because her kitchen is far too busy for me to be pottering around in.'

'That's no problem. You can bake them here. In the middle of the day you would have about five hours of total peace and quiet and if you do ever get round to making the bigger cakes again then you can use this place for that as well.'

Lucy's eyes sparkled and Camilla thought about how much fun it had been baking with Jackson. 'Are you sure you wouldn't mind? I would have to pay you to contribute towards bills et cetera.' Her mind began whirring with ideas.

'Of course I don't mind. Our little wedding planner family needs to stick together and you're my number-one cake maker. Everyone misses you.'

Camilla smiled. 'It's a deal.' And she chinked coffee cups with Lucy just as Jackson burst through the whooshing door and ran straight into the kitchen to wash his hands.

'I'm ready, Camilla,' he shouted before arranging all of his superheroes on the counter ready for her to show him how to sculpt figurines.

'Ah, I've just remembered, Camilla,' Lucy whispered, 'and please say no if you'd rather not but Jackson was wondering if you would mind him filming you both whilst you make the icing figures as part of his school project?'

'Oh, I don't know. What would it entail? Who would see it?'

'I imagine it would just be his teacher and maybe the headmistress or whoever is judging it. But honestly if you'd rather not it's fine.'

She thought about it for a second, looked at Jackson's excited face and agreed. 'I suppose it wouldn't do any harm, but—' she held a finger up to Lucy before she got too excited '—first I need to do my lippy. I won't be a tick.' She pulled out her lipstick and a hand mirror from her bag, freshened up her lips and smoothed a couple of strands of hair that had strayed from the confines of her hair clamp.

Jackson punched the air with a resounding 'Yes,' when he heard Camilla agree and began to position Lucy's phone on the counter in front of them, using Blu Tack and a couple of books to balance it. 'I've got a remote control to switch it on and off and we'll probably have to stop a few times so I can zoom in if that's okay?' he said, his face serious as he concentrated.

'That's absolutely fine with me but just before we start shall we put on our Signal Box aprons and prepare everything we need? So it's all ready to grab quickly while you're filming.'

'That's a great idea. Mum, can you help us unwrap the packets?' he shouted into the café.

'What's the magic word?' asked Lucy as she swept through the swing doors carrying her empty cup.

'Pleeeeeeeeeeeeeeeeeeeeeeeeeeeeease,' he replied with his impish grin.

Lucy ruffled his hair on the way past, put the cup in the sink and washed her hands before she helped tear open the packets of icing and colourings.

'So, what is this project you're doing for school, Jacks?' asked Camilla as she opened her cake-decorating toolkit for the first time in ages.

'Well,' he replied, 'we have to choose a role model who we really admire and work together, showing teamwork and the ability to follow instructions.'

Camilla's hand flew to her heart and she mouthed, 'Aw how cute,' to Lucy who mouthed back: 'I know.' She thought it best not to overly fuss Jackson as he was at that age, but she wanted to squeeze him so much.

'Wow I'm so touched. Thank you, Jackson. I'm very honoured that you chose me.'

'That's okay. I think we're ready to go now. Action!' He pressed the remote and nodded to Camilla, rolling his finger round to let her know they were filming. Lucy darted out of the way and blew a kiss.

'Hi my name is Jackson and my role model is Camilla err Cupcake and today we are going to show you how to make figurines like these—' he scooped up his toy figures and held them up to the camera '—out of this.' He held up a lump of icing and let it splat onto the counter. 'Okay, Camilla, over to you. Let's start with Spider-Man.'

Camilla had not expected Jackson to go into full on TV presenter mode and looked like a startled deer for a couple of seconds until Jackson nudged her with his elbow. 'Hi, everyone, Camilla here.' She reeled off the list of ingredients they needed while Jackson pointed to each one. 'So first we need to dust our washed and dried hands with icing sugar so that the icing doesn't stick too much.' She held the box above Jackson's hands and began to shake it. As the fine dusting sprinkled down, he caught as much as he could and clapped his hands rather too enthusiastically, which caused a cloud of it to coat Camilla's face and Jackson's hair. His eyes met hers and they giggled, which relaxed them both.

Camilla soon forgot about the camera and felt very much at home in the warm ambience of the café as her nimble figures did what they had been doing for many years – bringing sugar paste to life in the form of people, animals, vehicles and buildings – and it came as naturally to her as breathing did. Jackson still needed lots of practice, but he was extremely happy with his sculpted superheroes, having to focus on him had kept unwanted thoughts at bay and she hadn't needed Auntie Edie's broom once. As they cleaned up together, he thanked her for taking part.

'It was my absolute pleasure; I hope you get good marks on your project and thank you again for choosing me.'

'Thank you for helping,' he replied as he carefully placed his icing figurines in the box she had given him. 'Last year I chose Dom and he was funny too; we went fishing and Dom only caught a tiddler, but I caught a massive one.'

Camilla laughed.

'Who's your role model?' he asked.

'Ooh now that's a question.' She stopped wiping the worktop to ponder. 'I would say it was probably my Auntie Edie because she's always been there for me.'

'Is she your real auntie? Because I've got one real Auntie Abbie – that's Dad's sister. And Auntie Rosie from the boat café, she just called herself Auntie Rosie when we met her but she's really Mum's friend.'

'Yes, that's the same for me. Auntie Edie was my mum's friend. Have you ever heard the expression: "Friends are the family we choose for ourselves"?'

Jackson repeated what she'd said, and his face lit up when the meaning clicked. 'Ah I get it now. I didn't realise we could choose our own family because I was wondering whether I could call you auntie. My mum hasn't got any sisters but if I could choose one for her then it would be you.'

His eyes darted up to her and she smiled. 'Come here, you.' And she pulled him in tight. 'I would be honoured to be your auntie. Thank you for asking me. I've never had a nephew before, and I think you're absolutely amazing.' She kissed his forehead and he went back to filling his box.

'Right that's the last one.' He carefully placed the lid on the box and made his way to the door. 'Bye, Auntie Camilla,' he said through his trademark cheeky smile.

'Bye, Jackson, see you again soon.' She watched from the door as he skipped back off to Railway Cottage. A wave of warmth swept over her. Losing her mum, her only relative, had made her feel as though she were lost at sea, adrift without a lifeline, her feet swept from under her. But the words of a ten-year-old boy and the actions of her friends were keeping her afloat and gradually building the ground beneath her so that she would soon have a solid base to stand on. All she needed now was an anchor to keep her grounded.

The next day Camilla came into work earlier again but this time to create her first batch of cupcakes for the Signal Box Café. Lucy had ordered twelve each of chocolate, coconut, vanilla and strawberry to start with but she anticipated that they would fly off the shelves as soon as the customers got word that Camilla Cupcake was back in action. Lucy had another request for her from a bride-to-be,

'No please don't look so anxious, it's still just cupcakes. This bride would like some exotic ones for her hen do and for her groom's stag do.'

Camilla giggled. 'What do you mean exotic exactly?'

'Erm, I think the word I'm looking for is erotic but that sounds far too kinky.' She laughed. 'You know the usual stuff: willies on the girls ones and boobies on the boys.'

Camilla laughed too. 'Well I can't say I've ever made them out of icing before but I suppose I can give it a go. Better make sure Jackson isn't around when I'm making those ones and I definitely don't want to be filmed.'

'Oh, can you imagine that?' Lucy giggled. 'And what if Jackson took the wrong one into school.'

Camilla shrieked with laughter too. It felt like the good old days. Her heart felt warmed. She pulled out her notebook and made a note of the date. She did a rough sketch of a willie and held it up to Lucy. 'Like this you mean?' Lucy hadn't expected to see that and snorted as they laughed till they cried.

'Also—' she nibbled on the lid of the pen '—because I haven't got a car anymore I suppose people will have to collect. I hope that doesn't make it more awkward.'

'I'm sure it won't be a problem. We can always work something out. If I'm free I can drop them off for you.'

'You're an amazing friend, Lucy. I'm so lucky to have you.' She squeezed her hand.

'And I'm even luckier to have you too,' replied Lucy.

56

Chapter 8

The next day Camilla was on her way back to the Signal Box Café after popping out for more icing sugar when she heard a familiar voice.

'Hi, Camilla, how are you?' asked Ron, his elbow sticking out of the window of his van.

'I'm good thanks, Ron. How are you?'

'All good with my lot,' he replied. 'Anyway I was hoping I'd bump into you again. I've been thinking about your predicament and I hate the thought of you losing your little car so I thought you could pop over to the dealership. I'm sure we could find a little runaround over there for you. I mean I got one in the other day. It might not be as good as your one but it will do the job.'

'Oh, I would love to but . . . well it's a bit embarrassing but I can't afford it at the moment. Thanks for thinking of me though.' Camilla smiled and went to walk away to try and preserve her dignity.

'Oh no, you don't understand. I mean you can use it free of charge – you know until you get back on your feet again.'

Camilla didn't know what she'd expected him to say but it hadn't been that. She looked away and back at him again. 'What do you mean?'

'Well there's no point in me having all these cars sitting on my forecourt waiting to be sold when you could be whizzing about in one, delivering your lovely cakes.'

'Oh, I see, but no thank you. I couldn't possibly put you to so much trouble.'

'It's no trouble at all, my dear. I'm sure you've heard the expression *one good turn deserves another*. I insist that you come and at least have a look. Why not pop in tomorrow afternoon. I'll be there till six. If you don't fancy anything then we can just have a cup of tea. What harm can it do?'

Camilla's heart melted at the hopeful look in his cheerful face. She couldn't possibly turn him down.

'That's really very kind of you, Ron. Okay I'll come and have a look,' she said to appease him but had no intention of borrowing one of his cars. What if she bumped it accidentally? She'd feel terrible. Ron was such good company that she decided a cup of tea wouldn't do any harm.

'And Camilla, I didn't want to say anything in front of the boy but I just wanted to say I'm sorry about your mum, I saw you on the telly. You should have won by the way, your cake was magnificent but then I'm sure that was the last thing on your mind.'

'Thanks Ron, I appreciate that.' Her cheeks burned.

'I'll see you tomorrow then.'

'Yes, see you tomorrow.' She replied.

When she mentioned Ron's suggestion to Lucy she insisted on giving her a lift and so the next day they arrived at the dealership. Ron's face lit up on seeing them approach and positively glowed when Camilla handed over a box of cupcakes.

'How lovely to see you ladies. Now before we demolish these delicious cakes let's have a look around and see which carriage milady would like. Maybe it's not a car but a cupcake-mobile you need.' He laughed. 'You know like the Batmobile.'

Camilla chuckled. 'That would be perfect, Ron. I can just see myself getting changed in a phone box before I save the world with my cupcakes.'

'Technically that's Superman, but I get your drift,' Ron answered. He led them around the forecourt, showing them around an array of second-hand cars of differing values, insisting that Camilla try various ones out for size.

'Here's an Audi TT. Could you see yourself driving round in this?' He opened the door for her, and she climbed inside.

'There's not much room in this, Ron. It's a gorgeous little number for a single girl about town though. Unfortunately, it's far too trendy for me.'

'How about this?' called Lucy from behind the wheel of a Land Rover.

'It suits you,' said Camilla.

'Bit too big for me,' replied Lucy. 'Dom is always trying to get me to upgrade my car, but I just love my little old Mini. She feels like home.' She got out and slammed the door shut.

Ron showed them a few other vehicles, which they admired, but Camilla thought looked far too posh and in too good a condition for her to drive.

'Oh, I've just remembered one I got from the auction, which came in the other day. Follow me round the back past the car cemetery.'

'Car cemetery?' Camilla repeated as she and Lucy locked eyes.

'Don't look so worried; it's just where the oldies go and get stripped for parts,' said Ron.

'Oh, I see,' said Camilla.

'Ah here it is, a little Fiesta. That will be just the ticket for you. Only one little old lady owner and only five hundred miles on the clock. That would be perfect don't you think?'

'It is lovely, Ron, but I really don't— Wait, hold on, what's that?' She pointed over to a covered area housing a mishmash of car parts, most of them rusty, one of which was much taller than the others and half covered in tarpaulin.

'Oh, what, the old ice cream van? It's been here years. It was great when I had apprentice mechanics as they used to practise on it, but I've got no need for it now. Can't bear to scrap it though.'

Camilla headed over to it. She felt drawn to it somehow, like a magnetic pull. 'Can I see it?'

'Yes of course you can.' Ron pulled the tarp away and Camilla gasped as the van was revealed to her.

'It's so quaint,' she exclaimed, running her hand over the smooth paint parts and managing to avoid the crusty orange bits.

'It's so rusty,' said Lucy, her mouth agape.

'I'd say more vintage,' added Camilla as she pulled a tissue from her bag and began to scrub at the window so she could peer inside.

'It's got an amazing engine if I remember rightly. The apprentices pretty much souped the inside up,' Added Ron. 'Here look, the hatch still opens and the ice cream nozzles are still in there.'

'Let's have a look,' said Camilla as Ron opened the door. She stepped inside it, being careful to avoid the cobwebs. Ideas spun round her head as fast as her heart was thumping. After a little effort she slid open the hatch. Her face glowed as she smiled at the others. 'I think this is it,' she announced, her hands outstretched to either side of the hatch.

'The way your face has lit up you'd think this was a prize on that programme *Bullseye* not a little old rust bucket.' Lucy laughed, completely bemused.

'No, it's not a rust bucket – well it is a bit but I'm sure that can be fixed.' She looked at Ron, desperate for him to agree.

He nodded. 'I've seen vehicles much worse than this being renovated into something much better if that's what you have in mind.'

'Yes, that's exactly it. Renovated. I've been trying to think of something unique to get my business back on track, something that other cake makers don't have. When I was on holiday in Canada with my ex many years ago, I remember seeing a little cupcake van and I fell in love with it. That's what this reminded me of. This could be the project I need to get stuck into, to stop me thinking of all the bad stuff around me. I remember showing my mum photos of the other one and she thought it was a brilliant idea. I really wanted one but it was something I never got round to doing and I'd forgotten about it until now. I think she has led me here.' She was breathless as the words poured out of her at once. A warmth emanated from her heart as the memories came back. She was secure then, in a loving relationship with her soulmate and she still had her mum. Now she was on her own and she had to grow up and fend for herself.

'How much is this, Ron? I could pay you monthly for it.'

'I haven't seen you this energised in ages, Camilla. Not since before . . . you know. But I can tell you're really serious about this aren't you?' said Lucy.

'I really am. I think this could be a game changer for me.' She kicked aside some rubbish from the floor in the van and began investigating the little cupboards and drawers on board.

Ron had been scratching his chin as he watched the two women communicate. He sucked air through his teeth before he spoke. 'I'm sorry, Camilla, this one really isn't for sale.'

Camilla's shoulders slumped along with her hopes and dreams. 'Oh no that's such a shame. My overactive imagination was running riot then.'

Ron cleared his throat and continued, 'Actually the reason it's not for sale is because I wouldn't ask you for a penny for it. You can have it.' He laughed. 'It's been taking up loads of space here, but I could never bear to part with it. I can see you've got a real soft spot in your heart for it so it's yours.'

'Are you serious?' Camilla's spirits lifted and soared as she reached through the hatch and gave Ron a huge hug. 'You must let me give you something for it.'

'No way,' he replied sternly. 'You helped me out when I really needed it and I never forget people like that. You're a good 'un. Having said that it feels like you're doing me the favour by taking it off my hands.' He laughed. 'I can get some of my lads to help out by getting rid of that rust for you and it could do with a lick of paint to spruce it up. It will be as good as new in no time.'

'Ah that would be amazing, thank you – as long as I can be hands-on too.'

'Count me in too,' said Lucy. 'I'm not afraid to get my hands dirty.'

'Oh, thank you, Lucy. I know how involved you were in the Signal Box Café renovations and that looks amazing.' Camilla sat in the driver's seat, her hands on the wheel, pretending to drive.

'I loved every minute of it too.' Lucy smiled.

'Let's see if the old thing still goes then,' said Ron as he threw the keys to Camilla through the hatch. She caught them, put them in the ignition and turned. After a few raspy coughs and splutters the engine fired into life and she reversed it out of the shelter to the sound of applause from Ron and Lucy.

She fiddled with all the knobs, trying to work out which was the one to turn the chimes on and off. She flicked a switch and the tune of 'Teddy Bears' Picnic' blared out, at which they all laughed. Ron took them to his office where they drank tea, ate cupcakes and discussed the next steps.

'So that's all sorted then,' said Ron between mouthfuls of cake. 'You can keep it here as long as you need to and you're welcome to come at any time to do bits and pieces. Me and my boys will be on hand if there's anything you need.'

Camilla hugged him. 'This is amazing. Thank you so much, Ron, I really appreciate it.'

'You're very welcome and just to let you know, when you eventually drive off in it, I'm giving you six months' tax and insurance – no arguments,' he said as she was about to protest.

'How can I ever repay you?' she said, with a tear in her eye.

'I don't think you quite realise how much it meant to me when you bailed me out,' he said softly. '*I'm* repaying *you*.'

Chapter 9

Camilla walked into Bramblewood Theatre and Arts Centre and after a quick scan of the room saw Jackson jumping up and waving to her from one of the middle rows. She waved back and made her way through the crowd to join him. He patted the faded red velvet chair next to him, which she sat in. She smiled over his head at Lucy. She had been thrilled when he rang her to tell her he'd been shortlisted in the role model project initiative and invited her along for the county finals. The theatre was buzzing with atmosphere as other excited children and parents called and waved to their relatives and friends.

Lucy's husband Dom stood up and asked Camilla if she wanted a drink. 'Just a water please,' she replied.

'Coke for me please,' shouted Jackson.

'Just this once as it's a special occasion,' replied Dom with a smile.

A few minutes later he was back with Jackson's great-grandparents. 'Look who I bumped into in the lobby.' He smiled as he dished the drinks out. Camilla waved to the older couple and Jackson jumped up to cuddle them hello. 'Good luck, son,' said his grandad and ruffled his hair. Jackson bounced back in his chair as the lights started to dim and a deep voice boomed out.

'Ladies and gentlemen, please take your seats as the awards will begin in five minutes.'

'That's Dad's friend, Gabe,' Jackson whispered loudly to Camilla. 'He's an actor. I've seen him in lots of shows here.'

'Oh yes I remember him from your mum and dad's wedding. He was lots of fun. It's all very exciting,' she replied. His enthusiasm was infectious. 'Anyway, good luck, Jackson. I hope you win but I'll be ridiculously proud of you whatever happens.' She crossed her fingers and held them up to him and he did the same.

The heavy red curtains opened and Camilla began to wonder what she had let herself in for as she saw the large screen behind it spring to life with music and a little bit about the company who had organised the awards. The compere arrived on stage and introduced the judges who sat at either side of the screen and thanked 'Happy Holidays' – the sponsors of the event. The audience clapped as he read out the names of the fifteen short listees and then came her worst fear: they began to play the videos one after the other. She really hadn't bargained on this and found herself sinking lower and lower into the seat.

'Look it's us!' Jackson exclaimed, nudging her arm so it fell off their shared armrest. Camilla cringed at the sound of her voice and watched with one eye closed. The audience were obviously enjoying it, judging by the laughter. She had expected it to be filmed from a distance but found her face filling the screen in a slow motion close-up after Jackson had clapped the icing sugar in their faces. He'd also somehow incorporated comical sound effects with words like 'Pow' and 'Bam' appearing in stars, and at one point they were wearing superhero capes and masks and it looked like they were flying.

She eventually felt her body relax and soon joined in with the hilarity of the film, as the audience members were in hysterics. She found herself joining in with the raucous applause, clapping at Jackson's editing skills more than anything.

'Jackson, that was amazing. How on earth did you do all that?'

'It was easy,' he whispered as the next film was about to start. 'I just downloaded a couple of apps and added filters.'

After all fifteen films were shown, the judging panel stood up and handed three envelopes to the compere.

Third and second places went to a girl whose uncle was a farmer and a boy with a mum who was a dog trainer. They'd even brought the little cocker spaniel in with them and he delighted the audience with his tricks.

'And the winner is . . . Jackson Cavendish and his role model Camilla Cupcake Lockley.' The audience erupted and music blasted from the speakers. A still from Jackson's film appeared on the screen with the two of them laughing and covered in icing sugar. Jackson stood and took her hand, leading her to the stage after being kissed by his family members on the way. Camilla had a flash to the future of Jackson collecting an Oscar one day. He was so confident and such a clever little kid. They were each presented with a trophy and a Happy Holiday voucher for £1000. Jackson's eyes shone as he thanked Camilla for her support. She exchanged proud glances with Lucy and could see her expression reflecting her own; as in, when did he grow up?

The excitement spilled over into the bar area and Camilla and Jackson were approached by two young women wearing lanyards.

'Hi, Jackson, I'm Eleanor Spencer.' She proffered her hand to him and he shook it. 'I'm a reporter from the *Bramblewood Echo* and this is our photographer Erin. We just wondered if we could interview you and maybe take a few photographs?'

'Oh cool. Does this mean we're going to be in the newspaper?'

'Yes, it does, Jackson. This is a really huge achievement. We'd also like to have permission to share your video on our online edition on the website if that's okay.'

'Yes.' He fist-pumped. 'That's awesome.'

'Are you happy with that, Camilla, as you're in it too?'

She blushed. She hadn't quite bargained for so much publicity but what could she do? The look on Jackson's face as he beamed with pride strummed on her heartstrings. 'Yes of course,' she answered.

After they'd posed for photographs Eleanor took them to sit in a quiet corner to ask questions. Erin brought over a tray of drinks and said goodbye as she was needed on another job. The interview took ten minutes by which time the rest of Jackson's family had turned up. 'And just one more thing, Camilla: can you tell me your website address, please? We'll share that at the end of the article.'

'Oh, I haven't actually got one. I did have a Facebook page once but that's been abandoned too.'

'My advice to you would be to set one up and fast because I have a feeling that you'll be pretty busy when this goes out.' She scribbled some notes on a piece of paper, tore it out of her notebook and handed it to Camilla. 'Here's some instructions on setting a website up. Also, you should vlog. You came across so well on Jackson's film. A cake-making and decorating vlog would be fabulous.' She clicked her pen off and clipped it to her notebook before putting both into her voluminous bag. 'Goodbye and well done again, Jackson.'

Jackson waved goodbye and said thank you before returning to the centre of his family who were currently admiring his trophy. Camilla looked thoughtfully at the piece of paper and shoved it in her bag. She must remember to google what a vlog was when she got home. She noticed Lucy calling her over so joined the celebrations with the family who had welcomed her as one of their own.

Chapter 10

Ever since Camilla sent Gracie the picture of the van, she had been eager to help her friend. At the weekend she turned up with disposable boiler suits and safety goggles for all three of them. Camilla and Lucy were using sandpaper to scrape off some of the smaller patches of rust.

'Thanks, Gracie.' She dangled the safety goggles from her finger. 'What are these for?'

Gracie opened the boot of her car and pulled out a chunky piece of machinery.

'They're for this baby,' she replied. 'It's a sander from the boatyard. Finn said we can borrow it. It'll do the job in no time. I can show you how to use it because he showed me when we repainted our boat.'

Camilla's eyes opened wide. 'That's so nice of him. Thank you. Now before we start, does anyone object to me filming this? I was thinking of doing a time lapse of the renovation so I can share it on my new vlog, which the lovely Jackson has set up for me.'

'No that sounds like fun,' said Gracie.

'Fine by me too,' added Lucy. Camilla set the camera to record and listened carefully as Gracie explained how to use the machine.

'Wow, I feel like one of those flame-thrower women you see in clubs on holiday with this in my hands,' she said as Gracie passed it to her. She switched it on and began tackling the more severe patches of rust. 'Ooh we should have got some headphones. It's a bit noisy,' she shouted over the din.

After a couple of hours Ron came to join them with mismatched mugs of tea on a tray and a packet of biscuits. 'You ladies have done a damn good job of this. Well done.' He looked over their handiwork. 'I think I've got some primer somewhere that you can put over where the rust was.'

'Oh, that would be wonderful,' said Camilla as she climbed down from the ladder after working on the top of the van. She put the sander down and stretched out her fingers, which had become stiff. The muscles in her arms were weary but she felt revitalised through achieving something positive. I've been searching the internet for some suitable paint; it has to be a special type, so it doesn't rust but it's all so expensive and as you know my budget is zilch.' She dunked a biscuit in her tea and ate it quickly before it dissolved into a soggy mess. Lucy and Gracie downed tools too. They sat on piles of tyres that Ron's workers used for seats during their lunchbreak.

'Would it be the same paint you would use on boats? As I'm sure we have some left from *Precious Moments*. Oh but then it's black burgundy and cream. What colour were you thinking of painting it?' She reached over to take a biscuit from the packet on the tray.

Camilla tilted her head as she thought. 'The cupcake van I saw in Canada was pink so I suppose that would be perfect, or any pastel colour would be good.'

'It's going to be adorable, Camilla; I can't wait to see the finished product whatever colour it is. Anyway, I'm going to have to go as I have to show a couple around the Signal Box.' She gave the goggles back to Gracie and hugged them both.

'Thank you so much, Lucy. You've been such a great help. It would have been back-breaking to do it on my own.'

'You're more than welcome. See you soon.' She blew kisses and left.

'Have you thought of asking Mr Ives from Odds'n'Sods?' asked Gracie. 'He's amazing at finding all kinds of crazy stuff.'

'No, I haven't actually but that's a great idea, thank you. I'll pop over and see him later.'

Gracie got up from her tyre stool and stretched her back. 'I'm afraid I'm going to have to love you and leave you too as I have to take Matty to swimming lessons, but before I go, I'll just show you how to change the sanding disc.'

'Oh, do I need to change it? I thought we were finished now the rust has gone.'

'I'm afraid not. You're going to have to sand down the rest of the paintwork ready to repaint it.' Gracie smiled. She replaced the sanding disc and hugged her goodbye. As she was about to drive off, she wound her window down. 'By the way, Finn said that there's room for you to park up at the marina for when you're ready to paint it.'

'That's fantastic. Please thank him for me and thanks again to you. You've been amazing.' Camila waved her off, swigged down the last of her tea and climbed back up the ladder to begin sanding down the paintwork. The sun had gone down by the time she'd finished, and the street lamps had come on. Ron had returned and primed the patches where the rust had been. Camilla had a banging headache and joints she hadn't known she had were aching.

'You look shattered,' said Ron. 'Why don't you finish up now. We can store the sander in the van until tomorrow.'

'Yes, I think you're right, Ron.' She cleared her throat, which felt dry and raspy from the paint dust, despite wearing a mask. 'It's been a long old day.'

71

'Come on, I'm off home. I'll give you a lift.'

Camilla wanted to cry from the weariness she felt in her bones. 'Thanks, Ron, that would be just terrific. Oh sorry,' she said covering her mouth with her hand as she yawned.

Chapter 11

A few days later Camilla sat behind the wheel of the van and cautiously drove to the marina. She had spent hours scrubbing and cleaning the inside of the van until she could have eaten her dinner off the floor. Having only been used to a tiny car before she accidentally bumped up and down the corners of a few pavements on the way but gradually got used to the size of it. She pulled into the back of the marina, then navigated her way around several cars and a large blue crane that was hoisting a canal boat from the river.

Gracie and Finn waved to her from outside the boatyard and gestured to show her where to park. She turned the chimes on to make them laugh and her heart melted as Matty kicked his legs and waved to her, a look of pure joy on his face.

Camilla greeted her friends warmly.

'So, you've got the paint then?' asked Finn.

'Yes, it's all in the van. Mr Ives came up trumps and got it for me for next to nothing as it was a discontinued colour. He really can get anything. Thanks for the tip-off, Gracie.'

'I'm so glad he could help you and I can't wait to see what colour it is.'

'It's my new favourite colour: peppermint green,' Camilla said as she gently bopped Matty on the nose, making him chuckle. She gave him a present, which he tore the wrapper off.

'Boh,' he said.

'Yes, that's right. It is a boat, you clever boy. Say thank you to Auntie Camilla.'

'Ta,' he said, throwing the paper at her for good measure.

Finn had unloaded the van, prised open the lid from one of the tins and emptied it into the paint sprayer.

'Oh, Camilla, what a gorgeous colour. I love it,' said Gracie.

'Isn't it beautiful?' Camilla gushed. 'Just looking at it makes me so happy; it lifts my soul.'

'I can tell,' said Gracie. 'Your eyes are shining.'

'Are you sure you don't want me to stay and help?' Finn asked.

'No, I'm fine thanks, Finn. You've done enough by letting me use the space. Besides I want this job to be carried out by girl power.'

He laughed as she flexed her muscles and waved to him and Gracie as they headed off along the river with Matty in his pushchair. Camilla took some masking tape from her bag and began protecting the lights and windows of the van.

Two hours later Camilla stood with hands on her hips and surveyed her handiwork. Her muscles were still throbbing from the strange positions she'd forced her body into whilst sanding and now everything felt as though it were about to seize up. The colour was delightful and made her heart sing. She took out a flask of tea and a sandwich wrapped in foil that Carrie had made her and sat on a tree stump overlooking the river. The air was crisp, but the sun shone from a cornflower blue sky and warmed her face. She threw her crusts into the still water and watched as swans and geese squabbled over them.

74

'Wow, it looks amazing.' Gracie appeared behind her. 'You should be very proud of yourself.'

'I really am. It's been a labour of love, as you well know.' She stood up, brushed twigs and leaves off the back of her joggers, and linked her arm through Gracie's. 'Thank you for everything you've done to help.'

'You're absolutely welcome. That's what friends are for.' They made their way over to the van.

'It's really starting to take shape, isn't it? Although—' She tapped her finger on her cheek. 'I feel as though there's something missing; maybe a little bit of sparkle.'

'Mmm I know what you mean,' agreed Gracie. 'Maybe it will look more finished when you take the masking tape off.'

'I'm sure you're right. I'll have to find some sort of sign for it; maybe one of those stick-on graphics but they're so expensive.'

'I'll see if I can think of any ideas, so leave it with me.'

'Will do.' She yawned. 'I must get back as I need a nice hot soak in the bath.' She scraped at her hands. 'I just hope this paint comes off. I'll be back in a couple of days.'

'No problem, see you then.'

'See you and thanks again.'

Camilla headed back to the B&B feeling lighter than she had for a long time. The walk along the river added to her feeling of contentment as colourful canal boats glided by, cheery passengers waved to her and dog walkers smiled hello. It was a complete contrast to where she lived in her flat, which had been in a built-up area where nobody really knew their neighbours as they were out at work all day. Although she'd popped in and out of Bramblewood she'd never really appreciated the true beauty of it. Maybe when she could afford to, she should look for a place here. That thought warmed her heart immensely.

A couple of days later whilst Camilla was caught up in a whirlwind of icing sugar, cocoa powder and desiccated coconut, she heard a commotion outside. It sounded like a car horn beeping. She washed her hands and was wiping them on a towel as she headed out of the kitchen towards the door, just at the same moment as Lucy and Gracie appeared inside the café.

'What's going on?' she asked, not terribly worried now as she could see the expressions on their smiling faces.

'Wait a minute, you can't look just yet.' Lucy took the towel from Camilla's hand and tied it around her head like a blindfold. 'Now walk carefully this way.'

Camilla trod as carefully as she could as Lucy and Gracie took an arm each and guided her outside. 'What are you two up to?' she said. The cold air bit at her hands, though her face was nice and warm from the towel.

She could feel them gently untangling the knot in the towel, trying not to pull her hair and they shouted, 'Surprise!' in unison. When the material fell away and after blinking a couple of times, her eyes focused on the cutest thing she'd ever seen in her life. Ron was sat at the wheel of her little van. The peppermint green paint had transformed it and looked wonderful now the masking tape had been removed but the icing on the cake for Camilla were the delicious sparkly pastel-coloured cupcakes painted all over it.

She looked up to see a sign saying *Camilla's Cupcakes* that lit up at the top of the van.

'Well isn't that just the cherry on the top.' Her hands flew to cover her open mouth; she could register Lucy and Gracie's ecstatic faces and was completely speechless. Ron got out of the driver's seat and walked towards her, holding out the keys. 'There you go, you've now got your very own little cupcake van.'

Thank you so much, everyone. It's just absolutely perfect. Better than I could ever have imagined. Her eyes brimmed with tears of joy as her friends hugged her. They said goodbye to Ron, and Camilla climbed into the back of the cupcake van. Lucy joined her whilst Gracie stood outside and knocked on the window. Camilla slid it open, a huge smile on her face.

'Can I have a ninety-nine please?' Gracie laughed.

Camilla lifted the lids off the refrigerated part where the ice cream would normally go. Ideas were flying around her head like clothes in a tumble dryer.

'I've just had a brilliant thought,' she said.

'What?' said Lucy who was now in the driving seat.

Gracie was too cold outside so had joined them in the van. 'Ooh it's so cosy in here, isn't it?'

'It really is. It's my cosy little cupcake van and I love it. Thank you, ladies, so much,' said Camilla warming up as the heater was now on.

'Don't even mention it. We thoroughly enjoyed it. Now what was your idea?' Lucy asked.

'I was thinking that I could take this to events, school fetes, et cetera and I could offer a choice of toppings on the cupcakes. The buttercream could go in those two boxes where the ice cream is meant to go and I can swirl it onto the cakes.'

Lucy clapped. 'That is such an amazing idea. I love it. So, it's official then: Camilla Cupcake is going mobile.' She switched the 'Teddy Bears' Picnic' chimes on and laughed as they sang along to the tune, replacing the word 'picnic' with 'cupcakes'.

Chapter 12

As part of her meditation and relaxation process, Camilla had been getting into the habit of thinking of what she was thankful for. Sometimes it was something as simple as the sun shining for her or a beautiful sunset the night before. Other times she was thankful for having had such a wonderful mum, even if it was for only a short time. When her mum had lost her own mum, she told Camilla that grief was the price you pay for having loved so greatly. Camilla understood that now and knew that the price she was paying, though unbearably painful, was testament to how much she had loved her mum. She knew if she could go back and love her mum less to minimise the pain of grief that she wouldn't and couldn't do it; she had been truly blessed.

This morning she was thankful for the wonderful people she had in her life and was at a loss to know how to repay them for what they had done for her. She picked up her phone and flicked through the photos of her cosy little cupcake van, which brought a huge smile to her face.

She had loved her little pink car with everything she had and had been broken-hearted when she lost it, but this one was her precious baby, made with pure love. She clicked on the video and watched and listened to the three of them singing along to the chimes. They all looked so carefree and happy.

This was the first morning where she didn't have that awful gnawing at the pit of her stomach. She had been offered two lifelines here and she wasn't going to pass either of them up. Lucy had had to double her order of cupcakes for the Signal Box Café already as customers were buying enough to take home for their families. Lucy had also been taking more orders for bridal cupcakes as people were starting to hear about Camilla being back. She knew she would have a job on her hands to win back all of her customers as other cake makers had taken over when she had to let customers down. However, her beautiful little cupcake van would now introduce her to a whole new customer base.

Jackson had given her a leaflet about their upcoming school fete as they were always looking for interesting new stalls there. Camilla had decided it would be the perfect first outing for her little cupcake van. She had finished working at the Signal Box Café now but Lucy had given her a set of keys so that she could use the premises during the day when they were closed. She couldn't thank Lucy enough for helping to get her back on her feet slowly but surely; she had been so kind and patient with her.

She decided she had better start making a list of things to do. First and foremost, would be to get some new leaflets printed up. Gracie was a professional artist and had pre-empted this idea for her and had drawn a cartoon sketch of the little van and across the top had written.

'The Cosy Little Cupcake Van'

presents

Camilla's Cupcakes

Available for parties, fetes, weddings and all your celebrations.

Call now for details.### ####

'Gracie, these are amazing. The picture looks just like her. You've even got the sparkly bits on the cupcakes.'

Gracie laughed. 'She is definitely a girl isn't she. Have you named her yet?'

Camilla replied with the first thing that entered her head. 'It has to be Cora doesn't it? Cora the cosy little cupcake van.' She nodded her head decisively.

'Perfect,' agreed Gracie.

Camilla popped in to Odds'n'Sods, the shop opposite the B&B, which sold absolutely everything and had a photocopier. The leaflets were printed in no time and Sandra Ives – one of the owners – asked if she could keep one to display in her window. 'Of course,' said Camilla, 'that would be wonderful. Thank you so much for your support.'

On her way round to the Signal Box Café she popped into the shops along the high street and all were happy to display her leaflet. She also delivered them through letterboxes of all the houses she passed.

Lucy had allowed her to park the van outside the Signal Box Café for now until she found a better place for it. She crossed over the railway track and her face broke into the hugest smile when she saw it sitting there. Her heart fluttered with joy; it was the prettiest vehicle she had ever seen. She still had some pictures of what it looked like when she had first set eyes on it. Seeing such a rust bucket, unloved and abandoned, really tugged at her heart. From first sight she had felt an affinity with this vehicle and luckily after a lot of blood, sweat and tears, and Gracie's incredibly artistic touches, the cupcake van was restored. It was now even better than the one she'd seen in Canada.

She stroked her hand lovingly along the pastel green bonnet and admired the sparkle on the various cupcake toppings when she heard a window opening and someone call her name. She looked up to Railway Cottage to see Lucy hanging out of her bedroom window waving to her.

'I'm so glad it's parked here because I can't stop looking at it. Hasn't Gracie done a marvellous job with those finishing touches.'

Camilla grinned at her. 'You did too. It's amazing and I've got to admit I feel like I'm cheating on my old car but I'm totally in love with this one.'

'Have you got a name for her?' asked Lucy.

'Yes, I do, she has to be called Cora Cupcake don't you think? There's just no other name for her.' She laughed.

'That's perfect and you're so right – no other name could come close. Can you put the kettle on and I'll come over and have a cuppa with you? That's if you've got time of course.'

'I've always got time for you, Lucy, and then maybe we could go for a spin later.'

Lucy gave her the thumbs up and shut the window.

Camilla entered the café and headed straight for the kitchen, put the kettle on and lit the ovens; she washed her hands, put on her apron and began weighing out the ingredients for her cupcakes. The familiarity of the cake-baking mode helped her body to relax. She could cope with cupcakes. Lucy came over soon after and she sat on a stool watching Camilla at work, totally in her comfort zone. They enjoyed a cappuccino together and then Camilla went to the van to collect the boxes that originally held ice cream. She cleaned them thoroughly and put vanilla buttercream in one and chocolate buttercream in the other.

'I want to test my theory to see if I can ice the cakes on demand.' She explained to Lucy.

'I cannot wait to see this,' she replied. They put the boxes back into the refrigerated part of the van. The nozzle had already been taken apart and gone through the dishwasher so they reassembled that too and packed some of the cooled cupcakes into a large plastic box and went back to the van. There was just enough room for both of them to stand inside it. The place had been scrubbed and was spotless and smelt lemony fresh.

'Right, here we go,' said Camilla as Lucy passed her the first cupcake. She held the chocolate sponge underneath the nozzle and pulled the handle down with the other. She looked at Lucy, puzzled. 'Nothing happened.'

'Try again,' said Lucy, 'maybe give a little jiggle.'

Camilla jiggled it, lifted it up and down a few times and just as she was about to give up there was a huge splat and vanilla buttercream practically farted noisily onto the cake, all over her hand and a bit on her face for good measure. She licked her cheek.

'Oh, yum it tastes delicious but isn't looking that pretty. I think it's an airlock.' After a few more farting noises and a little more splattering, which caused them both to jump and giggle, Camilla could feel pressure behind the handle and realised the buttercream was now coming through as she'd hoped it would. She quickly grabbed another cupcake and swirled it under the nozzle until it was covered with a perfectly piped buttercream rose on top.

'Hurray,' shouted Camilla gleefully, 'it worked.' She placed it on the small worktop and took another. She tried the chocolate one this time but now she knew she had to get rid of the airlock and then the buttercream piped like a dream.

'Wait a minute,' said Lucy as she jumped out of the van and ran round to the hatch. She knocked on the window and Camilla slid it open, smiling at her crazy friend.

'I want to be the first one to buy a cupcake from you,' she said. Can I please have three of your finest cupcakes:

two chocolate with vanilla icing and one vanilla with chocolate icing.'

'Coming right up,' said Camilla, so pleased with her new invention of a cupcake topper. She carefully swirled the cupcakes until they were covered with the creamy sweet topping.

'Oh I've left my bag inside. I'll pay you later.'

'You'll do no such thing,' replied Camilla. 'You are on my free cupcakes for life list, along with Gracie and Ron.'

'Aw thank you, that's so sweet, in more ways than one actually.' She laughed at her unintentional pun. 'I'm just going to pop in and get some cupcake boxes.'

'Okay, I'll carry on icing these.' Camilla was so absorbed in what she was doing that she didn't notice the lady standing at the window with a couple of toddlers until she cleared her throat to draw attention to herself. Camilla jumped, which resulted in a floppy piece of buttercream hanging off the cake like Wee Willie Winkie's hat. 'Oh I'm so sorry, I was in a world of my own there. Can I help you?'

'That's no problem at all. I was just wondering what this is as it's obviously a bit too cold for ice creams but one of my observant kids noticed that they were cakes and not ice creams. Is this something new?'

Camilla stood tall, her shoulders back. She took a deep breath. 'Yes this is my new business. Welcome to the cosy little cupcake van. Today we have chocolate or vanilla cupcakes with chocolate or vanilla topping. What would you like?'

The children began to eagerly shout what they would like and Camilla left it to their mum to decipher the instructions. 'So that's one vanilla with vanilla, one chocolate with chocolate and one vanilla with chocolate. Is that right, kids?'

'Yeeees,' they shouted. Lucy had arrived with the boxes and winked at Camilla when she saw that she already had a customer. Camilla smiled back and placed the cupcakes into the box and closed the lid.

'That's lovely,' said the lady. 'Now how much is that?'

'That is free to you, lovely, as we've not really set up properly yet but here – please take a leaflet and if you enjoy them then please tell all of your friends.'

'Oh, are you sure? Thank you so much – you've really made my day. It's been a horrible morning so far, so thank you for brightening it up for us.' The lady's previously exasperated-looking face was now smiling and her children skipped along obediently next to her as they headed home with their pastel pink cupcake box.

It was only as she moved along and another customer appeared at the hatch that Camilla realised that they had a small queue. She served an elderly couple, then four schoolgirls and a few people who had just stepped off the train. Camilla sprang into action, fulfilling their orders efficiently, her conversation adapting easily to each customer she served. As soon as there was a gap in the customers, she closed the window over and she and Lucy headed back into the café laughing.

'I'm going to have to do a few more batches now. I can't believe we had a rush on and I haven't even opened up shop yet.'

'Imagine how busy you'll be once those people have tasted them,' Lucy said as she put the kettle on again. 'Have you heard back from the council yet?'

'Yes, they're sending someone round tomorrow for the health and safety inspection so hopefully I'll pass with flying colours and then I'm good to go. I've also created new social media accounts called The Cosy Little Cupcake Van.'

'Well done. Here's to the cosy little cupcake van,' toasted Lucy as they chinked their coffee cups together.

Chapter 13

Having transport again was a joy for Camilla, especially such eye-catching transport that turned heads wherever she went in it. She had been putting off this visit for a while but decided she should make the effort to go and visit her Auntie Edie. As she pulled up outside her house, she couldn't help but see the SOLD sign standing in her mum's garden. Knives sliced into her stomach and took her breath away. She almost choked on the bile that rose in her throat on seeing the house that was rightfully hers but had been cruelly stolen from her. Her hands shook, rattling the keyrings as she turned the engine off.

Images of her mum looking out of the window before standing at the open front door eagerly waiting to greet her when she came to visit, flashed into her mind. She wished she'd known how little time she'd had left with her mum. Maybe they could have gone on more holidays together, had more adventures, maybe fulfilled her mum's dream of going to Hawaii or even just spent more time doing nothing but chat, drink coffee and eat cake.

Lost in her own thoughts she jumped as she heard a banging on the window and smiled on seeing the octogenarian's face peering in at her. She slid open the window so she could hear what Edie was saying.

'What's all this then? Are you an ice cream man now?' She lifted her glasses up to peer closer at the designs on the van.

Camilla laughed. 'No I'm a cupcake lady actually; and look, I've brought some for you.' She turned the chimes on and handed the old lady a box of assorted cakes through the hatch.

Edie laughed and took the box delightedly. She didn't have many visitors and even fewer presents so this was a real treat. 'It's a darling little van isn't it, love? And I'm hoping that this means you're baking again.'

'Just cupcakes for now but I'm getting there slowly.' She locked up the van and followed Auntie Edie into the small bungalow.

She could hear her African grey parrots squawking from the front garden. As she got closer, she could make out the profanities from one of them. 'Piss off, blue nose.' Camilla laughed remembering Uncle Albert telling her that Bertie didn't like Evertonians but as she got older, she realised it was he who didn't like them. After all, Bertie had to have learned it from somewhere.

She went up to the large cage and put her finger in. 'Hello, Bertie; hello, Bella.' Bella trilled tunefully, her head tilted to one side so she could see who was talking to her. Bertie did his notorious wolf whistle then turned his back to her. Although the loudest of the two he was the shyest.

'You can let them out if you want, love,' said Edie as she went through to the small kitchen. Camilla opened the cage and sat on the floral armchair with her back to the window, so she didn't have to look at her mum's house. It was simply too painful. Bella flew out and landed on the back of the chair. She sang to Camilla as she gently nibbled at her hair. Camilla relaxed; she found it so soothing. She knew they wouldn't hurt her.

Bertie eventually plucked up courage to fly out. He landed on the floor and began to push around a little plastic yellow ball. 'Goooaaaal,' he squawked every few minutes.

Camilla looked around the familiar little room with fondness. She and her mum had often had tea here with Edie and Bella and Bertie. The kind old lady had also offered for her to sleep on her sofa when she first lost her home and was still storing her things for her in a shed in the small garden. She had been so good to her. The fond memories brought tears to her eyes; she sniffed and took a tissue from her bag to wipe them away. She had to smile as she could hear Auntie Edie clattering about in the kitchen, putting cups and saucers on the tray. When she heard the kettle whistling, she knew the tea would be ready soon.

Auntie Edie entered the room, tra la la-ing to the tune of 'Teddy Bears' Picnic'.

'Oh you've got that song stuck in my head now.' She placed the tray on the coffee table; the teapot had a green tea cosy with crocheted peonies decorating the top of it. She placed a cup and saucer and a plate of chocolate biscuits in front of Camilla, tipped a drop of milk in her cup then topped it up with the tea. The noise of it sploshing into the cup always reminded her of Auntie Edie. 'Is that strong enough for you, love?' she asked.

'That's perfect thanks.' Camilla was usually a coffee kind of girl but always drank tea at Auntie Edie's. It was a childhood comfort. Edie poured out her own tea then sat on the couch, reaching over to the box of cupcakes. She opened them and her face lit up as though the box contained sunshine.

'Ooh, love, these look divine. Now what have we got here?'

'I've been practising with some autumnal recipes so there's two each of: pumpkin spiced cupcake with a cream cheese topping, spiced apple with salted caramel topping and blood orange with a marshmallow topping.' She pointed to each one as she described them.

'Which one do you recommend? They all look so delicious. Which one will you have?'

'Oh no, I couldn't possibly have one; I brought them for you. I've got cupcakes coming out of my ears so I'm going to have a chocolate biscuit instead.' She chose a biscuit, peeled off the wrapper and placed it on the plate.

After a long while contemplating, Edie chose the pumpkin spiced cake, she lifted it carefully out of the box as though it were something precious and fragile and placed it on a plate. She raised her fork and hovered it over the cake. 'It seems such a shame to break into it doesn't it?'

'Just go for it, Auntie Edie. There's plenty more where that came from,' said Camilla, excited to see her reaction. She wasn't disappointed as she watched Edie's face melt into a look of pure ecstasy.

Camilla spoke whilst Edie ate her cake slowly and luxuriously. She could see she needed a moment to enjoy it so was filling her in on how she came to be in possession of the cupcake van.

'You've done an amazing job and what lovely friends you have,' said Edie. She finished the cake, wiped her mouth with a napkin and topped up their tea.

'Yes I do and you are included in that sentiment. I'm very lucky to have you all and will be eternally grateful to you for what you've done for me.'

Edie looked sad. 'I'm sorry for what happened to you, darling. No one deserves to be treated like you were but I'm sure karma will catch him and bite him on the arse one day – just you wait and see.'

'I hope so, but anyway I can't dwell on all that anymore, otherwise I'll get ill again, and I won't let him affect me in that way. I just wish my mum had never met him in the first place.'

'You and me both, love. Ooh anyway before I forget I've got a message for you. Now where did I put that piece of paper with his number on?' She stood up and began to search through the drawers in the sideboard. 'No, it's not in here.' She started to pull the contents out and was sifting through various bits of paper, receipts and flyers. 'Ah wait, I think I put it on the fridge behind that magnet you got me from France.' She disappeared into the kitchen, her slippers shuffling along the floor as she went.

'Who was it?' Camilla called to her.

'Oh you know, now, whatshisname?' Edie shouted back. Camilla could hear her filling the kettle again and had a feeling she'd been distracted. She gathered the tea things together on the tray and carried it out to the kitchen, being careful not to trip over Bertie as he continued his game of football. Edie lit the gas and began to fill the sink with soapy water to wash the cups and rinse out the teapot.

'You know the one I mean; I always used to say he had those come-to-bed eyes.'

Camilla laughed at the old lady as she fluttered her eyelashes behind her glasses.

Edie rinsed out the cups and headed to the fridge where she found the note. She looked through the bottom half of her bifocals. 'That's it, Blake, Blake Daniels – the one you were sweet on many years ago.' She crushed the paper into Camilla's hand and squeezed her fingers closed over it. She continued preparing the pot of tea while Camilla's world stood still for a little while.

It had been years since she'd heard his name. Just hearing it now made her heart want to burst out of her chest. She felt inanimate, almost ghostlike, as though she wasn't part of the real world. She remembered vividly the feel of his lips on hers, a softness surrounded by stubble, which scratched a little, the feel of his hands on her body, her hands on his body, the contours of him, the broad back and muscular arms, his skin on her skin. Those brown eyes with flecks of hazel, dark and brooding, could always see through her.

She unfurled the note in her hand and looked at it. The handwriting she could never forget, as she still had letters from him from long ago, though she hadn't read them recently. Questions spun around her head: what was he doing back here? Why would he be getting in touch with her? The last she'd heard he was married – that was through a friend of a friend of a friend. She was so lost in thought that she hadn't heard what Edie was saying. 'Sorry, Auntie Edie, what was that?'

Edie was carrying the tray back into the living room, once again laden with tea things.

'I said he's still bloody gorgeous. I don't know why you ever let him go. He'll always be your one that got away you know. That's why it never worked out with whatshisname.' She placed the tray on the coffee table and began to pour. 'You know I don't know why this is called a coffee table. I don't ever drink coffee; it should be called a tea table. I don't know why it's taken me eighty-odd years to work that one out. But anyway, as I was saying, that's why it never worked out with . . .' She paused to think again.

Camilla helped her out: 'You mean Freddy I think, and I don't know, after losing my mum I wasn't in a good place and things just didn't feel right with Freddy.'

Edie rolled her eyes. 'They don't make men like they used to you know, not like my Albert. Now he was almost my one that got away but he saw sense and came back for me and we were married for fifty very happy years. God rest his soul.' She blessed herself as she said it. 'He got my lovely Liver birds for our tenth wedding anniversary. Rescued them from a container on Liverpool docks he did when he worked for Cunard.'

Camilla shrieked with laughter, causing the two birds to fly back into their cage in a flurry of feathers. 'I can't believe you're dropping the F-bomb again, Auntie Edie.'

'What do you mean? A what bomb?'

'The F-bomb,' Camilla replied. 'You just said Uncle Albert worked effing hard.' She stood up to lock the cage door as Bertie and Bella were back on their perches.

'Did I? I don't remember that.' Edie frowned before realisation hit. She cackled. 'No I said he worked for Cunard – C. U. N. A. R. D – not fucking hard. Oops I suppose I did drop the F-bomb then.' She chuckled. 'Well if you can't drop it when you're in your eighties then when can you drop it?'

Camilla was howling. Oh how she loved coming to Auntie Edie's. She always did cheer her up.

'Anyhow, enough of these swearing shenanigans. You get on and ring your Blake before he changes his mind or sods off back to Canada again.' She ended her conversation abruptly by biting into the moistness of the salted caramel topping of a cupcake she had cut in half. Camilla was glad of the silence, as the thought of ringing him, hearing his voice – so deep and with that Canadian lilt that she'd always found so sexy – reduced her insides to mush. She plucked up the courage to find out more.

'So, what did he say exactly?' She held the cup to her face, trying to act nonchalant and hide her blushes.

Edie licked her lips. 'You know I swear you whip up a little piece of heaven in every cake you make, Camilla love.' She wiped her hand on a napkin. 'He was shocked to see your mum's house was sold and was hoping to see you just to catch up. I didn't tell him too much, as I know you prefer to keep things private.'

'Yes I do, thank you for that. Did he say why he was here and for how long for?' She fiddled with a chocolate biscuit on the plate, almost unwrapping it but deciding against it. The thought of seeing Blake again made her instinctively hold her stomach muscles in.

Edie sipped her tea and placed the cup delicately back onto the china saucer. 'Ooh let me think. I think he said he was here on business but didn't say how long.'

'How did he look?' Camilla looked into her cup, as she couldn't bring her eyes up to meet Edie's.

'Put it this way, with that gorgeous thick dark hair and those mesmerising eyes I wouldn't kick him out of my bed.' She chuckled.

Camilla's eyes opened wide and she almost spilt her tea. 'Auntie Edie, you're so bad.' She laughed at her antics. Edie may be in her eighties with a pink rinse on her hair, but she still had a twinkle in her faded green eyes, and she loved to shock.

Camilla pushed the note into her jeans pocket where she could feel it burning into her skin. Could she ring him? Was his marriage over? How would she feel if she saw him again?

For a long time after he left, she'd felt as though a piece of her was missing. Whilst her mind was reluctant and frankly too scared to contact him, she remembered how she had longed for him. Her eyes desperate to see him, her ears wanting to hear his voice just one more time, her lips needing to feel his kiss and her body . . . well that was another story, her body had craved every inch of him. But that was ten years ago, a whole decade. They must surely be two different people now. No one ever stays the same;

of that she was certain. Her heart agreed with her mind and was on high alert. She could almost imagine it flashing red warning lights, shouting at her through a megaphone: 'Please don't put me through that trauma again.'

Still deep in thought she placed some of her cake-making equipment that had been stored at Edie's in the van and waved to her old friend who would stand at the door until she was out of sight. She always did that. Camilla smiled as she saw her through the rear-view mirror, still waving; both had thoroughly enjoyed the visit. Camilla felt loved; she might not have her childhood home anymore, but Auntie Edie was a precious link to her mum and to Blake and carefree times.

Chapter 14

The Charming Man was a quaint establishment a couple of miles away from home. Before being converted to a restaurant it had originally been the gatehouse for Belvedere Manor, a mansion house that had been around for hundreds of years. It had once been the residence of the Belvedere family but generations later the family occupied only part of it, and they hired out the function rooms for parties and celebrations.

The restaurant was renowned in the area for its steak, which was from cattle reared on the immense grounds of the manor house, and venison from the red deer that roamed wild through the woodland that was also part of the acreage.

'So, when are you going to ring him then?' asked Lucy as she cut into her juicy steak and stabbed some mushroom onto the fork with it, dipping it in the Béarnaise sauce.

'Oh, I don't know if I will. I haven't seen him for years and as far as I knew he was married.' Camilla pushed some broccoli around her plate and gulped down some wine. 'Besides we're probably both completely different people to the ones we were then. I mean, we were young and stupidly in love.' Her eyes glazed over as she looked out of the window where the outside light had just come on. 'But when he left it hurt me like nothing else ever had and I couldn't go through that pain again. Especially not now that I've been through even worse pain since losing my mum and am only just about managing to get back on my feet again.' She cut into her fillet, the knife gliding through it like it was butter, and after adding a piece of onion ring to her fork she popped it in her mouth and chewed on the succulent meat, savouring the moment as the delicious flavours introduced themselves to her taste buds.

'So tell us about him: where did you meet, how long were you together and why did you split up?' Carrie didn't beat about the bush. She liked to get straight to the point.

Camilla's eyes began to drift again as she dipped into her bank of memories. Her time with Blake had been tucked away in her heart and mind, locked in a box that she had gift-wrapped in her imagination with shiny gold paper, tied with ribbon and topped with a huge red bow. It was the best time of her life; she didn't open the box very often, as it was hard to do up the bow in her mind as perfectly as she had done it before. She took a large gulp of merlot.

'We met at college actually. I was doing a catering management course and he was doing business. I'd seen him a few times around the building. There had been a little bit of eye contact and a double take every now and then.' She looked at Carrie and Lucy. 'You know how it is when you see a good-looking guy and you pass him but then look around to check him out again and then he's looking back at you too.' The two friends nodded to her in encouragement. Camilla laughed. 'I feel like Sandy in *Grease* telling the friends about meeting Danny.'

Lucy and Carrie giggled and started singing the song from the movie before Lucy nudged Camilla. 'Sorry, carry on.'

'Well we'd never spoken to each other. Then there was a Christmas party at the college and we all went out to a pub afterwards. I had a part-time job there and the boss asked me to do a couple of hours as someone had let him down. Blake came in with his friends. He seemed so confident with them. They were laughing and being a little bit loud. But when he came to order their drinks, he wasn't so sure of himself. I remember he couldn't stop smiling at me. That was the first time I heard his sexy Canadian accent. He took the drinks back to his friends but left his pint on the bar near me.' The memory caused her lips to curl into a smile, as though she could see him right now, and he was the recipient of it.

'It was manic in there at first so we couldn't talk much but as the queue died down, we were able to speak. He told me he'd seen me around and asked my name. He bought me a drink and we chatted. The first thing that struck me about him was his smile and the fact that he made me laugh. We had exactly the same sense of humour and there were countless times in our relationship that we would howl together over really stupid things. I remember one time we were getting off the tube and he reached round for me and accidentally grabbed an old lady's hand, and she was delighted. He'd gone a good few steps before he realised and I always referred to it as his granny kidnapping phase. Anyway, his friends called him as they were going to the next pub. He asked me for my number and I noticed he was blushing slightly. He looked so cute. I was used to real idiots trying to chat me up at the bar, usually legless, so unusually for me I gave him my number and he left.

'Shortly afterwards I finished my shift and joined my friends on a pub crawl. Two pubs later I walked in and he was standing there staring at the door. Our eyes locked like magnets. One of my friends was talking to me but I couldn't hear anything; I didn't want to hear anything. I just wanted to gaze at this gorgeous man.

'His face lit up when he saw me. It was as if he'd been waiting for me. He bought drinks for me and all my friends too. We had a brilliant night, ended up in the local Indian and our friends got on really well together too.

'I was a little worse for wear and felt a little hot, so he asked if I wanted to go outside for some fresh air. His dark hair curled messily just past his collar and his brown eyes were looking deep into mine, then he held his hand out to me and I took it. He led me outside and then leaning against a tree that was festooned with fairy lights, his lips met mine. I had never been kissed like that before and I've never been kissed like that since we broke up. He was a one-off. I swear we kissed for over an hour non-stop but then everyone began to pile out of the pub as it closed and it got a bit lairy. He offered to walk me home, and that Canadian accent turned my knees to jelly.' She took a sip of her wine as the memories came flooding back.

'It's quite a walk but you can if you want,' she'd replied.

His face had broken into a wide grin. Laugh lines appeared by his eyes and down his cheeks. She could imagine him when he was older as one of those handsome men who get even better-looking with age. He took her hand and put it with his, deep in the pocket of his thick coat, and they walked along together. His thumb stroked her palm gently, which sent shivers through her body. The cold air was fresh and clean but biting on their faces, which were the only parts of them that were exposed.

'So I hear you've got an accent. Where are you from?' she asked him shyly.

'I'm from Ontario. We moved here a couple of years ago for my dad's business. We've got one more year left and then I go to college over there to do my degree.'

Even though she'd only just met him she felt her heart sink as though it were made of stones. She wanted to ask him to stay but how could she? They'd only just met, yet she felt as though she'd always known him and not just in this lifetime, in many lifetimes. They walked past some shops and she thought she was imagining it at first when she saw white speckles in the air but as they got bigger, she realised it was snowing. As it began to get heavier, he pulled her into a shop doorway and they sheltered from it Snowflakes landed softly on his jacket. Close up she could see each individual shape. Some looked like flowers. She had to be quick to see them as they dissolved after a second or two.

Oblivious to the many people who hurried past, he took her in his arms again; their noses were cold at first but soon warmed up with the heat from the closeness of their bodies. Between kisses he carried on the conversation, the words disappearing into each other's mouths.

'I've only just found out your name and yet I already feel I've known you forever,' he whispered.

'Me too,' she murmured giggling as he interrupted every other word with a kiss. 'It's nice to meet you.'

'Camilla, I can honestly say I never expected to meet anyone like you.'

A jolt of electricity bolted through her body just from the way he looked at her.

He leant back from her as if to study her face better. He was bathed in an amber glow from the street light; his dark velvety brown eyes shone brightly, the pupils dilated as he looked at her in awe. He stroked the silky soft almost platinum hair that fell in waves around her shoulders. Her lips were open, waiting for his to join them again. She leaned towards him; his dark unruly hair tickled her forehead as he moved towards her, then the heat of his mouth found hers again.

Eventually and with much reluctance he pulled away from kissing her. 'I'd better get you home – you're shivering.'

'It is a bit cold,' she said with chattering teeth.

He opened his coat and pulled her into him so he could warm her with his body heat on one side and his coat on the other. She snuggled into his chest as they walked the rest of the way home.

Camilla sighed; a shiver went through her body like someone had walked over her grave as she brought herself back to the present.

Lucy and Carrie had finished their meals and Lucy topped up their wine, emptying the bottle.

'He sounds gorgeous, doesn't he, Carrie? And your face absolutely lights up when you talk about him.'

'He certainly does,' she replied, then pointed to Camilla's dinner. 'Come on eat up, love. You need to keep your strength up.'

Camilla enjoyed the rest of her steak whilst Lucy called the waiter over by waving and pointing to the empty wine bottle and Carrie popped to the loo.

As soon as the wine arrived and Carrie sat back down she asked Camilla to carry on. 'So what happened next?'

Camilla took a sip of the deep berry-flavoured wine and continued. 'Well from then on we were pretty much inseparable; that is, until he had to go to uni.'

'Did he go back to Canada then, the next year?' asked Lucy.

Camilla shook her head. Her mouth curved into a smile. 'His mum, dad and sister moved back to Canada the following year as planned but he wouldn't go with them as he didn't want to leave me. By that time, he'd researched the best business courses and decided to stay in this country to do his degree. He was only an hour and a half away from me so we made it work. We saw each other every weekend and sometimes in the week on special occasions. I was working hard in London as a pastry chef and he completed his degree at Cambridge. Afterwards he was meant to go back to Canada to work for his dad's business, but he decided to stay here with me. He got a really good job but always had a cloud of guilt hanging over him and so I promised him that one day I would go with him to live in Canada. We rented a flat together in London for a few years. It was impossible to buy somewhere, especially as the plan was that we would be going to Canada.' She swallowed as she neared the heart-breaking part. Lucy put her arm around her, and Carrie topped up their glasses.

'Stop if you want to,' said Carrie. 'We don't want you to be getting upset.'

Camilla took a tissue out of her bag and blew her nose. 'No, don't worry, it's fine. Mum hadn't been feeling so good and the GP had referred her to a specialist so I took a day off and went to the hospital appointment with her, and that's when we found out she had cervical cancer.' Lucy's arm tightened around her and Camilla patted her arm. 'Mum needed a hysterectomy and chemotherapy, so I packed up my job and moved back in with her.' She shifted uncomfortably in her chair.

'I'm so sorry, Camilla. I would never have asked if I'd known that it meant you had to relive all this again,' said Carrie as she held on to her hand.

'No please don't worry; it'll do me good to get it all out. Blake was amazing in helping me care for my mum, he insisted on driving her to her hospital appointments, organised shopping to be delivered and fresh flowers. He was a tower of strength for both of us, Anyway as if that wasn't bad enough then Blake got a message from home to say that his dad had suffered a heart attack and he had to get there immediately. I assured him I would follow him if he went back but really I knew I wouldn't be able to. There was simply no way I could leave my mum. She had a few complications following the operation and she took months to recuperate so I decided to stay at home with her and I got a job as a pastry chef in a local hotel. I began making cakes for people privately and stayed there until I met Lucy and the wedding cakes just took off.'

'I had so many recommendations for Camilla Cupcake,' said Lucy.

Camilla smiled. 'Yes and I got to keep my mum for almost ten more years, which seemed like a miracle at the time. So although I would have loved to have gone to Canada with Blake I would never have forgiven myself, and so I don't regret it because I was able to be with my mum.' She sniffed again. 'Sadly Blake's dad died a couple of days after he got there but at least he got the chance to say goodbye to him and I know he was grateful for that. Of course then he had no choice but to take over his dad's company and look after his mum and sister.' She glugged some more wine. Lucy was stroking her arm gently as if to ease the story out of her.

'So did you ever see him again?' asked Lucy.

Camilla shook her head. 'No, we tried to keep in touch with phone calls, Skype and letters but eventually he stopped all contact with me and the last letter I sent came back with "Not known at this address" written on it. The last time I physically saw him was when I said goodbye at the airport and both of us were crying. He felt so guilty for not going back to work with his dad when he wanted him to and I know he found that very hard to live with.'

'It must have been awful,' said Carrie. 'I can't imagine how you must have both felt.'

'That was a huge part of the problem: we'd both had our hearts broken so couldn't really offer the other any support. The last I heard was some years later when a friend of a friend mentioned he'd married an Englishwoman but that's all I know. I've had a few boyfriends since then but only one serious one and he never ever made me feel like Blake did. I don't think anyone else could.' She shrugged.

'Right, enough of my little trip down memory lane. Who fancies a liqueur coffee?' She patted both their hands, sat up straight, exhaled deeply and threw her shoulders back.

When the waiter brought the drinks over, he placed an Irish coffee in front of Carrie and Calypsos in front of the others. Camilla raised her tall glass, holding it by the tiny handle.

'I'd like to raise a toast to each and every one of you, without whom I don't know what would have happened to me by now, but I can tell you I was not in a good place. So, here's to friendship.'

'To friendship,' repeated the others, carefully clinking their glasses with Camilla's.

Camilla motioned to the waiter to bring the bill by writing on an imaginary pad in mid-air. He swiftly brought it over, trying to hide a yawn behind his hand. Lucy and Carrie picked up their bags to retrieve their purses and Camilla stopped them. 'No, I really must insist – this is my treat because you've both been so wonderful to me. Neither of you have charged me rent so this is the least I can do with my first lot of cupcake profits.' After a little resistance the two friends knew they would be defeated and so thanked Camilla for the lovely meal.

Chapter 15

Winter had arrived with a vengeance; the ground was wet with large puddles gathered in dips in the pavement, which were a huge indicator of how uneven the paths were. Luckily the early morning rain had cleared up now and a burst of December sunshine had broken through the grey sky. Rainbows always reminded Camilla of her mum as Iris was the name of the goddess of rainbows. Today a stunning arch of iridescent colours added to the cheeriness of the day It almost looked like it was touching the ground just in front of Camilla as she drove into the car park of Flowerpots Garden Centre.

Her trip to the school fete had been hugely successful. The children and their families had loved her cosy little cupcake van and she'd sold out of bespoke cupcakes within an hour. She'd had to borrow some of the Signal Box Café's stock and then work in the evening to make more for them. She'd completely underestimated how popular her cupcakes would be. She'd also added some extra bits and pieces such as sprinkles and small chocolate flakes, just like an ice cream van.

The fete had also provided her with a huge opportunity to network, which is how she found out about the farmers' market being held at Flowerpots. It was a monthly occurrence and the farmer who supplied her free-range eggs told her about it. One of the teachers had also told her about a part-time vacancy in the local college for a cake-decorating teacher, which she'd plucked up the courage to apply for.

A part of the car park had been sectioned off for the market stalls to set up and the mobile stalls such as hers were guided into place by marshals who waved her into a spot next to a hot drinks van. A hot dog van parked up after her. She jumped out of the van and introduced herself to the other stallholders: Ged on the coffee stall, and Angie and Bob on the hot dogs. She ordered a cappuccino from Ged and clung on to it to warm her hands, which were stinging from the cold due to her gloves being fingerless. She went back to her van and pulled out two little foldaway tables, each with two foldaway chairs, one pink set and one cream. She had bought them from a stall at the school fete and thought they would be ideal. She set them out in front of her van and climbed back inside to get ready for the onslaught. The sun was shining on her and seemed to be chasing away the chill from the air.

Once all the stallholders had been served their hot drinks, Ged came over to her van and tapped on the window. She turned around, smiled at him and slid open the hatch. He looked cute. Strands of deep chestnut hair had escaped from under his bobble hat and his green eyes were twinkling at her. He handed her a fresh cappuccino.

'Thought you might like another coffee?' He smiled at her.

She smiled back. 'Oh thank you let me get my purse.'

'No, that's on me just to welcome you to the farmers' market.' He winked at her, which made her insides jump.

'Well thank you, if you're sure. That's very kind but let me offer you a cupcake instead then.'

'Now that sounds like an offer I can't refuse.' He winked again, she blushed and he laughed. He had a Belfast accent, which she found very endearing. She giggled.

'I have gingerbread with cinnamon-spiced topping.' She pointed to a tray of read- iced cupcakes. 'Or we have Christmas tree cupcakes in either vanilla or chocolate sponge, like so.' She picked up a chocolate sponge, swirled the green icing on the top to look like a Christmas tree, then sprinkled it with multi-coloured hundreds and thousands, and added a glittery sugar paste star on the top. His head tilted sideways, and he nodded his approval as she placed it on the counter in front of him.

'That is one of the most amazing things I think I've ever seen. So what's in the other nozzle?'

'I'll show you.' She smiled, picked up a vanilla sponge and swirled the topping perfectly onto the cake, placed it on the counter next to the other one and added a candied orange to it. 'It's chocolate orange flavour. So which one do you fancy?'

'That's my favourite so I'll take that one, if that's okay. I mean they all take my fancy; in fact everything in this van takes my fancy, but—' He heard a shout from his van as some more stallholders wanted a drink. 'Oh I'd better get over there to this impatient lot. I'll catch you later yeah, and I'll make sure I send all my customers over to you for one of these?' He raised his cupcake and made his way over to his van.

She covered her face with her hand to hide her blushes; he had made her a little hot under the collar and she could feel little bluebirds twittering away in her stomach.

The next couple of hours passed in a blur as customers and stallholders were bowled over by her delicious and inventive cupcakes. She'd had business cards made and left a little pile of them on the counter, which she'd had to top up on numerous occasions. In amongst the succession of customers she heard her name being called and leaning out of the hatch she looked over at Ged and saw him pointing to his blackboard. On one side he had the prices of his drinks and on the other he'd drawn a big arrow pointing to her van with the word 'Amazing' written on it and a picture of a cupcake drawn in coloured chalk. He put his thumbs up to her and she laughed at him and shouted thanks. He mimed the action of drinking coffee to her so she nodded and shouted, 'Yes please.'

She returned the favour by cupping one hand and then mimicking a swirl on top of it with the other. He put both thumbs up to her again and within three minutes had appeared at her hatch with a steaming cappuccino in a paper cup. I take it you were telling me to stir it well,' he joked as he repeated the action she had done with her hands.

'I've never had to do an impression of a cupcake before.' She giggled. 'So what's it to be this time, Christmas tree or gingerbread spiced?'

He put his elbow on the counter and rested his chin on his hand. 'Why don't you surprise me?' He looked deep into her eyes before closing his and opening his mouth a little. She gulped down a mouthful of air and quickly grabbed a chocolate sponge and topped it with the Christmas tree icing and placed the little glittery sugar star on top.

'Are you sure about this?' she asked.

'Go ahead, just do it,' he replied.

She slowly peeled off the paper wrapper and held the cake to his mouth. He took a big bite and she managed to get the buttercream on his cheeks and on her fingers. She squealed at the mess she was making of him.

'Oh that's got to be the Christmas tree one, for sure.'

She pulled out some wet wipes from a container and handed him a couple.

'I'm sorry, I was just playing with you. Are you all right?' He looked genuinely concerned.

'Y . . . yes I'm fine,' she stammered. He was having a strange effect on her. He was flirtatious and cheeky, and he made her laugh.

'A few of us normally go out for a drink after the market. Do you fancy coming? It's just to the pub round the corner.' She wanted to say no and just go home and snuggle down. But then she realised she'd been doing that most nights so to shake herself up a bit she agreed to go with him just for one. He smiled a cheery smile at her and jogged back over to his van where he had more customers waiting for him. Camilla was pleased to see she had more customers too and served them swiftly.

Later on just as she was about to close up she saw a familiar face appear at the hatch.

'Auntie Edie, you made it. How lovely.' She grabbed the old lady's hand and held it in both of hers affectionately. 'Ooh your hands are cold. Now what can I get you: pumpkin spice, chocolate orange or a vanilla or chocolate?'

'Ooh I'll have a chocolate orange please, dear. Anyway you'll never guess what.' She was interrupted by the next customer who had a wailing child in her arms.

'Oh dear. What's happened?' Camilla soothed. She turned to Edie. 'Sorry, Auntie Edie, you go and get comfortable on the chair over there and I'll bring your cupcake over.' Edie seemed pleased to take the weight off her feet and snapped up the chair quickly as one customer was leaving and another lady was eyeing it up.

'I'm so sorry, she's just dropped her cupcake,' said the mum. 'And it's obviously the end of the world. So could

I please have another one?' She held a five-pound note out to Camilla whilst rocking the child up and down in an attempt to make her smile again.

Camilla gestured with her hand for her to keep the money and looking at the green buttercream around the little girl's mouth, she said, 'Now let me guess, I think you had a Christmas tree cupcake. Is that right?'

The little girl nodded, wiping her eyes with the back of her hand, the remnants of the cry caught in her throat. 'Yes please,' coaxed the mum.

'Yes pweeze,' repeated the little girl.

Camilla swirled the green buttercream onto the cake, added the glittery star and held it up to the little girl who reached over with both hands to take it.

'Thank you so much,' said the mum. 'You've really saved the day.'

Camilla smiled and waved goodbye then slid the shutter window closed and prepared Edie's cupcake. She placed it in one of her little personalised boxes and climbed out of the van, walked around it and over to Edie. She could see the back of a dark-haired man handing her a hot drink and talking to her.

Edie looked round. 'Ah here she is now,' she said.

The man turned, his eyes met hers, locked. Her stomach lurched and she froze on the spot. She could vaguely hear the music from the carousel playing nearby, the hubbub of a hundred conversations around her. His eyes, those flecks of hazel surrounded by darker brown, seemed to search hers for a sign of how she felt about seeing him again. His hair so dark and sexy the way it curled around his collar and occasionally caught on his eyelashes as he blinked. She remembered the feel of his thick dark hair between her fingers as she had grasped it in ecstasy; she blushed at the thought. It was still the same but maybe a bit shorter. She had to stop herself from reaching out and touching it. He had a beard now too; he'd always tried to grow one but had only ever managed a little patchy fuzz. She wasn't really a fan of beards but it made him look even more of a man than he had before, if that were possible.

'Cami, hi, it's good to see you.' His voice, thicker, more mature, the Canadian drawl more pronounced, did things to her insides, awoke memories within her that had been hidden away for so long. She could visualise the red ribbon on her gift box of memories slowly unravelling in her mind.

'Blake popped round again to see how I was and to see if you had got his message. I was on my way here so he kindly offered to bring me to save me getting the bus,' Edie explained.

'Oh, that was nice of you,' Camilla replied, her throat dry.

'It was no trouble,' he said, 'though the parking was a bugger so I dropped Edie off here to save her legs and I'm at the far end of the car park.'

Camilla pretended to fold her arms but really she was pinching her underarm to check whether she was awake. She didn't know what to say to this man who had been her everything at one time and whilst his presence was having the exact same effect on her body as he always had, which was completely unnerving, she had to persuade herself to slow down. After all, they were practically strangers.

'I was so sorry to hear about your mom. She was such a lovely lady.'

Her heart jolted at the mention of her mum. 'Thank you,' she replied. 'As I'm sure you know from your dad, the pain never goes away.'

He nodded in sympathy.

'How's your mum?'

He looked down. 'Ah, she died a couple of years after my dad actually. She pretty much gave up after we lost him.'

Camilla's hand flew to her chest. 'I'm so sorry.' She touched his forearm and even through his coat she could feel how taut it was; he was solid. Electricity flooded her body. He put his hand on hers; the softness of his touch turned her knees to molten chocolate. She looked into his eyes and saw her own pain reflected there.

'Thank you. At least I can hope that they are together again now,' he said.

Camilla nodded. 'That's a lovely thought. I really loved your mum and dad.'

'And they loved you too, as did . . . well you know.' He looked at the ground and shifted, his foot kicking an imaginary stone. 'Listen, I was wondering whether we could . . . that is if you wanted to . . . if we could maybe get together for a catch-up sometime?' He looked up to meet her eyes once more.

Her insides were dancing around doing a jig but she daren't let it show on the outside. She was far too nervous to actually smile at him.

'How about tonight or is that too . . .'

'Oh no, sorry, I can't make tonight, I'm afraid.' She interrupted in a panic. A thought entered her head loudly. Her conscience screamed at her: *"Ask him about his wife! He has a wife, you know."* She couldn't bring herself to ask him. It seemed more awkward. He was probably only asking her to meet up as friends anyway and surely if she asked him about his wife it would look like she had romantic intentions towards him. She couldn't even see if he was wearing a wedding ring because he had thick gloves on. She was torn but then thankfully Edie, having just eaten the last of her cupcake and wiping her mouth on a napkin, helped her out.

'It will do you good, Camilla, to get out and about again.'

'Maybe a coffee or something sometime,' he suggested. 'Call me please; you've got my number haven't you?'

She instinctively patted her coat pocket where she had put the piece of paper with his number on. It had been burning a hole in it ever since she'd put it there. It had already etched itself into her brain as she had read it so many times and now knew the number off by heart. She felt overwhelmed by shyness. This man knew everything about her once upon a time but now they were virtually strangers. She nodded to him and stared deep into his eyes. 'Yes, I will.'

She was jolted out of her dream-like state by a northern Irish accent behind her. 'So, cupcake queen, are you ready? Do you wanna hand with putting these tables and chairs away?' Ged had started collapsing the chairs that Edie wasn't sitting on and then closed down the other table too.

'Oh, right yes, thank you. Sorry, is it that time already?' She felt flustered. She hadn't even noticed that the other stalls were closing, and it was getting dark already.

Blake was eyeing up Ged, obviously trying to work out what his relationship was with Camilla.

Camilla turned to Edie. 'Will you be all right getting home, Auntie Edie?'

'Yes, I'll be fine, thank you. Blake is going to run me back aren't you, dear. And it's not often I get an offer like that from a handsome Canadian.' She rubbed her hands together and blew on them. 'I wish I'd remembered my gloves. My arthritis is playing up today.' She slowly pulled herself up out of her seat, groaning as she did so, her bones clicking noisily in various places. Ged returned from putting the tables and chairs in the back of the cupcake van.

'I'm sorry,' he said to Camilla. 'I didn't realise these were friends of yours. I thought they were just ordinary customers.'

'Oh no, we all go way back,' she replied, pointing to each of them as she said their names. 'This is Ged and this is my Auntie Edie and Blake.' Saying his name again out loud in a matter of days seemed so alien to her and yet it had been the name that fell so easily off her tongue once upon a time. The name she had uttered far more than any other name in her life. She used to get gentle butterflies in her tummy when saying it but now her whole insides were flipping over and over.

'Pleased to meet you,' said Ged, shaking Blake's hand.

'You too,' said Blake, unsmiling.

Camilla kissed and hugged Auntie Edie goodbye and allowed Blake to brush the gentlest of kisses against her cheek. His beard was soft and ticklish. Her eyes closed involuntary. He smelt the same, a comforting blend of warmth and musk, which allowed her mind to drift back to those happy times. But all too soon he was gone. As he walked away he pulled his gloves off with his teeth and offered them to Edie, stopping to help her put them on. Camilla's heart plunged through her stomach as she caught the glint of gold on the third finger of his left hand. With a sunken heart she knew then that she wouldn't be calling him.

Ged had told her to follow his van, so she drove out behind him, ready to meet all the other stallholders in the pub.

Chapter 16

The car park of The Unicorn looked like another farmers' market, as most of the stallholders had parked up their vans. Camilla pulled up behind Ged whilst he was helping another van to park up by gesturing to them how much space they had. Camilla was admiring the pub sign, which had a picture of a unicorn on it with a wonderfully coloured mane and a matching tail. The words *The Unicorn* were written underneath it in gold lettering, which matched the unicorn's glittery horn.

'That has to be the prettiest pub sign I've ever seen,' she said when Ged joined her. 'You know I've never seen this pub ever and yet I've been to the garden centre lots of times.'

'Ah yes, it's a hidden gem isn't it. The line of fir trees was planted many years ago by the owner of Flowerpots as it's all their land but I don't know if they realised how tall they'd grow, so this little area called Flowerpot Lane is completely concealed from view from that busy road.'

They walked into the pub and were immediately drawn in to the excitable ambience that was in the air. Chatter and laughter filled the traditionally oak-panelled room whilst the friendly bar staff tried to keep up with the demands of the thirsty customers. Because most of them were driving there was a large demand for hot chocolate and a non-alcoholic mulled wine, which filled the room with the smell of blackberry and cinnamon. Christmas decorations were swathed from beams and across the large open fireplace. Orange slices and frosted pine cones hung on invisible fishing wire in the windows and candles flickered in glass jars on tables and windowsills. It felt to Camilla as though she had just stepped into a magical world like something out of Harry Potter.

She ordered an alcohol-free mulled wine. Ged ordered a beer and led her over to a friendly group, some of whom she recognised from earlier in the day. She would have loved to have had a wander round the market but there simply hadn't been enough time. She recognised Frank, the farmer who provided her with the free-range eggs she used in her cakes and he waved to her from across the room. Ged introduced her to a jovial man called Stan who apparently produced the best cheese in the whole of the UK.

'Here try some of that, love.' He pointed to the board on the table, which had a variety of cheeses cut into little samples with cocktails sticks in them. She tried a white cheese with cranberries and she hoped her expression told Stan how delicious she'd found it. She then noticed that the other stallholders had brought some leftovers in to share too and was able to try scrumptious home-made sausage and apple rolls in golden puff pastry and pasties boasting of locally sourced ingredients. Fudge and coconut ice samples sat temptingly on long thin trays and gingerbread men lay alongside cinnamon stars.

'Won't be a sec.' She motioned to Ged and headed for the door. Ged raised his glass of amber liquid to her in acknowledgement. A couple of minutes later, carrying a box with six of her cupcakes in, she arrived back in the pub bringing a whirl of cold air in with her. 'I was saving these for my friend back at the B&B but I can always make more,' she confided to Ged. She reached for a clean knife on the table and carefully cut each cupcake into quarters so there was enough to go around. Soon the only evidence that any had ever been there was a smear of buttercream on an empty box and the sound of people admiring them. At least three people asked her for a business card and Angie from the hot dog stall asked her if she could make big celebration cakes as she needed one in a month's time.

She hesitated before answering; her heart beating rapidly. She still didn't know if she was ready to take on the pressure of being responsible for such an important part of a celebration. After all the cake was usually the centrepiece of any party.

'I used to but I haven't in a while. Also I don't have my diary with me so I'm not sure whether I can fit that in at the moment. But if it's cupcakes you want then I can certainly oblige,' she replied, hoping not to appear rude.

Ged waited until they were on their own again and motioned for her to sit with him on a comfy padded bench.

'So you're staying in a B&B. Are you just passing through this area then?'

Her face reddened; her eyes searched the bottom of her glass. 'No I've been staying there for a little while as I'm . . . I guess you could say, between homes at the moment.'

'Oh no, I'm sorry I didn't mean to pry. I'm not usually nosy but I had to stay in a B&B once as I went through a difficult time and ended up homeless for a while.'

Camilla felt able to look him in the eye. A flash of sadness swept over his face but it quickly dissipated as he asked her if she'd like another drink. She opted for another non-alcoholic mulled wine as the scent of it hung heavy in the air and added to the Christmassy warmth about the place. When he returned with the drinks she was staring into the embers of the open fire, enjoying the sound of it crackling cosily.

'Where do you live now?' Camilla asked him as she curled her hands around the warm glass and inhaled the blackberry and cinnamon aroma.

He took a sip of his shandy and licked the froth from his upper lip. 'About half an hour away from here in a place called Witchett. It's near the M1 so I can get to pretty much anywhere in the country, as I try to do as many of these fairs as possible. I'll always be a bit of a drifter, I guess, as I've never really had proper roots anywhere.' He gazed into the fire watching the flames leap and curl around the logs in there. Bits of white-hot ash fell out onto the hearth. 'I was much younger when I became homeless. To cut a long story short my da left my ma with four kids and she eventually took up with another loser who didn't want me around. Ya see he saw me as competition and he wanted to be the man of the house. So at fourteen I ended up on the streets of Belfast and eventually managed to get to London.

'I was saved by a homeless charity who gave me a bed and then a job working for them and then they supported me into buying the van so I'm now completely self-sufficient. I can support myself, pay my own rent and I even have enough savings to pay for a round-the-world trip, which I'm hoping to do next year.'

Camilla saw the reflections of the flames in his green eyes; she would never have guessed he'd had such a hard time as he'd seemed so cheery to her today. Then she realised that nobody would guess what had happened to her lately as she was also able to wear a mask in public.

'I'm so sorry you went through all of that.' She placed her gloved hand on his arm and he patted it gently. 'Do you ever see your mum? And what about your siblings?'

He took another swig of his drink and waved goodbye to some of the other stallholders who were leaving.

'I don't see her that often but I email and text her a lot. She's not with him anymore thank God and my brothers and sister are older now so she is working and much happier. She constantly apologises to me but I've told her there's no need. She felt she needed a man in her life at that time just for the security more than anything. I used to send her my wages but she doesn't let me anymore as they're all doing okay. What about you?' He tentatively tapped her leg with his knee.

'My story is quite complicated but the simplified version is that I lost my mum a little while ago and my world fell apart. Then as if that wasn't bad enough, her husband destroyed her will and basically stole her house. The legal fees were exorbitant, and I lost my car and having split up with my boyfriend we lost our flat as I couldn't afford it on my own. I was worried I'd have to sofa surf but then my friend offered me a room at the B&B in Bramblewood. I pretty much hibernated there for a week, drowning in my own sorrow, but then my other friend offered me a temporary job.'

She could see by the look on his face that he felt terrible at upsetting her and didn't want to push her.

'I'm sorry; but to be honest your mum's husband sounds like a right scumbag.'

'Yes, it's unbelievable isn't it. He told me he was sorting everything out and then did a moonlight flit. There are some very greedy people in this world.'

He squeezed her arm reassuringly. 'I've heard about cases like this before. It then becomes one word against another with no legal proof. Wills are so flimsy and it's unbelievable to think the most expensive thing you'll ever own in your life can be written on a scrap of paper. A friend of mine thought his will was safely at the solicitor's until he needed it and found that he should have been paying them annually to keep it otherwise it's just gone.

'Anyway, enough of this gloomy talk. It looks like you're not doing too bad for yourself now with your own business.'

She sniffed and nodded her head. 'I'm doing okay actually.'

'I know it won't seem like it now but one day you'll look back at all this and realise it's what made you into the fabulous person that you are. Sometimes shitty things happen to good people but it's how we deal with it that counts. You could hide away and bury yourself in self-pity or shrug it off and make your life the best it can be, knowing that you did it on your own.'

'I like the sound of that,' she said, 'but I didn't do it on my own, as my friends helped me a lot.'

'That's great but they could only do so much. Ultimately it has to come from you to work hard and carve out your own destiny and it looks to me like you've got that under control.'

Camilla nodded; he was right. She had never got as much satisfaction as she did when she stepped inside her cupcake van and delivered a little piece of happiness everywhere she went. She felt sad about the house for her mum's sake and tried hard not to dwell on that too much, but she had inherited her mum's get up and go and her work ethic and nobody could take those attributes away from her.

The bell rang abruptly for last orders and she stood up and put her arms in her coat and he helped her before he put on his own. He bid goodnight to the bar staff and held the door open for her.

'You know there's no shame in having been homeless; in fact don't they say that everyone is just a couple of pay packets away from it? So I think you should maybe not be so hard on yourself and make sure you hold your head up high.'

She smiled and nodded a thank you. She observed him looking at her face and self-consciously checked that her hair was tucked into her woolly bobble hat. He walked her to her van.

'You love this van, don't you?' He laughed. 'You just smiled at it like it was an old friend.'

'I really do. Every time I see her, she makes me smile. I think she's the first step to me gaining my independence back again and that feels good.'

'You make me smile,' he replied as he kissed her gently on the cheek. She felt the warmth of his lips defrost her cold skin.

'Hey, have you got plans for Christmas Day?' he asked after opening her van door for her. She hadn't really wanted to think about Christmas. Since losing her mum Christmas didn't hold the joy that it once did. Auntie Edie had invited her to Dorset to spend it with her and her daughter's family; Carrie had mentioned she would be doing a special dinner at the B&B; and Lucy had invited her to the Signal Box Café where she was having a private family dinner. Camilla had felt extremely grateful for all the offers but couldn't face the thought of bringing her sadness to other families who were feeling joyful.

'I haven't made my mind up yet. I've had lots of invites but I'm not really feeling it at the moment.' She started up the engine.

'How do you fancy spending it with me doing something worthwhile?'

'That sounds good actually,' she replied through lips that were now shivering in the cold. She passed him a business card. 'Here's my number. Just let me know where and when and I'll be there.'

He closed her door and waved her off out of the car park. She felt a warm comforting feeling inside and it wasn't because she had just put the heating on full.

Chapter 17

Christmas Day arrived in the twinkling of a fairy light. Camilla had wished Carrie and Jim a merry Christmas and had given them a present over breakfast. She also gave each of Carrie's cats a special new toy as she had become very fond of them; they were always there for a cuddle whenever she needed one. She hadn't felt this excited for months and wolfed down her salmon and scrambled egg on toast in no time. She had a tiny sip of Bucks Fizz and then headed round to the Signal Box Café to load up the van with her creations.

She drove the forty-five minutes to get to the leisure centre, which had kindly donated the use of their facilities to the charity. She was excited to see Ged in the car park unloading his van with some helpers. He waved to her and after passing a bin bag to another man he walked over to meet her.

'Hi, cupcake queen, merry Christmas!' he said kissing her on both cheeks.

'Merry Christmas to you too.' She smiled, feeling happier than she had done for a long time. 'Now where do I need to put these?' She gestured to some large plastic boxes in the van.

'Wait, I'll just go and get a trolley.' He walked briskly to the door of the leisure centre and returned soon after with a trolley on which they loaded the boxes.

'Looks like you've been busy,' he remarked with a smile.

'I think I got a little carried away.' She smiled back. They entered the sports hall and she was fascinated with the buzz that surrounded her. Long trestle tables were set up at one end, which some helpers were laying with tablecloths, cutlery and glassware. The other end had more trestle tables on which the volunteers were laying out clean warm clothing and shoes and coats. Camilla had added to the clothing by asking around her friends and neighbours, all of whom had contributed to the worthy cause. She had also been in touch with shops and asked for donations of underwear and toiletries. As they approached the dining tables Ged explained the procedure.

'The day starts early and our homeless guests can arrive from ten thirty. They are taken to the clothes tables where they can choose some new clothes, then through to the changing rooms where they can shower and change into the fresh new outfits, and if they would like their original clothes washed then we can do that too and have them ready for when they leave.

'We have so many volunteers here to help. We have legal people, people who can get them employed again and people who can help with paperwork and such like.'

Camilla was impressed and so proud to be among such a fascinating group of people. 'Is that a hairdresser setting up over there?' she asked.

Ged looked to the direction she was pointing. 'Yes we have lots of hairdressers and barbers and it's amazing the transformation you see to some of these people just with a bit of grooming and attention. D'you know I've met some of the most interesting people of my life in this place.'

They reached the tables and proceeded to open the boxes that Camilla had brought with her. Ged's eyes widened when he saw what she'd brought, and a sense of pride washed over her.

'These are amazing,' he said as he began to place them on the tables. A young woman with multi-coloured hair came over to kiss Ged hello. She had been placing Christmas crackers on the side plates.

'Hi, Ged, what have you got here then?' she enquired.

'Hi, Jess, meet Camilla, our cupcake queen.' Jess looked at her and nodded an indifferent hello. Camilla held out her hand but it wasn't reciprocated.

'So where are the cupcakes then?' she asked looking puzzled.

'They're here, you nit,' replied Ged playfully as he and Camilla placed the cupcakes, which were cleverly disguised as Christmas wreaths, onto the table. There were ten cupcakes in each wreath, Camilla had iced them so skilfully that it looked like ribbons and bows and even baubles were entwined with real fir leaves.

Jess couldn't hide how impressed she was. 'I honestly thought they were real,' she admitted.

Camilla opened another box, which had some simple Christmas cakes that she had made with iced snow scenes on them, decorated with little Father Christmases and snowmen. They looked jolly and festive. Camilla and Ged placed one in the centre of each of the wreaths. They received lots of compliments from the other volunteers as they went about their business.

Soon the hall was filled with people from all walks of life. A brass band and a choir had set up in the centre and they sang and played carols, which brought a tear to many an eye. Camilla was soon waiting on the tables and bringing food to hungry men, women and children. Some had dogs with them that they wouldn't part with so they were given food too. Camilla got talking to a lawyer who was there to offer free legal advice but also helped out with the tea trolley.

'What made you give up your time today?' she asked.

'I know what it's like,' he replied. 'I've been there and this charity helped me back on my feet again. I lost my wife and child in an accident and I literally fell to pieces, turned to drink and lost absolutely everything. These wonderful people picked me back up again and put me back together piece by piece.'

She gave him a hug and later mentioned her conversation to Ged. He wasn't surprised. 'Do you see that young man over there?' He pointed to a smart young man who was laughing and joking with some of their guests. 'He was made homeless because his family kicked him out for being gay.'

Camilla's hand covered her mouth in shock and pity for the young man. Ged continued, 'He now owns his own business with pop-up restaurants. He's amazing and he's supplied all the food here today. Pretty much all of the volunteers here have been through the same thing our guests have been through.'

'I feel so humbled to be here,' she replied. Her problems were nothing compared to these wonderful people and she vowed never to feel sorry for herself again. The man who Camilla had been talking to earlier motioned to Ged to come with him. Ged put his hand gently at the small of Camilla's back and led her toward the kitchen. 'Now it's our turn,' he said. 'And I don't know about you, but I'm famished.'

Camilla hadn't realised that she would get fed too and happily moved her tray along the canteen-style café and joined the first shift of the volunteers to have their Christmas dinner. Serving their guests had made her tummy rumble;

the roast turkey dinner with all the trimmings had smelt delicious and was fit for a king.

After they'd eaten and Camilla had heard more fascinating stories of how people had overcome adversity, they went back to the main hall where the volunteers were now laying out camp beds, each with a pillow and blanket.

'They'd love to do more,' said Ged, 'but there just isn't enough money to go round so at least they get a decent meal and a dry bed once a year and a chance to be treated like a human being again.'

Camilla was filled with admiration; she'd learnt that the charity provided a soup kitchen in London and a women and children's shelter local to her. She was determined to help out more often. She saw Jess hanging around Ged quite a bit and could see that she was completely in love with him. She wondered if he knew. She figured he would be a hard one to pin down as he was such a free spirit. She really liked that about him. He exuded an energy that seemed inextinguishable. Even though he'd been through a hard time he didn't have an ounce of self-pity.

She decided then and there that she would not be the victim anymore. If there was something that she could change to improve a situation she would do but if not she would learn to accept it and move on. She would be forever grateful to Ged for enlightening her to this situation. These people were to be admired for the challenges they had faced and conquered, and the fact that they wanted to pay it back was admirable.

As they parted later at the car park, she felt her emotions getting the better of her and planted a big kiss on his lips. His eyes widened and looked deep into hers but then they were interrupted by Jess who was calling for him to help her with something.

'I'm so sorry, Ged, I don't know what just came over me, I guess it's been an emotional day. Heat radiated from her face; she was sure she could give the Santa a run for his money in the rosy-cheeked stakes.

Ged squeezed her hand. 'No problem. Thanks for coming and merry Christmas.' He saluted to her then followed Jess back into the hall.

When she got home, Camilla relayed the whole day – apart from the kiss – to Carrie and Jim over a couple of brandies and when she went to bed, she fell into a deep and contented sleep.

Chapter 18

Flicking through the local newspaper over an early breakfast, Camilla noticed a delightful cottage available for rent in Flowerpot Lane; she circled it in thick black pen, tore it out of the paper and slipped it into her coat pocket. She would transfer the number to her phone later. Her cupcakes were in such high demand that she was having to go to the Signal Box Café as soon as breakfast was over and then stay until the evening rush, by which time they almost wouldn't know she had been there. That is of course apart from the delicious tell-tale smell of vanilla and chocolate that mingled in the air, along with the Signal Box specials of the day, which cooked in industrial-sized slow cookers.

At four o'clock she had loaded her wares into the cupcake van and began her deliveries. Once she had finished, she was able to call the estate agent and arrange for a viewing. Her heart raced with excitement as she made her way around there, past The Unicorn pub, which she was glad to see again as she almost believed that she'd dreamt it.

It would have been easy to imagine that she had been transported into the middle of the countryside, such was the rural feel of the leafy lane. Large, thatched cottages with extremely well kempt gardens lined the edges. After a little while the lane narrowed to allow only one car at a time and then she saw three cottages in a horseshoe shape. To the left was Angel Cottage, to the right Rose Cottage and straight ahead was the cottage with no name. It was painted white with black oak beams. The leaded windows were filthy and unlike its two pristine neighbours the garden was a tangled mess with some weeds reaching to her waist, but she didn't care about that because the flutters in her stomach assured her that she had fallen in love at first sight.

Relieved to be wearing jeans she tried to negotiate where once a path had been. Paint peeled off the unloved wooden front door and the window ledges, and she could see the remnants of a house martin nest in the eaves. She knocked on the heavy brass knocker though she was doubtful if anyone would answer as the place looked deserted. After waiting a little while she peered through the windows, wiping at the dirt with a tissue, then she heard voices coming from the garden. She went to the back gate, which had the same dried-up paint peeling off it and knocked on the wood.

'Hello,' she shouted.

The voices got nearer, and she could hear the bolt unlocking and a man and woman came out. The woman offered her hand and introduced herself.

'Hi, I'm Janet Ashcroft from Ashcroft and Barnes Estate Agent. You must be Miss Lockley. I'm so sorry but the previous appointment ran over a little and Mr Daniels has just agreed to take on the cottage I'm afraid so it's no longer available.'

Camilla's hand went limp in hers as she stood open-mouthed looking at Blake in disbelief.

He leaned and kissed her lightly on the cheek. 'Cami, hi, how are you? I didn't realise you were looking for somewhere to live?'

Her hand instinctively reached to touch the place where his lips had been. The skin tingled; his aftershave lingered in the air around her and she breathed it in.

'Well yes I am, or should I say was. I thought it would be perfect for me. I didn't realise you were moving back here,' she replied.

'I would love to move back here for good but at the moment I'm trying to build up a property portfolio so that I have something to support me. My company has been offered a takeover bid, which I'd be a fool to turn down, especially as they want me to stay on as a consultant to help them expand in the UK, which I could do from anywhere in the world. But I just need a base for now, so I don't have to keep staying in hotels.'

She replied quickly before her words got tangled up and she made a fool of herself. 'That sounds lovely. Good luck with that.' She held up the keys to the cupcake van. 'Oh well, I suppose I might as well go home. It's getting dark now and it seems like there's no point me looking at the cottage anymore.' She turned to fight her way back down the non-existent path.

'No please come and have a look round.' He turned to Mrs Ashcroft. 'You know I've been thinking, maybe the apartment in Nexton would be better suited for me as it's nearer to the train station and everything. I do need to commute every now and then, and I can get to the airport from that train line.' A look of sheer panic swept across the estate agent's face.

'Oh no, please don't change your plans on my account. I'm sure I'll find somewhere else. I mean who knows, I might hate it inside,' Camilla said.

'You won't – that I can promise you.' He grinned at her.

Intrigued. She returned his smile, noticing that his beard seemed to make his eyes twinkle more than they had before.

'Please allow me to show you around, if that's okay with Mrs Ashcroft?'

Mrs Ashcroft had been checking her phone messages. She looked up when she realised her name had been mentioned. 'Oh yes, would you mind? Only we've had a bit of a situation back at the office. Could you please ensure you lock up and return the key to the office. We're open till eight this evening.'

'Yes, I will do, thank you very much,' he replied as she handed him the bunch of keys.

'Brilliant, thank you, and I'll get started on the paper-work for the apartment if that's definite.'

'Yes, that's absolutely definite.' He gave Camilla a look that sent tingles down her spine. She looked away quickly to hide the flush that had started to creep up from her neck.

Mrs Ashcroft made her way to the side of the house where a couple of cars were parked under a pretty wooden pergola, which peeped out from its covering of ivy. Camilla hadn't noticed it before. She stifled a giggle as she heard the expletives whispered loudly as the woman snagged her tights on the overgrown weeds.

'Oh, what a lovely shelter. It's high enough for me to park my cupcake van in.'

Blake waved to the estate agent as she drove off down the lane. 'Yes apparently the previous owners had a camper van and built the shade due to complaints from a neighbour about it being an eyesore.'

Camilla pretended to gulp. 'Oh dear I hope they're not always so tetchy.'

Blake smiled, showing even white teeth. 'You sound like you've already begun to plan on living here. Come on, let's show you inside.'

He opened the heavy black door, which led straight into a tiny living room. Apart from dust and a few cobwebs it was pretty much habitable. The large mantelpiece provided the focal point of the room. Logs were stacked neatly either side of the open fire. The floor was laid with original earthenware tiles and the walls painted white. Camilla could imagine a couple of colourful throws draped over the battered brown leather couch and armchair, accompanied by a new rug and cushions to brighten the place up and provide a more feminine touch to the room.

Thick open beams separated the room from a small quaint kitchen with a large white Belfast sink under a leaded window that looked out into the side of the garden. Wooden worktops adorned a range of cupboards that cleverly disguised the fridge, freezer and washer-dryer. A cream-coloured range cooker stood proudly against the far wall. Beyond the kitchen was an addition to the house of a large orangery, the walls of which were painted a light dove grey. A heavy oak dining table and four chairs stood to the left, large patio doors led out to the garden.

Camilla gasped when she saw it. 'Oh wow I didn't expect that. What a lovely surprise.'

'Isn't it just,' replied Blake, 'I knew you'd love it.' he laughed.

'It's so lovely, and just looking at it my mind is whirring with possibilities as there would be plenty of room here to bake and assemble my cakes. I didn't think I would be able to when I saw the tiny kitchen but this is just amazing – and look at that view.'

Blake's phone rang, ''Sorry it's my sister, I won't be a minute.' he handed her the bunch of keys. She walked across to the French doors, which opened out onto a small patio area with a round café table and four chairs. An abundance of colourful plants burst from pots. They were obviously low maintenance as they just needed a little tidy-up. The grass on the lawn was overgrown but that looked easy enough to resolve, not like the front garden, which was a tangle of weeds and a daunting prospect. The small garden was surrounded by a tall fence; some of the panels had trellises on them with ivy growing up. A small rickety shed stood at the bottom of the garden. Camilla smiled as her heart swelled with delight. She could be so happy here. She imagined sitting on the garden chair, reading a book and sipping a nice glass of Malbec whilst her cakes cooled in the kitchen.

Blake joined her in the garden and interrupted her thoughts: 'So where do you bake at the moment?'

His voice startled her out of the blue. She still couldn't get used to hearing it after all those years. She gave herself a virtual hug as she thought of what might have been. They could have been living here together, maybe even have a couple of little ones by now. But that obviously wasn't meant to be. She wondered if he still felt the same as she belatedly answered him.

'Sorry. I've been working at my friend's place. It's called the Signal Box Café. Have you heard of it?'

'Oh yes, I've noticed it as I've been driving through the town. Last week I got the train into London for a meeting and bought a delicious bacon and sausage roll from there. Are you not happy working there?'

'I've loved working there but it was only ever a temporary measure until I found somewhere else. Shall we look upstairs?'

'Yes of course, but just before we do there's something I want to show you.'

Her eyes met his and she felt slight trepidation at what it could be.

'Don't look so worried. Here, come this way.' He took her hand and led her to the bottom of the garden. 'As soon as I saw this I immediately thought of you.' He covered her eyes with his hands.

'What are you doing?' She laughed, placing her hands over his. A ripple of desire shot through her body and took her breath away.

'Keep your eyes closed,' he said. She felt him remove one of his hands and heard the latch of a gate that must have been hidden in the fence as she hadn't noticed it.

'Now what can you hear?' he asked, pausing to allow her to listen.

'Is that what I think it is?' she asked as the gentle sound of trickling water filled the air.

'It sure is,' he replied as he removed his hands, reluctantly as if he'd enjoyed touching her again. 'It's your very own babbling brook; I remembered how much you'd always wanted one.'

Camilla realised she was standing in a small clearing under a large willow tree. She gazed in awe at the small stream that wound through the rocks and created the sound she'd loved ever since she was a child and her mum had taken her to Wales for a holiday. Her mum had called it a babbling brook and she'd vowed right then aged six and a half that she wanted one in her garden when she grew up and got married. She blushed at the intimacy that this revelation showed they'd shared. He knew everything about her and she about him. She used to anyway.

'I can't believe you remembered that after all those years.' Her voice was soft.

'I remember everything about you. You're a very hard woman to forget.'

She blushed and he smiled and looked away. 'You could put a nice little chair out here or even just a blanket and some cushions and you can read and relax,' he said, breaking into her thoughts.

It's like he can see inside my mind, she thought.

'I love it. Thank you for showing it to me. It really is a dream come true.'

'Would you like to look upstairs?'

'Yes I'd love too.'

'Okay, I'll just lock up here. After you!' He stood back to allow her to pass through and locked the door.

'So how is Lottie?' she asked, 'it must have hit her hard losing your parents like that.'

'She's good thank you, and yes it did. She went through a really rough time which affected her schooling. I mean she was fifteen when we lost dad and almost eighteen when Mom passed. It's been tough but she's settled now, just moved in with her boyfriend and still crazy about animals. She works in a vet's which is her dream come true.'

'Ah that's lovely, she was always such a shy young girl.'

Blake laughed, 'She is the exact opposite of shy now, she's so confident and fearless.'

'Well I'm glad she's happy.'

She made her way back to the living room and climbed the stairs. She felt self-conscious as he was close behind her. She was sure her bum was a lot bigger now than when she had last seen him and she hoped he wasn't looking at it. The thought of it made her want to giggle but she tried her hardest not to. There were two bedrooms upstairs, which were reasonable sizes, and a small bathroom.

The main bedroom looked out to the front of the house and her eyes opened wide as she noticed the focal point of the room.

'I've always wanted a window seat.' She skipped over to it, patted off the layer of dust and sank into the luxurious deep pink cushions that were fitted on the top of the seat and also on the sides of the walls surrounding the bay window. She couldn't see much outside because the dark nights were drawing in.'

'I can just imagine lazy Sunday mornings snuggled up here, reading or simply watching the clouds gently blow across the sky. This house makes me feel so content, like I'm really coming home at last, I haven't felt like that since moving out of my mum's place.'

Her excitement was contagious. Blake sat on the other side of the window seat and laughed affectionately.

'Remember when we moved into that old basement flat with the coal fire?'

'How could I forget, I nearly died when I opened the door to the coal shed and found the little old lady from next door in there with a bucket stealing our coal.' She giggled.

'Didn't she steal a couple of your bras from the washing line as well once or twice?'

'I'd forgotten about that.' She chuckled.

'It was a shame though, she didn't really have anyone did she? You used to leave her food parcels outside her door. You've always been a kind person.'

'Aw thanks. It's funny though how dank and awful that little flat was we were so excited because it was our first home together yet looking back it was so shabby.'

'It was but we didn't see any of that did we? We only had eyes for each other.'

Her heart missed a beat at his familiarity, his brown eyes were working their magic on her, she blushed as pink as the velvet on the seat. 'That's true, we did.'

'I take it you'll definitely want to move in then?' he asked.

'As soon as I possibly can,' she replied snuggling further into the seat. The estate agent had turned the heating on so the cold wouldn't put off potential tenants, and Camilla felt as though she could sleep very well exactly where she was.

'Are you sure you're happy to rent it? I assumed you'd want to buy somewhere, only I noticed your mum's house was sold.'

She jumped up abruptly from the cosiness of the window seat. Her stomach sank as though she'd swallowed a bucketload of pebbles. Some of the pebbles felt stuck in her throat and she couldn't speak.

Blake had been looking inside the fitted wardrobe but turned round to her when she didn't answer him. He closed the door and she could see his reflection in the mirror. He was devastatingly handsome, dangerously so. He took her breath away. She wondered if she were in a dream where the past ten years hadn't happened, and they were together and her mum was still around. But that was just wishful thinking.

'I'm sorry, I didn't mean to mention your mum. I know how raw the pain must be still.' He crossed the room and pulled her into his strong arms; she allowed her head to rest on his chest for just a second and then pulled herself away. He wasn't hers anymore. The position to be hugged by him had been filled a long time ago.

'Don't worry, I'm fine. It's just a very long story about the house, but suffice to say it doesn't belong to me anymore.'

Blake looked puzzled, but she didn't want to delve into it all and hoped he wouldn't push the matter. 'I need to go,' she said and left the room.

He followed her down the stairs. She was in a hurry to go but he looked as if he didn't want his time with her to end.

'So when can I move in?' she asked as he locked the door behind them.

'I'm not sure but I seem to remember the ad saying immediate occupancy available,' he replied.

'Oh hold on, I have it here.' She delved into her pocket and pulled out the piece of paper. 'Ah yes here we go: immediate occupancy.'

'Great, well I guess that means you just need to let Mrs Ashcroft know.'

She smiled and couldn't help watching his face as he spoke; he looked so grown up now. He'd been a boy when they'd been together all those years ago, from late teens to mid-twenties. The beard suited him; it made him look more rugged and handsome although she couldn't help wondering what he looked like without it. He bent down and she realised he was picking something up off the floor. It was the note he'd left for her at Edie's house. It must have fallen out of her pocket. His eyes looked sad when he realised what it was and he screwed it up into a ball.

'Why didn't you call me?' he asked with such tenderness that she felt she would break in two.

'I'm sorry.' Her cheeks were pink. 'I meant to but then I thought she probably wouldn't like it.'

'Who wouldn't like it?' He genuinely looked confused.

The light from the streetlamp wasn't very strong and she fought her way through the weeds and shrubbery in her haste to get away from the embarrassment of the situation. As she almost got to the path she tripped and shrieked as a piece of something spiky wrapped itself around her foot. He jolted forward and managed to catch her in his arms before she came to any harm. Feeling absolutely mortified she regained her footing as he stamped the offending flora away from its grip on her. She looked up into his eyes, which twinkled with the streetlamp.

'I mean your wife of course.' She pushed his arms off her and made her way to the cupcake van. Pressing her remote she heard two satisfying beeps and the indicators flashed. She would soon be away from him.

Her heart was beating rapidly. She didn't want him to know what he was stirring up inside her. He had someone new and she had spent so long trying to recover and get over that lost love, or – as Edie called him – the one that got away. It was easier to cope with that loss when he was out of sight but now he was standing here in front of her, living and breathing. Exactly the same in some ways but completely different in others. He was a man now, a strong handsome man who once belonged to her and now belonged to someone else.

She opened her van and tried to get in but hesitated as he called her name softly. She was torn apart all those years ago by her love for him and her love for her mother. She knew that as painful as it had been, they had both done the right thing when they'd parted, even though their hearts had been so badly broken.

'I'm divorced,' he said, his hands holding on to both sides of her face. 'We split up a couple of years ago; there is no wife.'

'But you're wearing a ring,' she managed to stammer. 'I was going to call you but then I saw your ring and didn't think it fair to meet up with you if you had a wife.'

He sighed with realisation and, shaking his head from side to side, he lifted his left hand up to show her. 'That's my dad's ring; I've worn it since the day he died. Admittedly it used to be on my other hand but when I got married we thought we were all so hip and trendy so we decided not to have rings; we got these instead.' He lifted the ring up to show her a faded tattoo underneath of a Celtic band and the date of the wedding.

Camilla chuckled. She couldn't quite believe what he was saying. 'But you've always hated tattoos.'

'Exactly but without you I became a different person. I didn't care about much. I'll be honest I felt a bit trapped in the situation with Dad's business and especially being without you. That hurt like hell.'

'I know, I felt it too. That's why I don't understand why you broke off all contact with me. It was far too painful. Then a few years later I heard you'd got married to someone from England and I knew that was it. I really didn't think I'd ever see you again.' Her stomach churned remembering the bitterness she'd felt at that time.

'I'm so sorry. There are no words to describe how awful I feel about that. I haven't forgiven myself so there's no way I could ever expect you to forgive me. Everyone seemed to want a piece of me. I was pulled in so many different directions. I had to make very tough decisions. Letting go of you was the hardest thing I've ever done. I hated myself for a long time. It was just that—'

He looked down. His hand smoothed down his beard, before his eyes met hers again, imploringly. She could see pain in his eyes and whilst wanting to relieve him of that she needed to know why he'd called it off and why so cruelly without a word, just a returned unopened letter.

'Look, I don't like talking about those times; it was hard and I'm sorry. But do you think we can move on from it? It was so devastating for both of us. Can we try and forget it and pretend we've just met? Please.'

Her stomach, which was twisted up in knots just thinking back to that time, unclenched. She took a deep breath and nodded. Although she was desperate to know what had happened, she understood that it wasn't healthy to harbour bitterness and resentment. It really had been a no-win situation for both of them. She had got over it eventually but meeting him again had churned up all of those feelings and emotions that had caused her physical pain. She released them as she exhaled, allowing them to break down into little atoms and circulate in the air and release her from their hold.

'Okay,' she answered. 'I'll try.' He smiled at her and her heart sang with joy. She held her hand out to him.' My name's Camilla. How do you do?'

'It's lovely to meet you. My name's Blake.' He took her hand and kissed it softly without breaking eye contact with her. His touch sent tingles rushing through her body.

'So, Blake, is it true that you're not married anymore?'

'I'm really not and what's more I'm getting this tattoo removed, so there will eventually be no trace of it ever having happened. What about you? Was that your boyfriend the other day at the farmers' market?'

Her eyes were glued to his mouth as he spoke. She imagined his lips kissing hers but knew that would be like drinking from a poisoned chalice. The taste would be delicious and all-consuming but the consequences would be dire. She would be handing over the weapon of power that could crush her fragile heart once more and she knew she couldn't take that risk. She had to protect herself.

'Who Ged? No he's not my boyfriend. We're just friends. I've not long broken up with someone. After losing my mum my head was a mess and I couldn't cope with a relationship. Still can't if I'm honest.'

He looked down. 'I'm not surprised. It's all still so fresh for you and actually I have been—' He was interrupted by a bright light shining on them. Camilla realised it was the headlights of the estate agent's car.

'Oh hi. I've just come to collect the keys as you didn't drop them in. Is everything to your satisfaction?'

'Yes, thank you, I'll take it,' said Camilla.

'That's brilliant news,' she said, no doubt rubbing her hands together in glee, now that she'd managed to rent out two properties. 'Why don't you pop into the office in the morning and we can sort out the paperwork.'

They agreed a time, she collected the keys and left them to it.

Camilla shivered. 'Thanks for, you know, not taking the house so that I could have it.'

'Not at all. I didn't want you getting your hands on my super-cool bachelor pad in Nexton. Besides what would I do with a window seat and a babbling brook? They'd be wasted on me. You deserve something lovely.'

'I do appreciate it. Anyway I'd better get back.'

'Can we meet up again soon? Maybe for a coffee. I'd love to catch up properly,' he asked.

'Yes, I'd like that. Can I have your number back and I'll text you mine?'

He smiled and dug the screwed-up piece of paper out of his pocket. She took it from him, her eyes not able to meet his for fear of blushing furiously. She could hardly admit that she knew it off by heart. That would be far too embarrassing.

'It'll be a while before I call, as I have some business to sort out in Germany first.'

He hugged her and kissed her on the forehead then shut the door of the van as she put her seatbelt on. She tried to hide her disappointment; she had hoped she wouldn't have to wait. She waved to him and drove off. A shiver of delight swept through her body as she remembered how close they'd just been. It didn't seem real. Her heart was beating to its own rhythm, although a knot of fear twisted in her stomach, fear of being hurt again. She promised herself she would take this slowly and not give herself too quickly to the one man in this world who had the ability to break her heart again.

Chapter 19

Carrie's face was glowing as she looked at the beautiful bouquet that her friend had just presented her with. Pink and lemon roses bloomed alongside violets and chrysanthemums.

'These are so beautiful I can't believe they're made of cakes. If I couldn't smell the delicious hint of lemon in the air, I'd struggle to believe you.'

'They are quite cute aren't they. I've seen them before but never tried to make them. So, I bought some special nozzles and they were such fun to make. I did one for Lucy and one for Gracie too. I'm so thankful to all of you for helping me out at such a difficult time of my life.'

Carrie hugged her and put the kettle on. 'It's been an absolute pleasure having you stay here and you've really helped me out with the cattery. You are welcome here anytime. Now have you got time for a cuppa before you go?'

Camilla looked at her watch and sat down on the barstool in the kitchen. 'Yes, I've got time for a quick one; I'm meeting Blake soon at the cottage as he's borrowed a van to deliver some furniture for me.' She reached down to pick up Marmalade, her favourite of Carrie's cats who had come to say goodbye. The cat snuggled contentedly in her lap and she stroked her silky fur.

Carrie took the teabags out of the jar and popped them into the teapot, then stirred them round whilst pouring in the boiling water. 'That was a stroke of luck, wasn't it, him finding that house clearance,' she said as she put the pot down for the tea to brew.

'Yes, I bought a lovely couch and armchair as the one in the cottage was on its last legs; I also got some soft furnishings too. They were so cheap as the couple were emigrating and so really just wanted to get rid of everything quickly. Blake bought a few bits and pieces for the apartment he's renting too.'

'So, he's planning on sticking around?'

'For a little bit yes. He's looking at buying period properties that he can do up and sell on for when he steps down from the business. He's actually very hands-on.'

'Oh, is he now? Well I suppose you'd know.' Carrie pulled an innocent face as she poured the tea out, causing Camilla to laugh and blush.

'You're terrible, Carrie.' She picked up her tea and blew on it, her face beetroot.

'Well you know me; I love a happy ending. So, when are you getting back together?'

'It's really not like that, Carrie. I mean don't get me wrong he's absolutely gorgeous, but we were so young and stupidly in love and when we split we were both heartbroken. I'm not sure either of us could go through that pain again.'

'Has he asked you out yet?'

'No but he did ask if Ged was my boyfriend and I told him no and that I wasn't ready for a relationship. I mean my head is all over the place. I think I need to be me on my own for a little while. I'm not the same woman that he knew. After all she had a mum and a solid grounding in this world. I feel as though I've had the rug pulled from under my feet and I'm not sure which way to turn.' She hugged the cat tighter to herself. Marmalade miaowed her disgust and jumped down from her lap. 'Oh I'm sorry, Marmalade,' she said as the cat strolled out of the kitchen, her tail sticking straight up in the air.

Carrie sat on the arm of the chair next to her and pulled her into her arms. 'You are doing amazingly well, young lady, and you're going to be fine. Ooh talking of marmalade, here you are, a little housewarming gift from me.' Carrie bent down to a cupboard and retrieved a basket wrapped in cellophane. Inside was a selection of jars of Carrie's home-made jams, marmalades, pickles and chutneys, a biscuit tin and a matching teapot with two china cups and saucers. Camilla clapped her hands in delight.

'Oh wow it's the same as your tin except mine has cupcakes on where yours has cats. I love it,' she cried.

Carrie flushed with pleasure. 'I know how much you loved the style of mine so when I saw the cupcake one I just knew I had to get it for you and you'll never guess what's inside the biscuit tin.' She tapped the side of her nose conspiratorially.

'It's not my favourite Carrie's home-made chocolate chunk shortbread is it?'

'It sure is, honey.' She laughed as Camilla pretended to swoon.

'Thank you so much, Carrie. It's been so lovely living here with you,' Camilla said as she hugged her. Her phone buzzed with a text message from Blake. 'He's at the cottage waiting for me. I'd better go.'

'It's been my pleasure, love, and you are welcome back anytime,' replied Carrie as she hugged her back.

It only took a couple of minutes to walk to the station from the square. Camilla packed her suitcase and a bin bag, which had more of her possessions in, into the cupcake van and made her way round to the cottage. As she bumbled down the lane, she could already see the van parked outside and Blake and Tony, one of his contractors, were carrying the heavy stuff out of it. She could hardly contain the smile that threatened to take over her whole face as she parked up under the pergola and retrieved her things from the van. Was she really moving into her perfect house? And was a gorgeous man helping to unpack her furniture? Her life was certainly changing for the better. But it all seemed too good to be true.

The front garden was not as bad as it had been, as Camilla had been busy. She'd hired some machinery and Carrie's husband Jim had helped her to chop most of the weeds down to a decent level. It still needed digging over properly but they could get access with the furniture, which was the priority for now. The landlord had offered to cover the gardening but the rent would have been considerably more so she opted to do it herself and was looking forward to the challenge.

When Blake saw her approaching the cottage from the side he shouted for her to stop in her tracks. 'Just wait there for one minute,' he said. 'In fact close your eyes.'

'Again.' She laughed. 'What for? You couldn't possibly beat a babbling brook surely?'

'I'll show you in a second; just make sure you don't look at anything for one minute.' He held his hand up with his index finger indicating that she should stay where she was. His eyes were twinkling as they used to whenever he surprised her in the past. Smiling to herself she did as she was told and looked down at the suitcase in her hand and fiddled nervously with the handle. Blake had gone into the cottage with Tony and put the new couch down in the living room. As promised he was back out in a minute.

He stood behind her and covered her eyes with his hands then walked her a few steps to the front door.

'You're not peeking are you?' he teased.

'No, I'm not. I'm very intrigued though,' she said.

'Okay then here we go.' He removed his hands from her eyes and the first thing she saw was a sign next to the freshly painted front door. Her hand flew to her mouth in surprise. His eyes twinkled to see her so touched by his gesture.

She stroked the letters of the engraving and traced the words as she said them out loud.

'Cupcake Cottage – that's so perfect; in fact—' she took a few steps back so she could look up to the roof '—the cottage almost looks like a giant cupcake with its thatched roof with a chimney for a cherry on top. Thank you so much. It's delightful.'

'Well we couldn't have you being the poor relation could we? The other cottages have names and so I thought that suited quite well. I'm so glad you liked it.'

'I absolutely love it,' she said, smiling inwardly as she noticed a slight blush to his cheeks. 'It feels as though everything is falling into place finally.'

She kissed him on the cheek; his beard softly tickled her chin, causing fireworks to go off inside her. It was now her turn to blush.

Camilla walked into the living room and felt quite over-whelmed. The jade velvet two-seater settee looked perfect in the bay window and the matching armchair and foot-stool went in the corner with its back to the open beams. Blake had lit the fire for her as it was quite frosty outside. A fluffy and sparkly patterned rug lay in the centre of the room underneath the oak coffee table, which matched a new small bookshelf.

'Blake, I thought that bookcase was yours for the apartment,' she shouted to him as he and Tony lifted the shabby old sofa back in the van.

He shook his head. 'No I remembered how much you loved to read so thought it would be perfect for you.'

'Thank you, that's so lovely of you.' She was taken aback by such a thoughtful gesture.

Her mind drifted to a memory – the first Valentine's Day after they'd moved in together. She'd come home from work aching all over and found rose petals leading to a hot scented bubble bath surrounded by candles. She stepped into it and felt the weariness slip away from her muscles as she relaxed. He brought her a glass of rosé and a box of her favourite chocolates. New pyjamas and cute fluffy slippers were warming on the radiator. After a long soak she put them on and went into the bedroom. On the bed was an envelope, which contained a clue.

She'd told Blake once that she loved treasure hunts, as her mum did them when she was little. Each of his clues led to a beautifully wrapped book: contemporary romantic novels by her favourite authors, as well as *Romeo and Juliet* – her favourite play, classics including *Jane Eyre* and Elizabeth Barrett Browning – her favourite poet. The idea for each book had evolved from snippets of conversations that they'd had over the years. The treasure hunt culminated in a delicious meal for two, which he'd had delivered as cooking was never his strong point.

She laughed as she remembered he told her he was going to call it a book hunt but thought better of it as it sounded like a profanity. She snapped out of her daydream and ran upstairs to one of the boxes that she'd stored at Auntie Edie's house. After three trips up and down the stairs, her arms laden, she filled the empty bookshelf.

She'd placed the poetry book on her bedside table. She'd forgotten how much she loved to read; her mind hadn't been able to settle on anything lately but hopefully with this reminder she could get back into it. Her heart felt lighter at the thought.

When she was losing her mum, she was aghast at not being able to find words strong enough to describe the depth of feeling she had for her. 'I love you so much,' or 'I love you more than words can say,' just didn't seem to cut it. When she opened the book by Elizabeth Barrett Browning just now she had found a sonnet describing that love perfectly. She wished for a moment that she'd read it out at the funeral but then realised that this way it was just for her. Maybe it was a sign from her mum delivered through Blake. Whether it was or not didn't really matter because it brought her comfort and that's what was important right now.

She put the kettle on and went out to ask the men if they'd like a coffee. They put their order in and Blake followed her back into the house, carrying two stripy deck chairs.

'What's this?' she asked.

'The people we bought the furniture from didn't want them so I thought you might like them for over there. He gestured towards the patio doors in the orangery. 'Just until you get some decent ones to sit on. He unfolded them and set them next to each other, facing the view of the garden. She smiled at how amusing but very relaxing they looked there.

She opened a bag that contained three fluffy and sparkly cream-coloured cushions with teal, beige and dark green patterns on them, which matched the rug perfectly, and she placed them on the couch and the armchair. It was starting to look like home.

She made coffee for the men and then went upstairs to check out her bedroom. She unpacked her clothes and found the picture she loved of her and her mum. She stroked her mum's face but still couldn't bear to look too deeply into her eyes as it hurt so much. It felt as though someone had reached into her chest, snatched her heart out and squeezed it until there was not one drop of blood left in it. She clutched the picture to herself tightly. It was undoubtedly the most important possession she had. She ran down the stairs and into the kitchen where Blake and Tony were drinking their coffee. She spotted Blake's toolbox on the floor.

'Have you got a hammer I can borrow please?' Blake glanced at the back of the picture in her arms and she could see from his caring expression that he'd guessed why she wanted to put it up as a matter of priority, even though so many other things needed doing. He opened the lid and gave her the hammer. She took it from him and he stroked her hand gently with his thumb.

'Are you okay?' he asked.

She nodded, her mouth set in a straight line. She went to the living room and hung the picture where she could see it both as soon as she walked into the house and from her new couch. She leaned against the opposite wall with her arms folded and had a comforting sense of satisfaction at the perfect positioning. She felt a warm glow in her chest as though her mum was with her and happy for her.

'Right these are the last of the boxes that we picked up from Edie's house,' said Blake as he carried them into the kitchen, 'Where would you like them?'

Her stomach sank on seeing them, they were her bits and pieces from her mum's house, she didn't feel ready to go through them yet.

'Oh can you just put them in here please,' she opened the large cupboard door and Blake put the boxes on the floor.

'Are you okay,' he asked, his eyes full of kindness. He stroked her arm gently and she was surprised she couldn't hear the crackles of electricity as his skin touched hers. She could feel goosebumps standing to attention.

'I'm fine thanks, it's just that they're from my mum's house.'

'I see well if you ever want me to go through them with you I will, just give me a call anytime.'

'Thanks, I will.' She replied, knowing that she wouldn't, she felt that this was something she would need to do alone, just her and her thoughts.

She soon thanked and waved to Tony as Blake gave him a lift home in the van. It felt good to have the place all to herself. The house creaked in various places as if to say "welcome home" to her. She wandered around the rooms to get a feel of the place; its convivial warmth seeped into her bones.

Whilst waiting for Blake to return, she spent the time fussing around with the cushions, plumping them and rearranging them until they looked simply perfect and homely.

Chapter 20

Awakening to the sound of birdsong, Camilla took a second or two to remember where she was. It was such a contrast to the noises she heard in the B&B – the sounds from the market setting up on the square every Monday, other guests moving around their rooms, doors slamming – and that delicious smell of bacon and sausages cooking, which would creep under her door every morning. She had loved staying there with Carrie as that was the place she'd been when her friends had helped to put her back together again. She felt so much stronger but knew that the emotion was still raw and near the surface.

She bounced down to the kitchen to make a cup of coffee and poured some cereal into a bowl. She went to the fridge to get the milk and laughed at herself as she opened the freezer door by accident; she would get used to the place soon enough. She poured the milk onto her cereal and in her coffee cup and carried them upstairs. Lucy had bought her a darling foldaway TV stand, which was basically a tray with legs, and she had set it up next to the window seat. She placed her mug and bowl on the tray, which was covered in little cupcake images and matched the gifts from Carrie perfectly. They must have gone shopping together, she thought, along with Gracie who had bought her oven gloves and tea towels in the same design. She was blessed to have such kind and thoughtful friends.

She snuggled into the window seat and gazed out into the picturesque scene in front of her. The day was frosty but the sky was mostly blue; it was a perfect day. She gobbled up her cereal and as no one was looking, she drank the excess milk straight from the bowl, wrapped herself up with a throw and picked up her coffee. Her mind fluttered back to last night, sitting in the deck chairs with Blake, eating fish and chips out of the paper and drinking beer. She'd offered to treat him to dinner as a thank you for helping her to move in and he'd chosen the menu. He was on his way back to Canada now. He'd said he would be backwards and forwards a lot as he was working on the future expansion of the business.

'Edie told me what happened with your mom's house. If there's anything I can do then let me know. I have a kick-ass solicitor who might be able to help.'

She stared at the dreary sky through the window as she recalled the worst time of her life. 'Everybody gave me advice at the time and even the solicitors were annoyed for me but there was nothing that I, or they, could do and even if there was I was grieving for my mum. I couldn't have fought my way out of a paper bag.'

'I wish I'd been here for you.'

'Me too,' she replied. 'Anyway, I later found out that because there was no will, he registered her death as intestate and that meant that everything went to him. I wrote to him asking for sentimental items and he said unless I had a receipt then I was getting nothing.'

'But this was your mum's house; she worked all of her life to pay for it and to raise you. Did he contribute anything to it?' His hands were forming into fists.

'Not a thing, apart from a bit of rent from when he was a lodger, but my mum always said he ate more than he paid in rent.'

Camilla stood up to throw away the chip shop papers and to put the kettle on. 'Anyway, Auntie Edie always said to me he'll get what's coming to him.'

'I know what I'd like to give him,' said Blake, nodding to her as she held up the coffee jar to him.

'He's not worth it. I couldn't believe he'd abused my mum's trust so badly. That's what breaks my heart the most – not the house or the money but the fact that he has denied her lifelong wish to leave me an inheritance. I actually hate him. To be truthful I never did like him that much anyway, but I did think he would be companionship for my mum at the time and she seemed happy enough.'

Blake admitted that he didn't have any words to help make this better; he just pulled her into his arms and let her talk. She could feel his heart beating like a jackhammer as he listened to the infuriating story.

'Auntie Edie has been my rock. She hated him too after what he'd done. She was so worried when she saw the sold sign going up at the house; she knew I wouldn't have sold it. Also, she was there when he promised me that he would fulfil my mum's wishes, but he put the final nail in the coffin when he transferred the house into his name. Legally of course he was entitled to do that but morally it was completely the wrong thing to do. I know he destroyed her will. The next-door neighbour found burnt bits of documents blown into their garden but none of this is tangible proof I've been told.'

She felt a little uneasy being in his arms as the reality of their situation burst the bubble they'd been hiding in and so she wriggled out of his embrace to finish her coffee. She took a couple of salted caramel cupcakes out of a tin, put them on a plate and carried everything into the living room. 'Come on, let's go somewhere more comfortable,' she said, before continuing.

'I'd been away for a couple of days on a trip I'd won and by the time I got to the house everything was gone. There had been a removal van, a skip and a charity van and between them they'd emptied my mum's house. I thank God that Edie managed to rescue that picture of me and mum from the skip as it was the only copy of it and it's of one of our happiest times together.' As she spoke she nodded to the picture she'd hung on the wall.

'What if he died?' he asked between mouthfuls of coffee and cake. 'You must surely have rights then as his stepdaughter.'

'You would think so wouldn't you? But no, stepchildren don't have any rights. I've looked into everything and spoken to so many solicitors that I reckon I actually could be a solicitor myself. All were very sympathetic but all were of the same opinion: that I don't have a leg to stand on. It's cost me . . . well more or less everything in legal fees, which is how I became homeless.' She took a sip of coffee and leaned back to look at him. 'Why? You're not thinking of doing him in are you?' She chuckled.

'No of course not but I certainly wouldn't shed any tears over the baldy bastard. Why did he do all this?' Blake was shaking his head.

Camilla laughed again. 'That's exactly what Auntie Edie calls him. I personally think it was just one huge power trip. He had achieved nothing in life, couldn't hold down a job or a relationship. He was with my mum for just a few years and I don't know why she felt the need to marry him. Suddenly he's her next of kin and got everything, including her house.'

'Let me talk to my solicitors.'

'I do appreciate you wanting to help but I think for my own sanity I need to move on. Greed is a horrible thing and it really brings out the worst in people. I'm doing okay now; I need to admit defeat. My friend's husband Dom is a solicitor and he looked into the solicitor who this guy used to sell the house and sort out the probate and apparently he's not the most scrupulous.'

She took a sip of her coffee and watched his broad back move as he threw logs onto the fire and began to light them. She wished she could stroke it and feel the warmth of his body against hers again but he was strictly out of bounds. He looked around at her. She reddened at nearly being caught ogling him, as if what she was thinking had been written across her face.

'I think he had a grudge against me because he once overheard me asking my mum if she was sure she wanted to get married. I was about to move in with my boyfriend at the time and I offered to stay home if she was just looking for companionship but she said she was fine. As I said she felt sorry for him in some sort of weird way but I don't believe she ever loved him.'

'I'm sorry you had to go through all of this, Cami, and I'm sorry for reminding you of it. I promise I'll never mention it again. But I don't think you should look at it as you being defeated. You're a strong woman and you will recover from this and come back even stronger. By the sound of it he's a thief and a liar and a fraudster. You're a lovely person with a big heart. He'll come unstuck one day. Anyway, changing the subject, these cakes aren't going to eat themselves.'

His gorgeous face helped to chase away the physical pain she felt when talking about her mum's house. It felt like someone juggling with daggers in her stomach. She smiled and stood up to go to the kitchen. 'I made them especially for you as a thank you so please help yourself.' He followed her and tucked into one of the cakes.

She bit into one and realised he was looking at her and smiling.

'What?' she asked, wiping her face with a paper towel. 'Have I got buttercream all over my face?'

'No,' he replied. 'I'd almost forgotten how beautiful you are and I'm so glad I got a chance to see you again after all this time. He gently stroked her cheek with the back of his fingers, causing her to close her eyes briefly and inhale deeply.'

'Would it be okay if I contact you next time I'm over?'

'Yes of course,' she said. 'I'd like that.'

Even though they weren't in a relationship her stomach churned when saying goodbye. He kissed her lightly on her cheek, just a fleeting moment like a butterfly's wing. Part of her wanted to hold on to it forever; the other part wondered if it had actually happened. The hug that followed took her breath away it was so unexpected. His strong arms around her rekindled memories of a time when she felt safe and loved. Her face was snuggled into the warmth of his chest; she breathed him in. She could only imagine how devastated she would have been had she become heavily involved with him again and then had to say goodbye to him so soon. Especially as last time he'd left her for Canada it had taken him ten years to come back.

But the chances of that were zero now anyway, as he'd mentioned earlier that he had started seeing someone in Canada. Someone named Dawn who his sister had been trying to set him up with for some time. He'd been about to tell her when they first looked around the cottage but the Estate Agent had turned up and interrupted them.

'It's been so good seeing you again. Thanks for dinner,' he said.

Feeling far too comfortable she broke away first. Like tearing a plaster off quickly, it seemed to get the pain over with. She patted him on the back as she would any male friend.

'Thanks again for helping me move in. It was really kind of you.'

'No problem – anytime.'

Chapter 21

Since moving into Cupcake Cottage, Camilla's feet had hardly touched the ground. She'd got the job in the college teaching cake decoration one evening a week, which was helping her to get back into the swing of things and provided a boost to her savings. The council had approved her premises which had lifted a huge weight off her mind. She had then been able to approach local supermarkets and garden centres, including Flowerpots, with samples of her goods. Her orders were increasing every day, not just for cupcakes but for regular-sized sandwich cakes too. The cupcake bouquets had really taken off as well and were in huge demand. It was as she was delivering one of these in the cupcake van that she saw Ron coming out of a house a couple of doors away.

'Hello, love, how are you? I've got to say it's been such a pleasure seeing and hearing your little cupcake van delivering sweet treats all over the place.'

'Hi, Ron, I wondered whether I would see you today when I saw the address. I really want to thank you as having this van has changed my life completely. You and the girls have done such a great job. I was at rock bottom when you did this for me and now I can hardly remember that girl I was.'

'You look so much better my dear. You've got some colour back in your cheeks now. Anyway I'm glad I bumped into you as I was going to give you a ring but now you've saved me a job.'

Camilla knew what was coming and felt her stomach clench.

'I was wondering if you could dig us out of a massive hole and make that christening cake for me for Sunday? The wife's got all the details. She tried to have a go and she's bawling her eyes out in here. I'll be honest with you, it looks like a bloodbath in our kitchen. She wanted a certain shade of pink and kept adding more and more food colouring until she ended up using the whole bottle and it really doesn't look good. Please just take a look and if you can do it, this time I'll be paying you full whack for it.'

Camilla went to protest but he held his hand up. 'No I insist, we are square now and so any cakes I order will be paid for. Have you got time to pop in now?'

Camilla looked at her watch and realised she could spare fifteen minutes before her next delivery. As soon as she saw the state that Ron's wife was in she knew she would have to help them out. The poor woman had bright red hands and patches of red on her cheeks and as for the cake it really looked like it should have police tape around it. It might take a little practice to get back in the swing of things, but she really needed to help. Ten minutes later she came out of Ron's house filled with tea and biscuits and armed with a rough sketch of what she had to create by Sunday. A fizzle of excitement swept through her veins. It made her feel stronger than before. Even if she had to make ten practice cakes, she felt she owed it to Ron to make a success of this one. She continued her deliveries with renewed vigour.

The look of pure joy on the faces of the people she surprised with cupcake bouquets built up her confidence bit by bit. She needed to push the black cloud of what happened with her mum's house behind her and start to look at the blue sky and sunshine that was her future. Thanks to being surrounded by amazing friends who picked her up when she was down and sheer hard work, of course, she now had a beautiful home, a job she loved and her amazing, cosy little cupcake van. She was surprised how many good things she had going for her.

Like her mum she worked for everything she got, and she wouldn't let parasites like dodgy Rog get her down. She may not have the house her mum had worked all her life to give her. Nor the many sentimental things that were in it, but she had her mother's values and work ethic and not to mention a whole lifetime of amazingly happy memories and you simply couldn't put a price on that. Counselling had helped her to understand that she hadn't allowed herself to grieve properly, therefore when she lost the house it tipped her over the edge and the delayed grief combined with the anger at Roger consumed her like an avalanche. The bitterness she felt at the mere mention of his name left a disgusting taste in her mouth and made her think of despicable swear words that she'd never dream of saying out loud. She knew for her own sanity she had to move on.

She popped into the wholesalers on the way back home as she had a lot of ingredients to buy and lots of catching up to do on making icing figures.

She hadn't quite realised how much the anger had been bubbling just under the surface until she spent all night forcing herself to make this cake. After shouting and throwing numerous attempts at icing figures in the bin, and a couple at the wall in total disgust, Camilla was finally able to deliver the perfect christening cake to the Signal Box

Café, where the christening party was being held. Ron and his wife and daughter Becky gasped as they saw Camilla's creation come out of the box. The cake was made of two white-iced tiers with pale pink garlands piped around the sides and joined at the top by tiny pink bows. Sparkling pastel-coloured blocks surrounded the smaller of the tiers and each block spelt out a letter of the baby's name: Ava Grace. The top of the cake had a perfectly shaped baby, wearing a pink Babygro and holding a teddy. The cake was standing on a pastel-pink-iced board, upon which sat a lemon giraffe and a pink elephant, again made out of icing.

'This is amazing,' said Ron's daughter as the little chubby-cheeked girl in her arms squealed with delight. 'Oh look, Ava, isn't it beautiful and this lovely lady has made it especially for you.'

Camilla tickled the little girl under the chin and waved goodbye. Ron handed her an envelope with the money in and Camilla knew she was really back in business. The events of the previous year had been a nasty blip in her otherwise beautiful life. The only other thing she could wish for was that her mum could still be around but that was futile. Yet she couldn't help but feel that her mum was around her anyway and that gave her a comforting warm glow as though a candle was shining in her heart and warming her up from the inside out.

She had lost her mum and would grieve for the rest of her life. Her Auntie Edie had told her that she would never get over the loss of someone so precious in her life but that she would eventually learn to live with it. She knew that the grief was still hiding in the deep dark recesses of her mind and heart and tried not to delve too deeply because she knew that down there lay despair. She seemed to be treading a thin line and had been teetering about on the ledge of that precipice ever since she lost the precious woman who had given her life.

Thankfully her friends and her auntie were holding her hands as she tentatively stepped down from the blackness to join them. She could feel their strength pushing her forward and like a mother with a baby taking its first steps, their arms were outstretched, surrounding her, ready to catch her if she should fall. Their strength was starting to course through her blood; their belief in her was firming up her self-confidence, making her feel solid again, more grounded and ready to take on the world once more.

Chapter 22

The sound of knocking on her very own front door still sent a quiver of excitement through Camilla; she opened it to see Lucy and Carrie standing on the front step with huge smiles on their faces.

'Ah if it isn't the ladies who lunch,' she said as she opened the door wider and gestured for them to come in, hugging and kissing them each in turn.

'Well we are today anyway,' replied Carrie. 'What a lovely idea to sneak away from our normal daily rituals for a spot of lunch. I could certainly get used to this.' She handed Camilla a bottle of prosecco and a bunch of sweet-smelling freesias, took off her coat and hung it on one of the hooks to the side of the front door.

'Me too,' said Lucy kicking off her shoes and hanging her coat up next to Carrie's. 'It's been ages since I've given myself the afternoon off.' She retrieved a bag from the floor and handed it to Camilla.

'Ooh thank you,' said Camilla, her eyes lighting up as she saw the bottle and a luxurious box of chocolates. 'So which one shall we have first — the pink or the white?' She held up both bottles and waved them up and down.

'Don't mind,' they said in unison.

'In that case I suggest we go for white then pink as I've got another bottle of pink in the fridge.' They exchanged mischievous glances.

'Looks like we're here for the night then, ladies.' Carrie laughed.

'Oh goody, so you're not driving then. Did you get dropped off?' Camilla spoke to them from the kitchen. Through the open beams they could see her put the bottle in the fridge and take out three glasses from the cupboard.

'No we walked. It only took us just over half an hour and the weather was lovely and mild,' Carrie replied as she couldn't resist stroking one of the fluffy cushions on the couch.

'Dom is picking us up later and Jackson is having a sleepover at a friend's straight from school so I'm free,' said Lucy as her eyes danced around the room. 'I love what you've done with the place; it's beautiful.'

'Thank you. It was lucky that Blake found this furniture going cheap for a quick sale or I never would have been able to afford it all.'

'So, talking of Blake,' said Carrie as she followed Lucy into the kitchen, 'when do we finally get to meet him?' She helped herself to a crisp from the bowl on the worktop. Lucy was waiting eagerly for an answer too.

'I'm not sure you will as he's back in Canada,' Camilla replied, trying her best not to think of him with someone else even though it was none of her business. She opened the bottle of prosecco and they cheered and tried to hold their hands steady as she poured it into the glasses they were holding.

'Cheers,' they said as they clinked their glasses together.

Camilla led the way to the orangery and her two friends oohed and aahed at how pretty the table looked.

'I love the candles and they smell divine,' said Lucy.

'Thank you. These are pomegranate ones I bought from Flowerpots this morning.'

'That's so handy having a garden centre practically on your doorstep. Just a five-minute walk away.' Carrie pulled out a chair and sat at the dining table.

Lucy joined her and Camilla went back into the kitchen to bring the food through, shouting over her shoulder, 'Yes it is handy and there is a lovely hidden pub too. I don't know if you spotted it; it's called The Unicorn.'

'Yes we passed it on the way. It looks lovely and I never even knew it was there,' replied Lucy loudly so Camilla could hear her over the sizzling noises coming from the kitchen. A delicious aroma soon began to waft out into the orangery and was followed by Camilla carrying a tray with three small plates on it. She placed a dish in front of each of them and encouraged them to tuck in. Lucy inhaled the delicious smell before even taking a bite.

'So this is a sort of bruschetta but I basically just make it up as I go along, so you have toasted granary bread brushed with garlic-infused oil and topped with tomatoes and red onion, fried in olive oil then mixed with chopped avocado and sprinkled with grated mozzarella and a pinch of herbs, then drizzled with a balsamic glaze. Enjoy.'

'You sounded just like Nigella then.' Lucy smiled before she cut into the lunch enthusiastically. 'Oh this is delicious. The flavours just burst in your mouth.' She wound a stretchy strand of mozzarella around her fork before popping it into her mouth.' Camilla pouted in her best Nigella impression.

Carrie agreed as she tried to balance a little bit of everything onto her fork to optimise the flavours.

Camilla looked around at her friends and smiled a genuinely huge smile. She raised her glass.

'Here's to special friends. I don't know where I'd be without you all.' She could feel herself glow with happiness.

The others raised their glasses too. 'To special friends.'

'And ladies who lunch once in a blue moon.' Lucy laughed.

'Is Gracie still coming?' asked Carrie as she took her last forkful, her face stretched into a look of ecstasy.

Camilla stood up and began to clear the plates, gesturing to the others to stay seated as they attempted to help her. 'She's really sorry but she couldn't make it for lunch. Apparently little Matty had a musical movement class to go to, but she hopes to pop in for a bit of pud later.'

'It will be good to see her and that scrumptious little boy.' Carrie smiled.

Lucy agreed. 'Ooh he makes me so broody; he's adorable.'

Camilla returned with steaming dishes and placed one in front of each of them. The delicious smell swirled around them.

'If this tastes as good as it smells then I'm moving in,' Lucy said with a laugh.

'It's a veggie lasagne so a bit lighter than a normal lasagne, I thought. I've used aubergines instead of pasta sheets so I hope you like it.'

'My mouth's watering just at the sight of the crispy cheese on top,' said Carrie. She cut into it. Her fork sliced through layers of peppers, onions, aubergine and sweet potato all coated in the creamy sauce and topped with the cheese topping. She nodded at Camilla in appreciation as she chewed.

Camilla smiled at the looks on their faces and the groaning noises they made. They were clearly enjoying it. She topped up their glasses and the bottle ran out as she tried to fill her own glass up.

'That's one down.' She laughed. 'I'll just go and get another.' She soon returned with her own lunch and a fresh bottle. 'Pink this time – wahoo!' She popped the popper to the traditional cheers that follow every bottle of bubbly opening, gulped down the drop of white that was already in her glass and refilled it. Then she was able to tuck into her lunch, which, even if she said so herself, was delicious.

'So come on then tell us more about this Blake of yours,' said Carrie as she picked through her side salad whilst waiting for the delicious lasagne to cool a little.

Camilla reddened. Her heart played hopscotch every time she heard his name; she too was munching on the salad and eating around the edge of the lasagne where it was a little cooler, impatient to get to the good stuff inside.

'He's not my Blake anymore. That was over a long time ago and even if he were free, I really don't think it would work between us. I mean he's lovely but we're two completely different people now. It took me far too long to get over him last time to even contemplate such a thing. He lives in Canada and is only here sporadically at the moment. He does love England and always wanted to live back over here, but he's probably settled there now.'

'Oh, is he with someone then?' Carrie did inverted commas with her fingers at the word "with".

'Yes, he's just started seeing someone called Dawn – a friend of his sister's apparently. So how have you ladies been?' she asked innocently.

'Oh, I'm sorry,' said Lucy. 'I was hoping you could rekindle your relationship.'

Camilla took a deep breath, which she blew out slowly.

'I can't deny that he was the love of my life, and always will be. Part of me thinks that getting back together would make all my dreams come true and I would float on a cloud of happiness for the rest of my life. But I do have some . . . actually a lot of trepidation about it all. If you can imagine what my heart looks like now after the way we split up, think of something precious like a broken Ming vase being held together with a couple of plasters. I don't know if I could put myself or my fractured heart back together again if it all went wrong.' Her throat felt thick with emotion. She gulped more water down.

'You poor thing, you must have been heartbroken.' Carrie stroked her arm across the table.

'Oh I was. I was a walking cliché really. I either couldn't eat or I'd eat too much; couldn't sleep, crying all the time but the sad thing was that my mum was almost more devastated than I was. She blamed herself the whole time and could have done without me being such a mess.' She laughed scornfully. 'I was so pathetic and wasted so much precious time by being miserable. I had a couple of boyfriends after that but nothing serious and then I met Freddy and fell in love or so I thought, but it was more a bit of reckless fun, which was great at first. However, our ideas of having fun were very different and, well, you know the rest.'

'There's someone special out there waiting for you, Camilla; maybe you just haven't met him yet,' said Lucy.

'That's the thing though – I'm not sure I want to meet anyone, not just yet anyway. Because for the first time in my life I don't feel like I'm just plodding along or a walking disaster area. I feel as though I have ambition and a real focus. I want my business not just to succeed but to excel. I think before I mostly felt as though I was doing a favour for a friend. I could relax and do the odd wedding cake here and there but I never really had that sense of urgency that I have now.' She took a sip of her drink and the bubbles fizzed on her lips. 'Losing absolutely everything has made me realise what's important in life and has forced me to take things a lot more seriously and to grow up.'

'I would like to raise a toast,' said Lucy holding up her glass. 'To Camilla Cupcake, the best darn cake maker in the world.'

Carrie raised her glass and repeated the toast whilst Camilla raised hers and giggled. 'To me and the best darn friends in the world – and not forgetting Cora, my cosy little cupcake van,' she added.

'To Cora the cosy little cupcake van,' they chorused.

She cleared away the lunch dishes and popped into the kitchen again just as the doorbell rang.

'Perfect timing,' said Camilla as she placed the dishes in the sink and headed for the front door, wiping her hands on a tea towel. 'You're just in time for pud. Oh—' On opening the door she expected to see Gracie and Matty but instead saw a pair of friendly green eyes and a cheeky smile.

'Ged, hi, how are you?' She felt a little light-headed thanks to drinking in the afternoon.

'Hi, I was passing through and thought I'd pop in and say hello,' he said in his cheery Irish accent, 'but if I'm interrupting something then I can come back another time if you like.'

She could sense her two friends pottering about the kitchen doing non-existent errands; they'd obviously heard the male voice and come to investigate.

'I've just got a couple of friends round for lunch but you're welcome to have some pudding with us.'

He turned to go. 'Oh no don't worry, I'll come back another time.'

Lucy had appeared at Camilla's shoulder and pushed her hand out to him. 'Hi, I'm Camilla's friend Lucy and you are?' she said, in the tone of a disapproving mother.

Ged shook her hand. 'It's good to meet you, Lucy. I'm Ged, also a friend of Camilla's.'

Carrie pushed her way through the two women to get to him; she pulled her glasses down from on top of her head so she could get a proper look and raised her eyebrows in admiration. She too shook his hand and introduced herself.

'Ah look here's Gracie, so you can't go yet as she's blocking your van in.' She smiled as Gracie got out of her car and reached into the back to get Matty out.

'Sorry I'm late, girls. I hope there's still some cake left for me.' She approached them carrying a bundle of arms and legs and all his paraphernalia in a huge changing bag. As soon as Matty saw Carrie he stretched himself forward to get to her quicker, almost toppling Gracie over.

Carrie stepped out of the house to take the little boy into her arms. 'So we've now got two handsome men at Camilla's door, have we?'

Camilla nudged her and put her finger to her mouth to shush her.

'What?' Carrie smiled with a mischievous wink at Camilla. She pulled Matty into an embrace and he allowed her to kiss him all over his face.

Ged and Camilla's eyes locked over Carrie's comment and they smiled shyly. Camilla held the door open wider and gestured with her head for him to come in.

'Come on in – the more the merrier. I hope you like lemon meringue pie,' she said.

'It's my favourite.' He winked at her. 'And it doesn't look like I'll be going anywhere for a while.'

She wondered, not for the first time, whether she should have set her sights on someone uncomplicated like Ged, who had a clean slate as far as hurting her was concerned. He didn't do relationships though; he would be strictly a no-strings-attached fling. Sometimes she wished she could be like that too. It was simple maths: no expectations equals no broken heart. Blake had the potential to destroy her and she didn't feel that she was strong enough to deal with that again. She wished her heart didn't race just at the thought of him, but it did and she needed to protect herself.

Within five minutes she had made coffees for Gracie and Ged, topped up the drinks for herself, Carrie and Lucy, and everyone had a succulent and tangy piece of lemon meringue pie in front of them. She had only just taken it out of the oven, so it was still warm when they ate it. Matty sat on Carrie's knee, bashing his spoon into the little piece he had been given and they laughed as he screwed his little face up from the bitterness of the lemon.

The girls had given Ged a good grilling about what he did and where he was from and Lucy indiscreetly put her thumb up to Camilla when he wasn't looking.

'That was so good, Camilla, the best I've ever tasted to be sure,' he said. Camilla smiled and tried to ignore the sneaky glances from the others. 'So the reason for my visit,' he said after scraping the last of the meringue from his bowl, 'was to ask you a huge favour.'

Carrie nudged Lucy but missed her arm and dug her in the ribs causing her to squeal and then try to stifle her giggles. Matty got overexcited and bashed his spoon louder, causing most of his meringue to fly around the table.

'Oh I'm so sorry, Camilla.' Gracie jumped to attention and tried to wipe down the mess with a couple of baby wipes.

'Don't worry about it, it's fine,' said Camilla. 'Nothing that can't be wiped away.'

Gracie began to wipe Matty's face and he started grizzling, which soon turned into a full-blown cry.

'Sorry, everyone, he's really tired so I'm going to have to go and put him to bed, and myself too come to think of it. I'm knackered.'

Carrie reluctantly gave him back to his mum and Gracie packed all of his things back in the bag. Gracie turned to Camilla.

'Oh yes I wanted to say well done to you. I saw Ron the other day and he told me you'd made his granddaughter's christening cake and they were all delighted with it. He showed me a picture of it.'

'Thank you,' said Camilla. 'It took a few attempts and a lot of tears but I did it eventually and I must admit it felt really good.'

Carrie and Lucy clapped.

'Does this mean that you're back?' asked Lucy hopefully. 'Have I got my champion cake maker back in business?'

'Baby steps,' said Camilla. 'I don't want to take on too much straight away in case I let you down again. I don't want a repeat of those awful panic attacks.'

'You didn't let me down. You suffered a devastating loss and then had to cancel a couple of jobs. It happens all the time. You're a human being and there were plenty of decent cake makers out there who filled in for you, so no harm done. Anyway do you have a picture of this masterpiece?'

Camilla glowed with pride as she found the photo on her phone and showed everybody. Lucy punched the air. 'Yes! Camilla Cupcake is back in business.'

Matty squealed louder as Gracie zipped up his coat and she hitched him up on her hip. 'I'm so pleased for you, Camilla. Thanks for the delicious food and the lovely cup of coffee I managed to drink while it was still hot for a change. Wave bye-bye, Matty. See you all again soon.'

Gracie and Matty did the rounds of kissing and hugging everyone goodbye. Ged shook Matty's hand and then he stood to go too.

'I'm going to let you get on with your girly day.'

'But we haven't finished interrogating you.' Carrie laughed.

'Maybe next time,' he said. 'Nice to meet you all. Bye for now.'

He stood at the front door with Camilla.

'I'm sorry it was such a mad house in there today.'

'Nonsense,' he said. 'I had fun.'

'So what did you want to ask me?'

'Oh that, nothing important. I just wondered what you thought about helping me organise a fundraiser for the charity and dare I ask maybe if you could make a cake for it – no pressure of course, after what you just said.'

'That sounds like a great idea,' she said. 'Let me have a think about it.'

'I'll give you a call next week if that's okay,' he said, taking her hand and planting a chivalrous kiss.

Pink spots appeared in the middle of her cheeks and he winked again as he walked off to his van. Camilla waved to Gracie as she drove off. Matty was already asleep in the back. Then she waved to Ged as he drove off in his coffee van.

As she went back into the orangery she could hear the others laughing.

'So, where the hell have you been keeping him?' Carrie asked. 'He's frickin' gorgeous.'

'Full of that lovely Irish charm too,' added Lucy. 'So, which is it to be: Blake or Ged? Because he has got the hots for you.'

'Don't be daft,' replied Camilla.' Let me get some more wine. There's no such thing as an empty glass in my house.' She laughed.

When she got into the kitchen, she laughed to herself after once again mistaking the freezer for the fridge. She pulled out the bottle of wine and cuddled it to herself as she tried to dissect her friends' comments. She realised that since splitting up from Blake she had never felt that strongly about anyone. That is until she met Ged on the very day that Blake had come back into her life. Why did everything have to be so complicated? She wanted to hear Blake's voice again so checked her watch and guessed it would be roughly 8am where he was, so she might just catch him before work.

The wine had made her a little tiddly so she dialled his number, giggling to herself as she heard the ring tone. Just as she was about to hang up she heard a woman's voice answer, 'Hello.'

Her stomach clenched and she could feel the prosecco about to make a reappearance. She pulled the phone away from her ear and checked the screen in case she'd dialled a wrong number but no there was his name as clear as anything. 'Er hello, is Blake there please?'

'I'm sorry no – he's in the shower,' came the husky answer with an unmistakable Canadian accent, emphasising the r in shower. 'Can I take a message?'

'No, thank you, it's fine. Sorry, bye.'

Camilla hung up, took a deep breath and exhaled slowly to try and ease the pain in her heart. What an earth had she done that for? She must be a glutton for punishment.

Her thoughts were interrupted by Carrie and Lucy calling her, as it was apparently time to sing. Plastering a huge smile on her face, she shook off the negative vibes, re-entered the orangery and joined in with the singing, using the bottle as a microphone in between topping up her friends' glasses.

Chapter 23

As she pulled up next to Ged in the gigantic car park on the old airfield just outside Bramblewood, she could feel the strain on the cupcake van's engine as it croaked under the sheer weight she had packed into it. Boxes and boxes of cupcakes were stacked neatly in the back of the van and on the passenger seat in the front. Ged had warned her this was a remarkably busy day and great for business, so she had brought lots of flyers and business cards advertising her cupcake bouquets and celebration cakes as well as cupcakes.

It was only eight in the morning and the car park was almost full already. There was a special area for the trades vans and stalls. Delicious cooking smells filled the air, from sizzling bacon to the aromatic spices from the street food stalls. The sound of excited chatter added to the atmosphere, as stallholders greeted each other and gave helping hands to those who were struggling with setting up stalls.

Once again Ged seemed to know everybody and introduced Camilla to his friends who were all very welcoming. She set her table and chairs out at the front of the cupcake van and rubbed her hands together to try and warm them up. Ged had popped over to chat to another friend and came back with two steaming bags containing bacon rolls. She gratefully took one from him and held it with two hands to absorb the heat coming from it.

'Now that is what I call good timing. Thank you so much,' said Camilla as she sat on one of her chairs, peeled back the paper bag and took a generous bite, Ged went to his van and came out with two frothy cappuccinos in takeaway cups then sat next to her. They munched their rolls companionably.

'It's getting warmer already,' he said. 'Can you feel that sun on your face? It's going to be a bit of an onslaught as soon as the crowds get going so I will try and remember to bring you hot drinks at least every couple of hours. How does that sound?'

She washed down the final bite of her roll with the last of the cappuccino, tipping the almost empty cup so that the chocolatey froth slid into her mouth. Midway through the manoeuvre she noticed Ged looking at her. His face cracked into a wide grin, his friendly eyes teasing her. 'Is that your favourite bit then?'

She teased him back, patting the bottom of the cup till the last bit slid into her mouth.

'If I'd known that I'd have just given you a babycino.' He laughed.

She looked puzzled and screwed up the empty cup ready to go in the bin.

'You know it's literally just milky froth with cocoa on the top,' he clarified.

Camilla screwed her face up. 'Oh no that would be like me giving you just the buttercream and sprinkles. Although it might seem like the best bit, it goes much better with a delicious feather-light sponge, and anyway by the sounds of it I'm going to need plenty of caffeine to get through this busy day.' He laughed then had to go as some customers began queueing for hot drinks. She hopped back into the cupcake van and took two cupcakes, a lemon meringue and an ice cream one. She climbed out again and popped to the side of Ged's van.

He noticed her whilst he was serving a customer.

'Well fancy seeing you here,' he joked. 'See you later, Andy.' He waved to the man he'd just served, then turned his attention to Camilla. 'Your face looks so fresh and bright, I'm glad I told you about today as you seem to love getting out and about and meeting new people.'

'I really do. It's quite a solitary job making cakes all day so doing my deliveries and getting out and about in the cupcake van is exciting and it seems to bring about such joy in people, judging by the smiles I see when I'm serving customers.'

'That's because it's such a novelty and really popular everywhere we go. There aren't many cupcake vans about, especially not any as unique as yours where customers can choose their own toppings.'

'I guess I'm just a unique sort of person. Anyway, I'll swap you for another cappuccino,' she said as she placed the two cupcakes on his counter,' and smiled at him.

'Oh my God, woman, what are you doing bringing me an ice cream in this weather?' he joked.

Another customer had appeared behind her, an old lady. 'He's right, dear,' she said, 'far too chilly for ice cream.'

Ged turned away laughing to himself as Camilla tried to explain that it was in fact a cake.

'Are you sure?' she asked screwing her eyes up in disbelief.

'Yes I'm absolutely sure. I baked them myself.' She laughed. 'Come and try one if you like.'

She took the cappuccino from Ged and he winked at her cheekily as she made her way back to the cupcake van.

No sooner had she opened up her hatch than she was inundated with customers, many of whom said they came to the market on a regular basis and were excited to have a new stall offering such unique goodies. The old lady had come straight over from Ged's stall and was intrigued with the ice cream cupcakes, she asked Camilla how she made them.

'It might seems strange,' answered Camilla, 'but you can actually bake the sponges directly into these flat-bottomed ice cream cones, then the topping is buttercream and I just add a chocolate flake and some sprinkles. I can even add strawberry or chocolate sauce too if you like.'

'Oh they are just marvellous,' answered the lady. 'I want to get some for all of my grandchildren. Do you have a box or something I can carry them in?'

'Yes of course.' Camilla reached into the cupboard below the hatch and retrieved a box. 'How many would you like?'

'I'll have ten please.' She was joined by an old man who took one of the hot drinks from her. 'Look at these, Alf, aren't they delightful? I'm getting them for the kids.' The man smiled wearily at Camilla. 'They're lovely, dear.'

Camilla had been taken aback at such a huge order; she hadn't expected that. She pulled out another box and put ten of the cupcakes inside, which left two spaces.

'I tell you what,' said Camilla, 'as you've been my best customers so far I'd like to offer you and your hubby a cupcake of your choice – on me.'

The old couple looked delighted. 'Isn't that lovely of the young lady, Alf?'

Alf nodded in agreement with her.

As Camilla reeled off the different flavours she had on board that day the lady seemed spoilt for choice but then decided on a lemon meringue one. Camilla had described it as a light lemon sponge filled with lemon curd and then instead of buttercream it was topped with a swirl of meringue, which had been baked to perfection. The ice

178

cream cupcakes and the lemon meringues had been pre-made and the elderly couple and the others in the queue behind them, who had been listening carefully to what was on offer, seemed intrigued with the bespoke cupcakes.

Today she had brought some vanilla and some chocolate sponges, one nozzle was for chocolate buttercream and the other was a new idea she was trying out. She had managed to put vanilla, chocolate and strawberry buttercreams into one of the chiller boxes and as it swirled out of the nozzle it piped out the three separate colours perfectly. She made one up and some of the customers clapped as she held it up and showed them.

'I call this one the Neapolitan,' she said, and proudly put it in the box with the others. Looking at the smiles on the faces of her customers brought her even more joy than she seemed to bring them. Here there were people of all ages and every one of them was enjoying her crea-tions. She seemed to absorb strength from every person whose face she brought a smile to. A cupcake may be just a little trivial thing in the grand scheme of things and yet they brought so much pleasure.

The rest of the day passed in a blur. By the time she had tried to take a sip of her coffee it was stone cold and she had warmed up so much she'd had to take her coat off. Ged turned up at about three with a hot chocolate for her and she managed a sip every now and then between excited customers. She had given out all of her flyers already and only had a few business cards left. By three thirty she had nothing left and began to pack away her things. Ged still had a long line of customers, so she popped over to his van and offered to help.

'Yes please.' He opened the side door and reached his arm down to her to help her up. She took the order from the next customer, keeping an eye on how Ged used the hot drinks machines, and it didn't take her long to get in the swing of things. As they worked together they were able to chat between customers and dance around each other to move around the van. It felt quite intimate but not uncomfortable. At one point she leaned out of the van to give a customer his forgotten change and she almost fell but Ged caught her, and they laughed. He still had his arms around her as he pulled her back into the van and upright when they were interrupted by a not very happy voice.

'Well it didn't take you very long to move on did it?'

Camilla looked to see a pretty woman standing in front of them wearing a peaked cap, red curls bounced around her shoulders as her head moved up and down when she shouted at Ged. Camilla gently unhitched his hands from her and began to serve the next customer, causing him to look at her intently and not the spectacle that was playing out before them. Her cheeks were burning, which made her look much more guilty than she was.

'Oh, Gina, you can't keep doing this to me.'

'You're a user, Ged. I wish I'd listened when everyone told me what you'd be like. I hate you.'

'You know I don't do relationships. I told you at the beginning,' he shouted after her as she stomped off. Camilla felt mortified and tried to pretend nothing had happened, which was extremely difficult given the close proximity of the van and the fact that some of the customers were winding him up.

'Oh you're in trouble, son.' And: 'You'd better watch him, love,' they said loudly.

Ged was looking very serious. 'I'm sorry about that,' he murmured into her ear. He continued to serve customers but the banter between the two of them had stopped abruptly.

As the airfield emptied, Camilla packed up her van and sat in the driver's seat.

'Are you okay?' Ged knocked on her window, she gasped, and her hand flew to her chest.

'Oh you made me jump then.' She wound down the window. Her heart rate returned to normal after the fright. 'I was supposed to be having a girly night tonight but the girls can't make it. What are you doing?'

He leaned on the door of the van. 'Nothing that can't be cancelled,' he replied.

'Just wondered if you fancied joining a friend for a takeaway and a couple of beers back at mine.' She flushed slightly in case it sounded like a come-on. 'As friends I mean, of course.'

'So, what you're asking is would I like to join a friend for a takeaway as friends? Are you sure you've hammered the word *friends* down enough?' he teased.

She laughed. 'Hey I know your reputation, you heart-breaker you. So, what do you say, Friendy McFriendface?

He put his finger to his chin, his face serious as if in deep thought, then his mouth broke into that dazzling smile of his and he replied, 'Isn't that what friends are for?'

She drove home with the music from the ancient radio blaring out loud, pushing unwanted thoughts from her mind.

By the time she finally pushed the key in the door she realised how exhausted she felt. Her legs were aching and her back throbbed from standing all day. Ged had pulled up just behind her and followed her into the cottage. She put on the lamps, which instantly provided a warming ambience, reached into a drawer and pulled out the menu for the Chinese takeaway and handed it to Ged. She lit the fire whilst he perused the menu.

'Do you want me to pop round and collect it?' he offered.

'No don't worry, we can have it delivered. They don't take very long.'

She went through to the kitchen, turning the lights on as she went, and he could see her through the open beams. She opened the fridge door and took out a beer, flicking off the lid with a bottle opener that was attached to one of the kitchen cupboards. She handed it to him through the gap in the wall and he sat in the armchair, threw his head back and gulped down half the bottle in one glug.

'Ah, that's better. Are you not having one?'

'No I'm having this.' She held up a bottle of red, which had been stored near the boiler in the kitchen and was just the right temperature for her. Taking a wine glass from the draining board she filled it with the burgundy liquid, listening with satisfaction to the glug-glug sound it made.

She rejoined him in the living room and flumped onto the sofa, placing the bottle of wine on the coffee table. She took the menu he proffered to her.

'Ooh what are you having?' she asked as her eyes scanned the page for her favourite.

He smiled at her. 'I haven't had Chinese food for such a long time but it has to be mixed starters and crispy duck pancakes for me. After that nothing matters.'

Camilla's stomach almost answered for her, as it rumbled so loudly making her laugh and colour flood her cheeks. 'Ooh yes, same for me and how about we share a fillet steak Chinese style with egg fried rice.'

His stomach answered hers with a gurgle, which made both of them laugh. 'I think what my stomach is trying to tell you is: add a chicken chow mein to that and it's a deal,' he replied.

Camilla pulled out her phone. After she'd spoken to them, she turned to Ged.

'Can you manage to wait half an hour, or do you want some nuts or something?' She stood up to put a George Ezra CD on the stereo.

'I'm sure I'll manage,' he replied before finishing his bottle and placing it on the table.

'Can I get you another?' she asked.

'No I'd better not as I'm driving; I'll have another when the food comes.'

He stood up to flick through her small CD collection, groaning at the names of some of the artists.

'What, you don't like pop?' she asked pretending to be offended.

'I'm more into rock bands, I'm afraid. You can't exactly air-guitar to George Ezra.'

'Who says you can't?' She smiled as she played her invisible instrument. He laughed and shook his head. She topped up her glass too vigorously leaving purple blotches on the coffee table. 'Are you sure I can't get you a drink, a Coke or something?' she said as she mopped the spills up with a tissue.

'No, I'm fine; I'll wait for my beer, thanks.'

'Oh come on, you deserve a drink after the hard day we've had today. You can always leave your van and get a taxi or even stay over.'

His eyes shot up to meet hers, his eyebrows raised, and then she continued.

'I mean I know the couch isn't huge but it's big enough and very comfy. I always fall asleep on it and I guess what I'm trying to say is . . . I don't really want to be alone tonight. I could really use a friend.'

'Why didn't you just say that then?' He laughed. 'Go on then I will, but only on one condition.'

'Okay, try me?' she said inquisitively.

'That I can get my Queens of the Stone Age CD from the van and show you what real music is.'

'I'm not sure what I'm letting myself in for but okay we've got a deal. You get the music; I'll get the beer and plates.'

The food arrived at the same time as Ged came back in from the van, so he paid for it and tipped the delivery driver. Camilla spread the packages across the coffee table, and they tucked in hungrily as they listened to Ged's favourite band. Camilla was surprised to find that she liked them.

'I expected it to just be loud noise and screaming but I'm really enjoying it,' she said as she lifted a spring roll to her lips using the disposable chopsticks the restaurant had provided.

'I'm glad you like it,' replied Ged as he washed his prawn toast down with a swig of beer and picked up a chicken satay. 'So are you going to tell me what's wrong?' he asked as he dipped the satay into the peanut sauce.

'What makes you think there's something wrong?' she asked, not making eye contact with him as she watched the flames dance in the grate.

'Oh you know, because you said you could do with a friend and didn't want to be alone.' He held both ends of the satay stick and tore the chicken off with his teeth.

'It's a long story, but basically I've realised I'm developing feelings for my ex – Blake.'

'Is that the guy I met with the beard who came to the farmers' market?' he asked as he spooned some plum sauce onto a pancake. 'Here, do you want some sauce?'

She looked away from the fire and noticed he was offering her the teaspoon. 'Oh yes, sorry. Thank you.' She took the spoon from him and spread the thick sauce onto her pancake. He offered the spring onion and cucumber, which she took and arranged them over the sauce before continuing. 'How did you know it was him?'

Ged handed her the shredded duck and wrapped up his pancake expertly before preparing to take a bite. 'I could just tell the way you were looking at each other that there was definitely some unfinished business going on. He couldn't take his eyes off you and you looked pretty smitten with him too, if you don't mind me saying.' He bit into the pancake to let her absorb what he was saying.

'Was it really that obvious?'

'You couldn't miss it. There were literally sparks flying off the pair of you.'

She shook her head. 'Well there shouldn't have been because he's been seeing someone in Canada. I really don't even want to get back into it with him, as he broke my heart last time so this whole conversation is pointless.' She bit into the pancake, her hunger getting the better of her, and chewed quickly so she could carry on talking. The backs of her eyes were stinging, and the pancake had to manoeuvre its way past a lump in her throat. She felt foolish but didn't want to cry. 'I'm so sorry. I don't know why I'm telling you all this.' Thick tears ran down her cheeks and she swiped them away angrily.

Ged looked sympathetic and passed her a tissue from the box on the table. 'Because we're friends – that's why. Look, I'm not making any excuses for him but us blokes sometimes don't know how to handle situations so well. I mean I try and be upfront with girls I've been with when I say I don't want a relationship and they tell me it's fine. But then they can't handle it. Like Gina today, they always want more than I can give.' He rubbed his forehead with his hand.

I feel terrible about it, but I can't do the relationship and kids thing. I'm too much of a free spirit but I never hide it.' He took a swig of beer; she leaned forward and sipped her wine. 'If it's any consolation, judging purely by the way he looked at you and the way he looked at me like he wanted to punch me, I would say that it was far from over between you two.'

Camilla glanced at him; full of hope. 'Do you think?'

'Look, you're far too beautiful and intelligent and independent to be worrying about all this so why not just wait and see what he has to say for himself? This guy would be crazy to walk away from you.'

'He did it before,' she snapped but immediately felt disloyal to Blake, 'although that was because he was in another country and his dad died. I'm probably not being fair to him, but I just can't hide my disappointment.'

Ged sat next to her on the couch and put his arm around her. 'Look, how about we strike up another deal?'

She rested her head on his shoulder. He smelt delicious, like coffee beans.

'What sort of deal were you thinking of?'

'I was thinking that if you don't get back with him then you buy a round-the-world ticket and join me on my trip. I'll be going in a couple of months and it will be unbelievable.'

She lifted her head to look in his face. He was smiling. 'Are you serious?'

He nodded enthusiastically, brought his bottle of beer to his mouth and took a refreshing swig.

'I'm deadly serious. We can even go to Canada and blow raspberries at him and his stupid girlfriend if you want.' He blew a raspberry with his thumb on his nose, his fingers waggling above. She laughed at the display of childishness and copied him. He continued, 'We can have cocktails in Koh Samui, go dancing in Da Nang and scuba-dive in the Seychelles. It'll be so much fun. What do you say?'

The wine had already begun to infiltrate her brain so there was only one answer she could give.

'Yes, why the hell not.' She clinked her wine glass against his beer bottle and they both toasted their new deal.

He kissed her on the top of the head. 'Now I don't know about you but I'm ready for that fillet steak.'

Feeling happier, she jumped up and skipped into the kitchen to collect their main meals from the oven whilst Ged replenished their drinks.

'How's the charity event plans coming along?' She asked as she placed the dishes on the coffee table.

'Not bad thanks, although I've just been let down on a local venue, the village hall in Nexton has flooded apparently so all their events have been pushed back?'

'Oh no, would you like me to phone Lucy and ask her if we can use the Signal Box Café?'

'Yes please that would be brilliant if you're sure.'

'No problem,' Camilla called Lucy and after a couple of minutes chatting she hung up with a huge smile on her face. 'Right that's all sorted then, your charity event is being held in Bramblewood at the Signal Box Café. Lucy was delighted to help.'

'Thank you and thank Lucy too. I'm co-ordinating a few of these events in different areas and could do with some more volunteers to take over the organising. I don't suppose you'd like to get involved would you?

'I'd be honoured to and I'm sure the girls would love to help too.'

Camilla grabbed a notebook and pen to jot down a to do list as they bounced ideas around with one another.

Chapter 24

'Ah, I thought the smell and sound of sizzling bacon would bring you back to life,' said Camilla the next morning. Ged threw back the throw he'd used as a blanket, stretched his legs and stood up.

'Did you sleep well?' Camilla asked.

'Yes, fine thanks,' he said, although the way he was rubbing at his lower back told a different story.

The bacon spat noisily as she turned it over in the pan. She brought Ged a cup of steaming coffee. 'I know it's not as good as yours but this should wake you up, sleepyhead.' As she placed it on the coffee table for him her robe fell open. She wrapped it around herself again and did up the belt. Luckily she had her matching pyjamas on underneath so she didn't need to be too embarrassed.

A loud pop and the sound of the smoke alarm going off sent her running back into the kitchen where she removed the pan from the heat and wafted a tea towel underneath the detector until it was silent.

'Are you okay in there?' he shouted.

'All good thanks. Don't worry, it was just the pan smoking. The bacon is just right. You do like it crispy, don't you?'

'Is there any other way of having it?' he replied taking a mouthful of coffee.

'Red or brown?'

'Ah I see you are fluent in the international language of bacon sarnies; definitely has to be brown for me please.' Within seconds she handed him a small plate with a bacon sandwich oozing with melting butter and brown sauce. 'Thanks, this looks delicious.' As he bit into it she walked in with her own plate and a paper towel each.

'Ooh looks like I'm just in time with this,' she said as she wiped the butter from his chin.

His eyes rolled up to the ceiling. 'See now, here's me thinking you were just the cupcake queen when in fact you're the bacon butty queen as well. Who knows, you could be the one who finally makes an honest man out of me and marches me up the aisle.'

She laughed. 'What and leave a trail of heartbroken women in the world? I don't think so. Don't worry, I'm happy to be your best mate, aka cupcake slash bacon butty queen, aka possible travelling round the world companion.'

He winked at her and flexed his muscles. 'There's a lot of women who would love to get the shackles on this and my coffee is to die for so let me know if you change your mind.'

'Believe me I know how many women are after you. I've seen the trail of heartbreak you leave behind. And although those Irish eyes of yours are always smiling, I know that if we stay friends then I'll get to keep you for longer.'

'Oh yes and how do you work that one out?'

She smiled at him. 'Because the inevitable breaking up wouldn't have to happen and I can cry on your shoulder for evermore.' She took a hearty bite from her sandwich and giggled as sauce appeared on her cheek.

He looked at her and screwed his face up in pretend disgust. 'Oh if I'd known that I would have never offered to let you waltz me up the aisle.'

'Known what? That I'm a messy eater?'

189

'No! The fact that you're a red.'

She looked at the napkin she'd just wiped her face with to see the bright red sauce and pretended she was going to wipe it on him.

Laughing, he laced up his boots. 'Thanks for last night. It was lovely and relaxing. Thanks for sorting out the venue for the charity event and for your offer to help.. I'm sure it will be an amazing do.'

'No problem, it's such a worthwhile cause, I'm really looking forward to it. Thank you for keeping me company and for talking me down about Blake. Can you please forget everything I said. I realise in the cold light of day that I was just wishing for something that had long gone. It must be my hormones or something.'

'If you say so,' he replied, not looking a hundred per cent convinced.

'Oh, wait a minute.' She ran into the kitchen and pulled a carrier bag out of the fridge, which she brought through and handed to him. 'Leftovers from last night. There's another couple of meals in there.'

'Are you sure you don't want them?'

'No it's fine honestly; I'm going to Carrie's later for a roast so it'll only go to waste.'

'Okay if you're sure.' He shrugged on his coat, took the bag from her and opened the front door then leaned in to kiss her lightly on the cheek.

She threw her arms around his neck and squeezed him tight. 'Thank you again for the shoulder to cry on.'

'Anytime, darling. As I said that's what friends are for.' He returned the affectionate squeeze and as she opened her eyes, her chin snuggled comfortably on his broad shoulder, she could hardly believe the sight in front of her and her heart almost stopped beating.

'Blake,' she said weakly. She watched as he stood at the bottom of the path, his pained eyes darted from her to Ged then back to her. She looked down and realised that her belt had come undone again so she quickly covered herself and tried to tie it in a double knot. Her eyes locked with Blake's, she shook her head and knew it looked defensive. She also wanted to utter: "It's not what it looks like," but knew how clichéd that sounded. He stood still as though not quite being able to take in the scene.

Ged had started walking down the side of the house where his van was parked. He looked back and asked her if she was okay. She nodded to him and gestured with her hand that he should go.

'Don't go on my account, mate.' Blake handed her a paper bag 'I asked Mrs Ashcroft if I could get into your mom's house just to see if anything was left there.' His voice was thick with something. Was it anger or jealousy? She waited for his face to break into the usual beautiful smile he wore whenever he saw her. It was normally involuntary and accompanied by eyes filled with love and warmth, but now they were filled with accusation and hurt. 'I've got to go, bye Cami.'

'Blake,' she called, her voice croaky, as though she had forgotten how to talk. 'Do you want to come in for a coffee?' She faltered.

'No, thanks. I need to get back to work.'

He didn't even look back as he strode down the path to his hire car, jumped in and drove off. Camilla slammed the door shut so hard that the windows rattled. Hot tears of frustration and hurt streamed down her cheeks. He had no right to be angry when he was the one who had left her feeling lost and abandoned once more. Just when she thought everything was going to be all right there was another hurdle to get over. Her phone beeped with an incoming text. She dived on her bag to retrieve it and rummaged through it with shaky hands. She could never find the phone in this bloody bag. Running out of patience she tipped it out over the coffee table. The contents spilled over the table and clattered to the floor. Typically the last thing to fall out was the phone. She hoped the message was from Blake but when she saw Ged's number, she at least felt grateful that he cared.

'I'm parked just further up your road in case you needed me. Have just seen him drive off, are you okay? Ged x'

She quickly typed in a reply telling him she was fine.

Chapter 25

Organising the charity event for the homeless provided the perfect distraction and kept Camilla and most of her friends busy. The Signal Box Café had been booked for the night and all the tickets sold. A champagne reception and delicious hot buffet would be followed by a fun auction, whereupon guests were invited to bid for services that ranged from babysitting to gardening, photography to cake making.

Having advertised in the local paper they had received a fantastic response from people who were keen to help. A dance would follow the auction and continue until the early hours. Many of the local businesses had provided goods and services for free and it promised to be a brilliant night, which should raise thousands for the charity. The organising along with the cakes she was constantly making ensured that Camilla slept at night regardless of any worries she might have. Since her appearance in the newspaper with Jackson her workload was getting heavier and heavier and she knew she needed help in the kitchen. After a conversation with Ged, he had suggested she meet with a friend of his who needed a job.

At four o'clock precisely the doorbell at Cupcake Cottage rang and she answered the door to a pretty young woman holding a Quality Street tin in one hand and the hand of her young daughter in the other. Camilla flung the door open widely and welcomed them in.

'Hi, you must be Angela,' she addressed the woman, who nodded and released her daughter's hand so she could shake Camilla's. As she did so the little girl stamped her feet in protest at losing the comfort of her mummy's hand and she wrapped her arm around her mum's leg instead and gripped her little pink teddy tightly.

Camilla bent down to her level and spoke kindly. 'Hi, my name's Camilla. What's yours?'

The little girl didn't answer, instead hiding her face in her mum's legs.

'Don't be silly, Tillie, say hello to the nice lady,' Angela said as she tried to lift the little girl's face up to see Camilla.

'No don't worry she's fine. Anyway do come in. Are they your samples?' She pointed to the tin in Angela's arms.

'Yes, they are.' Angela looked nervously down at the tin before handing it over and walked into the cottage, dragging the leg with Tillie attached to it. She was very accomplished at doing so, which alerted Camilla to the fact that this was a regular occurrence. She beckoned them through to the dining room and sat them down so she could put the kettle on.

A few minutes later when she came through with the tea tray she saw Tillie sitting on a chair of her own with some colouring books and coloured pencils. She was concentrating very hard as she scribbled on the page, her tongue sticking out and hair flopped over her eyes. Her mum unclipped the slide at the top of Tillie's head, swept the errant wispy curls into it and clipped it shut again.

Camilla set out the cups and poured the tea. Tillie had her own water bottle so hadn't wanted anything else to drink.

'So, tell me all about yourself,' she said, placing a plate of her delicious lemon meringue cupcakes on the table between them all.

Tillie's eyes opened wide. The cupcakes were huge. She shook her head before looking down again, hiding her face with her hands when Camilla asked her if she would like one.

'Yes please, I'd love one,' replied Angela. Camilla placed one on the plate in front of her and another on Tillie's plate.

'I know you said you didn't want one, Tillie, so this one's for your teddy.'

Tillie's head shot up and she eyed up the cupcake again. She picked Teddy up from the chair next to her and sat him on the table in front of the cake where she proceeded to feed him with the spoon that Camilla had placed near the plate. As Teddy couldn't manage much to eat, Tillie had polished off the remnants of every spoonful whilst Camilla and her mum talked.

Angela picked the cup of tea up and sipped at it before speaking. 'Not much to tell I'm afraid. I haven't worked since I've had Tillie for various reasons, but one main one is because we had to relocate due to the nature of the relationship I was in with her D. A. D.' She spelt out the last word. Angela looked tearful so Camilla offered Tillie the chance to watch telly. She nodded shyly and allowed Camilla to lead her by the hand after first checking that her mum said it was okay, then she curled up quite contentedly with Teddy on Camilla's sofa watching cartoons.

Camilla rejoined Angela, placed a box of tissues on the table and they resumed their chat.

'I used to work in a busy office before becoming pregnant with Tillie but my ex made me quit because he didn't want "his woman being leched over by a bunch of pervs in an office".' She held her fingers up to represent quotation marks as she spoke then pulled a tissue from the box. 'He eventually controlled my every movement and even punched the doctor who was helping me to give birth.'

Camilla's hand flew to her mouth as her jaw dropped open. She also took a tissue from the box as she absorbed Angela's pain.

'He was in and out of jail for violence and when he hit me in front of Tillie just six months ago, I knew I had to leave once and for all.' She blew her nose, shrugged her shoulders as if to shake off her troubles and continued, her voice much stronger.

'So now I just need a job that I can do around Tillie and when I saw Ged at the shelter he mentioned you were looking for someone to help you. I thought maybe I could help with the dishes or something. I'll do anything. I'd really like to get out of the refuge we're in and find a decent place to call home.'

Angela's determination to do the best for her child reminded Camilla of her mum working hard all her life and she immediately felt a bond with her.

'I certainly need some help. I'm rushed off my feet these days as my business is growing so fast. It'll only be a few hours at first but will progress as things get busier, so yes I'd like to offer you the job.'

Angela shrieked, jumped off the chair and hugged Camilla hard.

'Thank you so much; you won't regret it I promise,' she replied.

'Oh wait, I forgot to taste your samples,' said Camilla reaching for the tin.

Angela's shoulders slumped. 'Oh don't worry about that; it's fine,' she said, about to snatch it away. But Camilla had got to it first and when she opened and saw the burnt offerings inside it she laughed until tears streamed down her face. Angela looked mortified but had to catch on to Camilla's laugh.

'I'm sorry but the oven was useless, and the truth is, I can't bake to save my life.' She was blushing furiously and looked about to cry.

'It's a good job for you that I'm an excellent teacher then isn't it? When can you start?' asked Camilla. She knew when somebody needed a chance in life and this woman wanted to work to get a home for herself and her child and there was much to be admired in that. She was determined to do what she could for these lovely people who had suffered awful abuse and needed help. Angela hugged her warmly and they made arrangements for her to start the next day and she was welcome to bring Tillie with her.

Camilla had stocked up on toys and puzzles for Tillie to play with when she came round and Camilla started by teaching Angela how to pipe the roses on top of the cupcakes that she'd prebaked that morning. She was pleased to see that she was a dab hand at that and picked it up really quickly. So, in the afternoon she shared her recipe for chocolate cupcakes and walked her through all of the instructions for making them and they turned out perfectly. Angela was delighted as was Tillie who became chief taster and declared them 'very yummy'.

Camilla laughed. 'I should use that as the tagline for my cupcakes: "Camilla's Cupcakes are Very Yummy".'

'I didn't want to blame my tools but the oven in the place where we're living is really bad and it's so lovely here to be able to use all the proper equipment and a good recipe, so I'm thinking maybe I'm not such a disaster area after all,' said Angela.

Camilla showed her how to assemble the cupcake bouquets. One set of cupcakes were decorated as daffodils and the other as red roses. Again Angela picked it up straight away and Camilla was delighted that the jobs were being done in half the time. She now felt able to make some cake deliveries knowing that she could leave cupcakes in the oven, other cupcakes being iced and a cupcake bouquet being created with beautiful pastel-coloured flowers. She was happy to be leaving her business in Angela's capable hands.

Having loaded up the cupcake van Camilla first headed into town to deliver the bouquets. When delivering her cakes she always turned on the chimes before knocking on the door. The novelty of the van and the beauty of the unique gift she delivered brought smiles to the recipients' faces and it warmed her heart to have brightened up their day. Next stop was to deliver the Signal Box Café's order of cupcakes, the number of which was growing day by day. Lucy had popped out of Railway Cottage to help her to unload the van.

'Oh that smell gets me every time. I just can't resist and I'm going to have to keep three of these back for after our dinner tonight,' Lucy said as she breathed in the sweet vanilla scent.

'As you know there's plenty more where they came from and I've now got some help so do feel free to increase your order at any time.'

'That's great and I must say you look like you've had a weight lifted from your shoulders.'

'That's exactly how I feel. It's like for the first time in ages I've been able to lift my head up and take a look at what's going on around me.'

'Okay well, I'm just testing the waters here, but I've had a request for a wedding vow renewal cake. I think only you will do it justice.' She bit her lip, obviously unsure of how her request would go down.

Camilla felt her heart palpitate and took a deep breath. 'Oh, I don't know if I'm quite ready, although I did end up enjoying doing Ron's daughter's cake.'

'Look, I completely understand and believe me if I thought it was too much or that you weren't ready then I wouldn't dream of asking you but I thought as you've got some help now you might be able to think about your masterpieces again. Remember how much you used to love creating them?'

Camilla nodded and smiled. 'Yes, they were my pride and joy and I could always get lost in my thoughts as I moulded and shaped those buildings and little people out of icing.' Her body fought against itself with the stress of letting people down versus the absolute joy she got from cake making.

Lucy continued, 'You would be doing me a huge favour as this cake is needed for the weekend and the lady who was meant to be doing it has taken ill.'

Despite the pterodactyls hatching in her stomach she spoke quickly, 'Who's it for and what sort of cake do they want?'

Lucy smiled at her. 'It's for Mr and Mrs Ives and they would like a replica of their shop: Odds'n'Sods.'

Camilla's heart fluttered and despite her nervousness she knew she couldn't turn it down. She had always been a huge admirer of the beautiful quaint Victorian shops in market square and she knew it would make a magnificent cake with its windows filled with all sorts of curios. It was a dream of a job and she could already see it in her head, complete with beams and a little version of Mr and Mrs Ives standing in front of it. Maybe he would be carrying his wife and she would have a tiny bouquet in her hand. She could probably even fit the fountain in Market Square in too. So, with nervous trepidation she nodded at Lucy.

'Well as that was my view from when I stayed at the B&B, I reckon I could manage it from memory. Okay. I'll do it.'

Lucy hugged her tightly. 'Thank you so much, my wonderful friend. You are a lifesaver and Mr and Mrs Ives will be so happy you've agreed as they wanted it to be you from the beginning.'

Camilla hugged her friend, climbed back into the cupcake van and tootled off to buy some supplies for the new cake. She felt a new sense of excitement with this job. Her mind was freeing up some space to enable her to think about other things.

Camilla was looking forward to getting into the habit of breathing a sigh of relief when Angela turned up for work. She still couldn't quite believe her luck that she'd got such a good assistant. She hoped that Angela and her little one would soon be able to move to a place of their own. Camilla had discovered how it felt to be homeless but was lucky enough to have been surrounded by wonderful friends who had helped her to not only get back on her feet but also to create a solid base for her feet to stand on and feel more secure. Helping Angela was good for her too as she felt she was able to give something back. This felt like a giant step on the road to her recovery.

She arrived back at Cupcake Cottage just as Angela was leaving. She thanked her for all of her help and Angela hugged her, her eyes glassy.

'You don't know how much you've helped me,' she said, her voice thick with emotion.

Camilla hugged her back. 'Ditto,' she replied.

Chapter 26

The sunshine brought a promise of spring as it poked its nose above the trees that Camilla could see over her garden fence. She'd made an early start today and was standing in the orangery putting together ten cupcake bouquets. They had really taken off and she loved creating them. She had a note pinned to the noticeboard with the requirements of each one and the table was completely covered in all varieties of iced cupcake flowers. She used green wooden skewers as the flower stems and then wrapped them in cellophane and pretty tissue paper in complementary colours. The one she was working on at the moment was made of large pink gerberas, but she also had daisies, one of pink roses, one of red and the majority were of a colourful selection of spring blooms.

Each bouquet would have one of her business cards displayed with the loving message from the purchaser written on it. Camilla felt a thrill when writing the messages out, as though she was party to hundreds of secrets: the start of new relationships, the affirmation of long-time love, apologies for stupid behaviour and cheeky messages from secret lovers. She could let her imagination run wild whilst writing these cards, imagining the stories that went on behind the scenes. She wished she could be a fly on the wall after she delivered them, but she was just a tiny piece of their lives and she was thrilled that her creativity could bring such happiness.

She sang at the top of her lungs to George Exra on the loudspeaker whilst baking and constructing her master-pieces. Luckily, she heard the dinger on the oven so went to retrieve her sponges. She still had to fulfil the orders for the Signal Box Café and the many supermarkets that she now baked for, as well as one day start back on the larger themed cakes, providing of course that she could control the anxiety she felt when making them. She was beginning to look forward to making the cake for Mr and Mrs Ives and had decided to film it for her vlog.

She set down her sponges to cool and replenished the ovens with the next batch of chocolate sponges. As soon as they were done she stored her bouquets carefully in large boxes and placed them in the back of the cupcake van, grabbed her delivery list and set off down the lane. Seeing the happy, surprised and amazed faces on the people to whom she delivered made all the hard work worthwhile.

Once all her jobs had been done, Camilla got ready for her new venture that she was stupidly excited about. Since meeting Angela, Camilla was in awe of her. She'd watched her grow in confidence with every day. Not just in personality but even in the way she held herself, she reminded her so much of her own mum for bringing her up single-handedly.

Angela had told her all about the other women in the shelter and their children and she really wanted to help. Whilst visiting Lucy one day they'd been discussing it and Jackson had piped up with the perfect suggestion. So today was the first Mother and Child Baking Session, and Camilla couldn't wait.

On the way there Camilla pulled up outside Railway Cottage and put the chimes on. The door burst open and Jackson flew out of the house shouting goodbye to his mum with one arm in his jacket and a biscuit hanging out of his mouth.

'Hi, Auntie Camilla,' he said as he jumped in the passenger seat.

'Hi, darling, I'm so glad you suggested this, Jackson. I'm really excited.'

'Me too,' he replied. 'I can't wait.'

They arrived at the shelter and began to unpack the two large-lidded plastic boxes of ingredients. Angela met them and introduced them to five mums and eight children ranging from eight months old to twelve years. Jackson was extremely helpful handing out the bowls and wooden spoons.

'Hi, everyone, it's lovely to meet you all. Thank you for allowing us to come and bake with you. Today we thought we would start with half of you making cupcakes and the other half truffles, then we can swap over so you all get a chance at making both. How does that sound?'

'Good,' came the replies in excited voices.

Camilla and Jackson helped the children to weigh out the ingredients for the cakes and place the paper cupcake cases on the trays. Angela had to light the oven because it was very temperamental. A sullen young girl walked into the kitchen to get a drink of water. 'Hi, Jenny,' said Angela. 'Are you not joining in the baking session?'

'Nah,' said the girl, 'I'm going to watch telly instead.'

'Hi, Jenny,' said Jackson, his cheeks flushed.

'Oh hi. I don't live here, you know. We're just staying for a while.' Her face was beetroot. 'I suppose you're going to tell all the other kids now?'

'No,' said Jackson. 'Why would I do that?'

Jenny shrugged but the look on her face showed that that wasn't what she expected him to say.

'Did you hear Miss Barton burp in class today?' He laughed. 'It was like this.' He made a fake burping sound.

'Yeah, that was so gross,' replied Jenny. 'She sounded like a warthog.'

'Oh, do you two know each other from school?' asked Camilla.

'Yes,' they both answered together.

'Do you want to help me show the little ones how to make the truffles? They're really easy to make and they taste delicious. We've got some of my Auntie Camilla's cake and we mix it with melted chocolate then roll it in chocolate strands or hundreds and thousands.

Jenny thought about it for a second, and glanced at her mum who nodded at her.

'Okay then,' she said.

'Okay first you need to wash your hands.'

Camilla met Jenny's mum's eyes and returned her smile as she bounced her two-year-old on her knee to the sound of Jackson and Jenny laughing and chatting away.

By the end of the session, despite the oven turning itself off three times, each of the children had half a dozen cupcakes, lots of truffles and huge smiles on their faces.

'Jackson was a real tonic for Jenny tonight. She had lots of fun. Thanks for doing this. It was like a lovely ray of sunshine for us.'

'You're absolutely welcome, Angela. Shall I come back in, say, a month's time and we can try biscuits or something?'

'That would be amazing. Thanks again.'

'Come on, Jackson,' shouted Camilla. He and Jenny came to the door still chatting non-stop and laughing.

'Jenny's mum said she can come to mine for tea in a couple of days,' he said, his face animated as he jumped back into the seat of the cupcake van.

'Oh, that's lovely, Jacks.'

'Next time can I bring my camera and film the session?'

'Ah I'm afraid not, Jackson. I don't think that would be allowed.'

'Why?' he asked, ever inquisitive.

'Because some of the children haven't got very nice dads and they've had to leave them for one reason or another, and they're not allowed to know where they live.'

'That's horrible,' said Jackson. 'I noticed that quite a lot of their toys were broken so I'm going to sort out some of my toys to give them when I get home.'

'That's really kind of you,' replied Camilla. Her heart melted at the tears she could see in his eyes. What a compassionate and caring young man he was.

Camilla had had her own taste of homelessness too. She felt she needed to do more to help those women and children. Maybe she could mention thecharity on her vlog, she'd had quite a few hits especially since she added the conversion of the cupcake van and the making of the cupcake bouquets.

Chapter 27

Distractions were plentiful: the cupcake orders, the charity event, attending fetes and farmers' markets in the cupcake van, and now with the strong possibility of celebration cakes being back on the agenda. Camilla realised she hadn't checked in on Auntie Edie for a little while, so she packed a selection of cupcakes into a box and set off in the cupcake van to her house. As she pulled up outside she turned on the chimes as she knew how it made Auntie Edie laugh to hear them. She knocked on the door and eventually heard slippered feet shuffling down the hallway. The door opened slightly, only as far as the chain would allow, and Edie's face came into view through the opening, she could hear Bella and Bertie squawking loudly from their cage. Bella shouting 'hello' and Bertie swearing like a trooper.

'Hello, darling.' She opened the door wider and pulled Camilla into a hug.

'Hi, Auntie Edie, special delivery – I've brought you some cupcakes.'

'Oh, that's lovely of you. Thank you. Let me go and put the kettle on.'

Camilla followed her down the hall to the kitchen.

'I've got a new flavour of cupcake I'd like you to try. It's called Tropical Tease and I think you'll love it.'

Auntie Edie made the tea and Camilla put the cakes on

a plate and followed her into the living room. The old lady looked out of the window at the cupcake van.

'Ah, remember when you were a little girl and the ice cream man would park outside and I would send you out with some pennies for a ninety-nine for you and an oyster shell for me? Seeing your lovely van has just reminded me. Where have the years gone? Then your mum would call you in for your dinner and I'd have to tell you to shush as I'd be in trouble if you didn't eat it all.'

'I do remember,' said Camilla. 'And I used to share my ice cream with Bertie. Those were happy days, weren't they? I remember we used to have little afternoon tea parties here with my mum and I would bake the cakes.'

'Yes, we did and now look at you: all grown up and those cupcakes smell delicious. Your mum would be so proud of you right now.'

'Thanks, Auntie Edie, I really hope so. You're my only connection to her so I'm sure you'd know.'

'I definitely do know, my darling. You've handled yourself with so much dignity about this whole debacle with the house and just look what you've achieved. A home and a business to be proud of; you're amazing just like your mum. Now, which is the coconut one? I'm going to have to try that first. And you will stay for dinner won't you?'

'I'd love to, thank you – that's if you don't mind.'

'Have you seen anything of Mister Gorgeous lately?' asked Edie with buttercream on her top lip.

'I don't know who you mean,' Camilla replied, a cheeky grin on her face.

'You know exactly who I mean, that Canadian hunk of a man.'

'I did see him briefly but it was a bit of a disaster if I'm honest.'

'Why? What on earth happened?'

Camilla filled her in on all the gory details whilst Edie ploughed through her cupcake.

'Well that will all blow over, it sounds like a storm in a teacup. So what was in the bag he gave you?' she asked.

Camilla rummaged in her bag and pulled out the cookery book that she and her mum had used for years and years, stained with butter, egg and cake mix, favourite recipes dog eared and the cover beaten. An item worthless to everybody else on the planet but to her it was priceless.

'Oh how lovely.'

Camilla's eyes had filled, 'I never thought I'd see it again, I burst out crying when I saw it, I could practically see the memories playing out in front of me like a hologram as I flicked through the pages.' She hugged it to her chest.

'I wonder where it was.'

'I presume it got stuck in a kitchen drawer or something, thank God'

'Ah you look exhausted love, you have a little rest and I'll go and make some tea.'

Camilla tucked the book safely back in her bag, she felt so cosy in Edie's living room; she had practically grown up there. She'd loved to play with the little animal ornaments on the top of the old-fashioned gas fire and recalled that underneath the shiny porcelain lion there was a little chip that nobody else knew about, from when she'd taken it outside to play and dropped it on the step. Luckily the whole thing hadn't broken. She enjoyed watching Bertie play with his ball and Bella flew to her shoulder and played with her hair, which she had done since she was little. Camilla loved the ticklish sensation and felt totally relaxed.

Her eyes began to close as she sunk into the couch. The old familiar sounds of Edie clanging the pans in the kitchen and preparing her speciality of boiled ribs and cabbage and lentil soup, which she cooked in the pressure cooker. Camilla had never liked the pressure cooker as it was so noisy, but the sound and the smell of the food that eventually permeated the air soothed her into a gentle sleep.

She was eventually woken by the sound of a deep voice with a Canadian drawl and realised that Blake was at the door. She straightened herself up; she probably looked a right mess. She glanced at the ancient clock on the mantelpiece and was horrified. An hour and a half she'd been asleep for and was completely curled up on the sofa. She could see the Liver birds were back in their cage, Bella trilling to her reflection in the mirror and Bertie pecking at the seeds in their food bowl, his ball lying abandoned on the floor. They had more energy than she did and yet amazingly they were fifty years old.

She pulled her own mirror out of her bag. Her hair was bedraggled after having been restyled by Bella and her eyes were bloodshot. Filled with embarrassment, she contemplated sneaking out of the living room window but thought the neighbours would think her odd, as would Blake if he happened to walk in while she had one leg in and one leg out. However, there was no way she could let the love of her life see her like this. It was bad enough that he thought she'd slept with Ged. A fresh wave of mortification swept through her at that thought. She also maintained, though, that she was well within her rights to have slept with anyone should she have wanted to.

Her fight-or-flight reflex kicked in; maybe she should just stay and square up to him. She took another look in her mirror, caught sight of the sleep creases still on her face and shook her head; the window it was. She pulled at the metal loops at the bottom of it and managed to drag it open.

She'd heard Blake go down the hall to the kitchen with Edie. He'd brought beautiful flowers by the sound of their conversation and she could now hear them on their way back to the living room. *Shit, shit, shit,* she thought, grabbed her bag, and sat on the window ledge her heart thudding in her chest so hard she could feel it in her ears. She kicked one leg out, ducked her head under the window and followed with her other leg. A trickle of sweat ran down her back as she heard the handle on the door being twisted. She shuffled her bum off the ledge and turned quickly to close the window when a flurry of feathers, swept under it and swore at her as he flew past.

'Bertie. Nooooo,' she screeched as she closed the window as quietly as possible. She could see Blake was now in the room, standing there looking out at her, his face equally as horrified as hers. She could just about make out him mouthing, 'What the f—'

Camilla quickly ducked down as she saw Auntie Edie burst into the room carrying a vase with a beautiful bouquet of colourful blooms in it; they lit up her face as though they were made of pure sunlight.

'Camilla, will you look at what your man has brought me. There's three more vases full out there.' She stopped. 'Now where's she gone? Shall I put them on the windowsill or the mantelpiece?'

'Mantelpiece,' shouted Blake. He cleared his throat. 'Sorry, I think they'll look lovely on the mantelpiece. Sometimes the sun dries them out on the windowsill.'

'Yes, I think you're right. There, don't they look beautiful?'

Camilla could see Bertie pecking at the shingle on the path. She looked back at Blake, put her finger in front of her lips to shush him then gestured for him to come outside.

'Ah, Camilla has just popped out to the van and she needs me to help with, erm, an engine problem. By the way I would love a coffee after all if you don't mind. I won't be long.'

'Okay, love,' called Edie as she traipsed back to the kitchen. 'The ribs and cabbage won't be long,' she shouted over her shoulder.

Bertie was strutting down the garden path, with Camilla hot on his tailfeathers, when Blake opened the door and closed it quietly behind him.

'I've just grabbed this from Edie's ironing pile,' he said in a loud whisper as he unfolded a pillowcase in a snapping motion. He held it out front and to the side like a bull-fighter. Camilla looked at him, puzzled but grateful for help. 'I've also got this,' he said, rolling the yellow ball around in his hand. 'I figure if you distract him with the ball and I come chasing up behind with the pillowcase and throw it over his head, it should work a treat. What do you say?'

'It's worth a try,' she whispered back, all thoughts of looking a mess having disappeared with this predicament.

Camilla wanted to cry but knew she had to stay strong and get Bertie back in his cage. He'd never survive in the wild now, which was why Uncle Albert had rescued him and Bella in the first place. 'Blake, I can't lose Bertie. He and Bella are Auntie Edie's pride and joy. Her husband gave them to her on their tenth wedding anniversary. They're so, so precious to her.'

'I know. Aren't they about fifty years old?'

'Yes. What are we going to do? It'll break her heart to lose him.' Camilla could feel her voice going wobbly as it caught in her throat.

'Don't worry, we'll get him back home before you know it. Here, show him this.'

He gently threw the ball to her but she missed and as it bounced on the ground, Bertie squawked, 'Piss off, Ref,' and took off, spreading his wings like he'd never done before. He soared above them, a flash of colour across the sky. Camilla shrieked as he revelled in his new-found freedom, her hands clasped to her face, her stomach plunged to the earth.

Blake ran his hands through his hair leaving it dishevelled, a look of hopelessness on his face. Bertie settled in a tall tree in one of the neighbour's gardens pecking at the berries.

'If you give me a leg-up, I reckon I could climb up that tree and reach him,' said Camilla.

'I don't think so because there's no low branches to climb up,' Blake replied. 'Although if you got on my shoulders, that might work.'

Camilla contemplated it. She was absolutely mortified. The last time she was on his shoulders was in a hotel swimming pool in Greece and she was at least two stone lighter then. She looked at him then up at Bertie and knew she had no choice; she had to catch this bloody bird. They opened the door of the cupcake van so she could step up a little higherand Blake stooped down in the doorway. After a couple of attempts he finally swung her up onto his shoulders and made his way over to the tree. Camilla wobbled all over the place, shouting out every now and again as she tried to get used to the sensation of being up so high. Her hands clung tightly to his forehead and occasionally blocked his vision.

'Left a bit, left a bit,' she instructed. 'No right, right.' Blake shifted along as requested and handed her the pillow-case. 'Okay come on, Bertie,' she said before a kerfuffle of squawks and a few grey and red feathers floated in the air as Camilla once again failed to trap him.

'Oh no, he's taking off again. Look at him swooping and soaring; he's having the time of his life.'

'Having you on my shoulders is reminding me of us having the time of our lives on holiday, except we had a pool to play in then. Do you remember?'

'Well that was a long time ago and we didn't have a crisis on our hands then.'

She felt guilty for snapping and completely awkward talking to the top of his head, which was still trapped firmly between her thighs. 'Erm I'm sorry but could you put me back down now please.'

'Yes of course.'

Blake backed up to the cupcake van and helped Camilla to step down to it. Every time Bertie swooped near them Blake tried to catch him with the pillowcase to the joyful sound of 'Piss off, Ref,' and 'Come on, you reds,' being repeatedly squawked at him.

Camilla tried to catch her breath and get ready to catch him again when a mewing sound came from the sky.

'Oh shit,' said Blake. 'It's red kites – they're birds of prey. There's two of them. We've got to get him away from them or he won't stand a chance. We need to tempt him with something.'

Camilla racked her brains. The ball didn't work but he did have a favourite toy parrot in the cage with a bell on it, he always came flying over for that but then by the time she went to get that it could be too late.

'Wait, I remember now, he loves ice cream. He's only allowed it once a year on his birthday, but he always went mad for it whenever he saw my ninety-nine from the ice cream van.'

The call from the red kites had become more urgent and they were swooping for Bertie. Camilla jumped into the cupcake van and tore open a packet of ice cream cones she used for her cakes. Blake swore as Bertie came flying past squawking, 'Penalty, penalty,' and yet again managed to avoid the Egyptian cotton trap. Camilla's hands were shaking as she swirled some vanilla buttercream onto the top of the cone and, for the pièce de résistance, she added the chocolate flake. She opened up the hatch and shouted to Bertie. She looked up and to her horror saw one of the predators hit him, which sent him spiralling through the air at breakneck speed.

'Noooo, Bertie, here's your ice cream,' she shouted to the bundle of feathers that appeared lifeless as it hurtled towards the ground but suddenly sprang to life and flapped his wings again. She stretched out of the cupcake van holding the ice cream aloft and remembering something else he loved, she grabbed a handful of chopped nuts and threw them on the top. 'And your nuts,' she screeched as she saw the two massive birds swoop down to catch him.

Bertie glided down to his favourite treat and landed on Camilla's arm, which she quickly swept back into the cupcake van whilst Blake slammed the hatch shut. The noise of which scared the two tormentors off. Bertie pecked at the ice cream whilst eyeing up Camilla and wolf whistling, Blake joined them inside, both he and Camilla had to catch their breath before either of them could speak.

'Thank you so much for helping. I would never have forgiven myself if anything had happened to Bertie and I don't think Bella or Auntie Edie would have done either. Do you remember Uncle Albert telling us about the Liver birds' statues in Liverpool and how Bella looks out to sea watching for the seamen to return home safely?'

'That's right, I do remember that. And Bertie looks out to the city, allegedly waiting for the pubs to open, but really to look after the seamen's families. Uncle Albert told some great stories of when he worked on the docks.'

'They are such a close link to Uncle Albert for Auntie Edie.'

'Hey look, don't worry about it. Bertie's safe now. But am I allowed to ask why you climbed out of the window in the first place?'

She blushed. 'I'd really rather you didn't.' As she shook her head a strand of hair fell across her face and his hand instinctively moved towards her, causing her to draw in a sharp intake of breath. He hesitated and put his hand back down by his side whilst she tucked the hair behind her ear herself.

He grinned at her and now that the crisis was almost over, she could appreciate again how sexy he was. She was lost in her thoughts when he spoke.

'You literally look like you've been dragged through a tree backwards.'

'Oi.' She laughed, slapping him playfully on the arm.

'I didn't get a chance but I wanted to let you know how grateful I am that you got my mum's recipe book back.'

'Oh that's okay, I didn't think I'd find anything but then I realised the kitchen drawer wouldn't open fully and there it was. I remember your mum's baking very well especially her speciality that she always made us on our birthdays.'

'Yes the choc chip sponge, always cooked in a loaf tin, that was my absolute favourite. Especially straight out of the oven.'

'Mine too.' Their eyes met and they smiled at their shared memory.

Whilst Bertie was enjoying his fake ice cream Blake sneaked up behind him and threw the pillowcase over his head like a kidnap victim. It was like a comedy sketch as

Blake wrestled with the wriggling bundle and headed back to the house. Camilla almost wet herself laughing with a mixture of relief and mirth.

'We always did make a good team, didn't we?' he said. Her eyes once again found his and she nodded, unable to find the words to answer him. The past tense of his sentence had unsettled her, reminded her of what could have been and what she'd wished for once upon a time. The panic now being over left the awkward situation with Ged hanging over them like a weighted blanket and she didn't quite know what to say to him. Blake had left Edie's door on the catch, so they were able to let themselves back in. Camilla walked straight through to the kitchen allowing Blake to smuggle Bertie back into his cage. Edie was doing a crossword at the kitchen table.

'Hello, love, is it all sorted now?'

Camilla looked at her blankly.

'The cupcake van – did he fix the engine?'

'Oh yes, all fixed now,' she exclaimed overenthusiastically.

'Well now it's time for your favourite dinner at mine. You do still love it, don't you?'

Camilla really did love it. It was wholesome and hearty, delicious, and tasted of her childhood. She had often sat in this very room with her mum and Edie enjoying this meal. The delicious aroma carried her back to carefree times.

'Right, I'm going to set up the TV tables so, Camilla, can you please butter some bread for us. You'll need to slice it first and, Blake, can you sort out that wine you've just brought please. The glasses are in the top cupboard.' Edie went to the cupboard in the hallway and retrieved three mismatched foldaway TV tables that she set up, one at her favourite armchair and the other two next to each other at the two-seater sofa.

Neither Camilla nor Blake spoke as they set about their duties. They wouldn't have heard each other anyway as the pressure cooker was whistling away, filling the room with steam as it did so. Camilla wanted to joke with him that she had been to saunas with less steam than this but she couldn't speak. She remembered the look of hurt on his face as she was saying goodbye to Ged and she knew what she would think in the same circumstances. She'd looked guilty as hell when he'd turned up at her house and she didn't quite know how to convince him of her innocence without using the old clichéd words: 'It's not what it looks like!' It shouldn't even matter anyway because they weren't in a relationship – well he was, just not with her.

He had his back to her and was uncorking the wine. His dark hair curled round the nape of his neck and she wanted more than anything to wrap her fingers in it and pull his face close to hers so that she could feel the warmth of him. She longed to feel his lips touching hers, his beard scratching at her skin, those strong arms holding her like he used to. Ged was a cute young guy who was looking for fun and he could provide her with a pleasant distraction, but it was Blake's arms she longed to be in. They had history. They were still growing up when they met and they grew together before circumstances pulled them apart so cruelly, each of them having no choice but to care for their parents.

Their lives probably would have been so different now had they been able to stay together. In an alternate universe maybe they would have been married for eight years with the three children they always talked about having and the little home near the babbling brook. At least they had achieved one of those things; Camilla loved living in Cupcake Cottage and liked nothing better than to sit at the bottom of the garden listening to the water trickle along. Weaving its way in and out of the rocks, each tiny drop seemingly insignificant on its own but as part of a greater entity, capable of etching a path through the solidity of stony ground.

When she had been with Blake she felt part of a much greater being and as though the two of them could achieve anything. Her body reacted like memory foam whenever she saw him and was desperate to mould itself around his familiar contours. She was proud to be an independent woman and, so far, she'd achieved so much, but her life would unquestionably be so much better with him in it.

The steam irritated her nose and she sneezed loudly over her shoulder whilst in the middle of slicing the bread, causing the knife to cut through her finger. She squealed and popped it straight into her mouth. Blake turned; his face full of concern for her injury.

He took her hand and led her to the sink where he poured cold water over the cut; the blood turned the water slightly pink as it ran down the sink. He reached for some kitchen roll and dabbed at it. She bit her lip to try and stop the flutters that she felt in every part of her body, especially as his hair softly tickled her face as he looked down to her hand. He pressed the makeshift gauze firmly over the cut with his fingers and took her other hand, which he placed over the folded kitchen roll; a patch of blood was starting to appear through it.

'Just press on this,' he said firmly as he placed her fingers over the cut. He opened the pantry door and she could hear him moving things around in there. 'Ah here it is,' he said and walked out with the green first aid box. After finding the right-sized plaster he cleaned the cut with an antiseptic wipe, which caused Camilla to wince and made her knees turn to jelly. He then placed the plaster over the cut and smoothed it down gently; her skin tingled at his touch. Camilla dared to look up into his eyes but before his could meet hers, Edie burst into the kitchen to switch off the pressure cooker.

'Why didn't you turn this off instead of standing there looking dopily into each other's eyes?' She swiftly turned off the gas, heaved the pressure cooker over to the draining board, and proceeded to take the lid off. She moved quickly and retrieved three soup bowls from the oven, which she ladled the wonderful-smelling lentil broth into.

'You two need your heads banging together,' she said as she carried the tray of soups into the living room. Blake and Camilla followed sheepishly. He carried the wine and she the plate of buttered bread minus the slice with blood on it.

'But—' Camilla started to say.

'No buts,' said Edie. 'Now will you two just sit there and eat your soup?' She gestured to Camilla to take the oven gloves from over her shoulder so she could lift the bowls onto the TV tables. Once she'd finished handing round the bread she was able to sit down and start her own soup. She blew quite loudly on the spoon.

Blake had tasted the soup and was spooning it up eagerly.

'This takes me back, Edie. I remember coming here on a Saturday and we'd have this with you and Albert and in all my years since, I've never tasted soup this good,' he said between mouthfuls.

Camilla nodded a silent agreement. She couldn't trust herself to talk; embarrassment swept through her in waves. He thought she had slept with Ged and even though they weren't together she could understand how bad he felt about it. They had been in love. They were soulmates at one time – no one could imagine one without the other

– and then they'd been torn apart and just when they meet up again, she had to go and spoil it all.

He wasn't totally blameless. After all he was the one who stopped contact with her, and it was the look of devastation on his face that made her feel so guilty for being with Ged. Yet he was the one who was seeing someone else. They were obviously just not meant to be. Her heart sank at the realisation that as much as she tried to deny it he had broken her heart again. She couldn't stop him from doing it. However much she tried, her heart belonged to him and no one else. She'd have to get used to that. She gobbled up her soup in silence as she pretended to be absorbed in Edie's favourite TV game show. Although, thankfully, they were sitting side by side so they didn't have to look at each other. However, she wasn't sure whether the heat pulsating through her body was down to the soup or being in such close proximity to him.

Once the soup was finished Camilla helped Edie take the bowls and bring in the hot plates with the boiled ribs and cabbage on. The memories of childhood flooded back and so she wasn't surprised to be chided once more by Edie as soon as her programme had finished.

'So, what have you got to say for yourselves then?' she asked before nibbling the salty meat from a rib bone and picking up another. 'Camilla tells me you saw her say goodbye to the young man from the coffee van and you stormed off.' She pointed at Blake with the bone and a piece of the delectable meat fell onto her tray table. She picked it up and popped it into her mouth, then washed it down with some of her wine. 'To me that suggests that you've got feelings for her.'

Camilla blushed violently; she hadn't expected Auntie Edie to blurt out this fact that she'd confided in her, but then she should have known better. Edie was a very forth-right lady. Edie continued her onslaught.

'I didn't get to the ripe old age of eighty-two without having the odd tiff with my Albert but one thing's for sure: we never went to sleep on an argument, so you two need to get over your egos and sort this out before you lose each other yet again.'

'Look I know it's none of my business but I was looking forward to seeing Camiagain and to give her the recipe book I'd found as I knew how much it meant to her. But when I saw her hugging and kissing him, that early in the morning, so he'd obviously been there all night. I was sorry that I was too late and I'd missed my chance.' He carried on munching on his food.

'Well from what I can gather Camilla is a free agent whereas you, on the other hand, have some explaining to do.' She sucked the meat off the bone and pointed it at him.

'Who me?' he said looking around as though she could be talking to anyone else. He stretched out his arms, palms open, facing upwards. 'What have I done?'

Camilla covered her face with her hand. She knew what was coming next and tried to avoid eye contact with Blake as he gave her a sidelong glance, she saw a familiar flicker of mirth cross his face and could see he was desperately trying not to laugh, she felt giggles bubbling up inside her like a soda syphon.

'Yes you – I thought you were meant to be a big intelligent businessman, so why are you getting jealous of Camilla with the other guy when you're actually seeing someone else? Donna, isn't it?'

'Dawn!' piped up Camilla, a little too quickly to appear nonchalant.

221

'I wasn't jealous.' He laughed. 'I was just—' He hesitated until he found the right word. 'Disappointed, I suppose.'

'You've got some nerve being disappointed in me for spending some time with a friend,' said Camilla, her hackles now raised like porcupine spines down her back.'

'No I wasn't disappointed *in* you. Look, can we start from the beginning please? The reason I was disappointed is that I finished with Dawn when I was in Canada and I was hoping to ask you out when I came to your house, then when I saw Ged. I just . . . I don't know it wasn't how I envisaged meeting you again.'

'Okay,' said Edie, 'thank God for that. Now can you two just apologise to each other, eat your dinner and get a bloody room? The sexual tension in here is enough to set my bloody curtains alight.'

Blake looked suitably admonished; his eyes wide open after Edie's comment. Camilla, who had been tucking into her meal with fervour was now choking on a piece of cabbage. He whacked her on the back.

'I'm so sorry for everything. Can I take you home for a chat? Edie's right; I've been such an idiot.'

'I don't know what to say,' said Camilla unsure as to whether she'd heard him correctly or whether it was just wishful thinking.

'You have been a bloody idiot but you're going nowhere until you've eaten pudding. Camilla, can you fetch those lovely cupcakes in for me please and some plates,' interrupted Edie.

Camilla smiled and left the room. She felt much lighter now that she'd heard Blake's news. She opened a cupboard and bent down to get the plates out. When she stood up again her spine tingled as she felt his presence in the kitchen behind her. She was tempted to spin round and pull him close to kiss him but then there would be no going back, and she still had questions that needed answering.

'Please . . . I need to talk to you.' His eyes sought hers and she could see her past reflected in them. They were the same eyes that had looked into hers all those years ago when they first met. The only difference being some extra lines at the sides. Crow's feet, Auntie Edie would call them, but her mum used to call them laugh lines, and oh how they'd laughed. The question was, could they ever possibly be happy again when the universe had treated them so cruelly? She needed to somehow find out whether her future also lay in those dreamy brown eyes, which now searched her face for something. What? She didn't know – forgiveness maybe?

They joined Edie for a cup of tea and a cupcake and then headed over to Cupcake Cottage.

Chapter 28

She arrived home twenty minutes later at the same time as Blake pulled up in his hire car.

'You really should call this the Cupcakemobile,' he joked, as he opened the door of the van to help her out.

'That's what Ron said. Who knows, maybe I will. If it's good enough for Batman then it's good enough for me.' She locked the van door and walked across the drive, the keys jangling in her hand. She was glad he couldn't hear her heart thumping as it was almost jumping out of her chest. She was eager to get this conversation over with so they could decide whether they would be able to resume or more accurately restart their relationship.

She opened the door, threw her bag on the coffee table and hung her coat up. He followed her inside and she walked through to the kitchen, turning the lights on as she did so.

'Coffee or wine?' she shouted through the open beams into the living room. He sat on the sofa watching her as she moved around the kitchen.

'Wine sounds good please.' She pulled two large glasses down from the overhead cupboard and reached for a bottle of red from the small wine rack on the worktop. She handed him the bottle and the corkscrew and walked back through the door from the kitchen. She sometimes just stepped through the gaps in the beams but decided it might not look very sophisticated if he saw her do it. Although she was sure sophisticated was the last thing she'd looked when escaping out of Auntie Edie's window. She cringed at the thought.

She joined him on the sofa but hitched away from him as she accidentally sat too close. The warmth from his body had felt nice but she needed to distance herself until she knew what she was dealing with.

She placed the glasses on the coffee table and Blake poured the wine. The glug-glug of the burgundy liquid was the only sound in the room. Blake cleared his throat and put the bottle back on the table. Some of the dark liquid had dripped down the bottle and was now forming a tiny pool on the wood. Camilla picked up the glasses and handed one to him. They tapped glasses gently and he said cheers before taking a sip.

'I like what you've done to the place.' He nodded to the new curtains, which matched the rug.

'Thanks,' she answered, taking a too big gulp of wine that she nearly choked on.

'Are you okay?' He passed her a tissue from the box on the side. They were decorated with cupcakes; it made him smile.

'Yes, I'm fine. she said quickly, dabbing at the droplets of wine that had dropped onto her jeans.

'Look I feel I need to feed the elephant in the room. I'm sorry about walking off but as I said it was disappointment rather than annoyance. When I saw him with you in his arms, it really hurt, but I had no right to storm off and leave you upset. That was wrong of me and I'm truly sorry. But I really need to know, is there anything going on between you and Ged?'

225

'Yes,' she cried, taking him by surprise, 'there is. It's something called friendship and yes I won't deny there is an attraction there but I'm not open to flings or one-night stands and I'll be honest, nobody else has ever felt right. Not since you.' She picked up her wine glass and took a large swig. He held her other hand and clasped his fingers through hers. She continued, 'The thing is you're the one who was seeing someone else anyway. I know we're not together but I felt as though we were starting to reconnect then you dropped your bombshell. How do you think that made me feel to find that out?'

'I don't know, tell me please. How did it make you feel?' His eyes searched hers, but she averted his gaze.

'I felt horrible and abandoned. Again. But if I'm honest a little bit relieved because it meant there was no chance that you could leave me again if we weren't together. I know that probably doesn't make sense, but I really couldn't go through that pain again. It took me years to get over you.' She untangled her hand from his as though to make a point, to keep herself separate from him.

He sat back; smoothed his beard with his hand.

He took her wine from her and placed both glasses back down on the table. He held her face softly with his hands; she relished the feeling of his touch, the rough skin from years of hard work. Even though he was a boss, an entrepreneur, he had always remained hands-on with the building and renovating. She closed her eyes and the last ten years disappeared as fat tears rolled down her cheeks. He gently kissed them away just like he did at the airport the last time she'd seen him. The feather-light touch set off feelings of longing inside her that caused her heart to race.

He wrapped his arm around her, pulling her close to him so she could smell that familiar scent of him. His aftershave may have changed over the years but that wonderful musky smell of him hadn't. She breathed it in. Her body relaxed into him, the familiarity was soothing, even though she knew that the next words he uttered could devastate her. She sat up to get her drink and also to face him.

'Is it really over with Dawn?' She had to know.

He cleared his throat. 'It was over as soon as I saw you again.'

The words he used along with the look of complete sincerity sent tingles all down her spine.

'We hadn't been together long; it was really early days so no hard feelings between us. In fact—' he laughed '—I think my sister was more upset than either of us were because she'd set us up in the first place.'

'When did you break up with her?'

'As soon as I got back,' he replied. 'I hadn't even unpacked but I felt she should know straight away.'

'Are you sure you're telling me the truth? Because I rang you a few days into your trip and a woman answered, she said you were in the shower.'

He contemplated for a while before his face registered the day she must have been talking about. 'Ah that would have been my sister. She came round one morning to give me a hard time for finishing with her friend. I'm sorry she never told me you rang.' His face looked genuinely concerned that she wouldn't believe him. His words seemed sincere.

'That's okay, I believe you.'

'Look, I can't tell you how sorry I am for everything. When I saw you in your amazing cupcake van, it took me back to that holiday we had. When I took you to Niagara Falls and we spent the weekend shopping in Buffalo. I remembered you saying how much you'd love to have one, all those years literally melted away and you were my Cami again.'

'That's just it though, I'm not the same and things aren't the same,' she countered.

'I realise that. Don't think I haven't noticed. You're now a confident, self-sufficient woman who has triumphed over adversity. You've overcome such huge obstacles and I'm filled with such admiration for you. I don't think you quite realise how amazing you are.' He nodded to the picture on the wall, at the two happy faces smiling back at them. 'Your mum would be so proud of you. I mean she was anyway but seeing what you've achieved, her face would be glowing with pride right now.'

'Do you think? I'd really like to hope she would be.'

'I don't just think; I know for definite and you look so much like her. I was a little taken aback when I first saw you in the cupcake van because you're the image of her.'

'I love that,' she replied. There weren't many people who had connections to her mum but when Camilla thought of them, she imagined them with long red silken swathes of fabric attached to memories of her. They formed an almost tangible bond to her, a special connection like ribbons to a maypole. She'd seen it when she bumped into an old school friend of her mum's a couple of months ago and always saw it with Auntie Edie. Blake was also one of those people. He had loved her mum almost as much as she had, and the feeling was mutual. Hearing him say her mum would be proud gave her a warm glow inside because she knew he was speaking not just from the heart but also from the experience of having known her so well.

'Cami, I would give anything to have the chance of getting to know you all over again. The past is behind us and the future is unknown but we've got the present, the here and now and we've got each other in this moment. I realise that you've got every right to hate me, but I really hope you don't.'

'I don't hate you at all. But it took me so long to get over you last time and if I'm honest I never really did.' Her heart plunged into her stomach as the realisation of how deep-rooted her pain was hit her slap bang in the solar plexus. He put his arm around her, but she shrugged him off, immediately missing his warmth. Guilt overwhelmed her at the look of rejection and hurt on his face. 'I don't think I can ever truly trust you a hundred per cent until I know the reason why you stopped contacting me all those years ago. Otherwise the fear will always be there that you can switch off from me again, so finally, leaving me with nothing but pain.'

He stood up and paced the room. 'It's really hard for me to talk about that time. I wasn't in a good place.' His facial expression changed, and he became distant. He ran his fingers through his hair, leaving it dishevelled. She was desperate to smooth it down with her fingers, longed to be able to touch him again and rediscover him. But not until they had cleared this up once and for all. She sat on her hands to keep herself from hugging him.

'Please just know that deep down I never stopped loving you.' His eyes were cast downwards, and he turned away, so his back was facing her.

'I'm actually ashamed of what happened back then. Everyone expected me to be strong. My dad died, my mom was devastated, my sister needed me – she was only a kid. I was the man of the house and Dad's business needed looking after. Then there was you. Losing you was more than I could bear. I went off the rails – smoking, drinking, and generally being a real asshole. It was all too much. Everything seemed so pointless. A long-distance relationship, Skype dropping out every five minutes, letters taking days, sometimes weeks to get there. Looking back now I was just too immature to deal with it all. It seemed easier, kinder even, to just break contact. If I'm honest, seeing your face or hearing your voice reminded me that I'd let my dad down. Seeing you stoked the flames of my guilt and I couldn't handle that on top of all the other feelings I was dealing with. I wasn't thinking of anyone but myself. I was a selfish little shit.'

She took a sip of wine and held it in her mouth for a little while before swallowing it, mainly to stop herself from letting him know how much it hurt to hear that.

'Did you blame me because you didn't go back sooner?'

'No, I didn't blame you at all. I think it was just the connection to you that did it. I didn't feel as though I deserved happiness because I'd let him down. When I couldn't see you, the guilt didn't cut so deep. I felt horrible for thinking like that and I'm truly sorry, but I just couldn't help it.'

'I thought you'd gone off with another woman,' she admitted.

'No, I didn't – I can promise you that. With hindsight I was probably depressed. I was angry with the world but never you.' He turned to face her. 'Ever since I went back the only thought that kept me going was that you would be joining me soon just like we'd always planned. But as the months went on that dream became less and less likely and when you told me for definite that it wasn't going to happen, I just switched off. Like I said I didn't know what to say to you. I wrote letter after letter but screwed them all up because the words just didn't come out right, in the end it seemed better to say nothing at all. I'm sorry for that, truly I am.'

She wandered to the window and gazed outside. The moonlight and streetlights had bathed everything in a golden glow. His explanation made a lot of sense but was it what she had wanted to hear? He sounded as though he'd gone through hell. He interrupted her thoughts.

'We were lucky as Dad's oldest friend helped out with the business and kept it going for the first year, then eased me back in slowly when I was ready. Uncle Stu was so patient and kind – not many people have friends like that.'

'He sounds wonderful,' she replied. Thoughts buzzed around her mind like a thousand wasps clamouring over each other to get to their nest. Could she let go of the hurt she'd felt knowing that they were so young back then and that he had been hurting as much as she had?

'It sounds like you could have done with some grief counselling.'

'My mom tried to get me to go but I was stubborn. However we did have a lovely old lady who lived next door, I used to do jobs for her and she was a huge help, I would sit and have tea and cake with her, she talked me through a lot of my grief. She made out that I was doing her a favour by keeping her company but if truth be told I think she saved my life.'

'She sounds just like Auntie Edie, I don't know where I'd be without her.' Said Camilla with affection. 'I just wish that you could have told me,' she couldn't help herself from blurting out.'

'I truthfully didn't know what to say. But now you know. I'm sorry for how much pain I've caused you. But I'm a million miles away from the idiot I was back then so please can we put all this behind us and move on. As Edie always says, life is far too short for these sorts of shenanigans.'

'Yes, and she's quite right. I'm sorry too, Blake, for everything you've been through. It just doesn't seem fair. Life has been so cruel to both of us, but I think we both deserve happiness from now on.'

'I completely agree.' He clasped her hand in his. 'And you're what makes me happy.' He stroked her cheek gently before his face came closer and his lips brushed hers lightly. It seemed the lighter the touch the more powerful the jolts of electricity that shot through her body.

'Please give me another chance. Let's start afresh with a clean slate and a new first date, let me prove myself to you. I promise you won't regret it.'

'Okay,' she breathed, 'let's give it a try.'

Chapter 29

Sitting at a table for two in Flowerpots garden centre the next day, Auntie Edie was as sympathetic with Camilla as she had been with Blake the day before. The waitress had brought over their jacket potatoes and removed the large brightly painted wooden flower they'd been handed when they placed their order. Edie sprinkled salt and pepper vigorously on her tuna mayonnaise filling; un-wrapped the little rectangle of butter and buried it deep into the flesh of the potato where it oozed delectably.

'Now then milady, what on earth is it that you want from this man, he hasn't actually done anything wrong and all he wants to do is love you.'

'I know, I just wish I'd known at the time.'

'Well by the sounds of it you wouldn't have been any help anyway, you would have put more pressure on him had you been there and he didn't want to drag you away from your mum, and the truth is . . .' she hesitated.

'What is the truth?' Camilla asked as she sloshed the balsamic dressing a little too heavy-handedly onto her tuna potato so that it splashed over the table, earning a dirty look from a passing waitress. Camilla used her napkin to wipe it up.

'You being there may have put even more pressure on him and maybe your relationship wouldn't have lasted. At least this way you get to start afresh. The man worships the ground you walk on; he does nothing but talk about you when I see him,'

'Wait. Hold on a minute,' Camilla interrupted, 'how often do you see him?'

'He's been popping in quite regularly and making sure I get to my doctor's appointments and he runs me down to the shops whenever I need to go and he takes me for the odd lunch.' She popped a forkful of the potato in her mouth.

'Oh, I didn't realise that you'd seen that much of him lately,' Camilla felt strangely jealous which was ridiculous, but Edie was her auntie not his.

Edie was never one to hold back, especially where Camilla was concerned. They had always been close but ever since Camilla lost her mum Edie had been fiercely protective of her. She put her knife and fork down and there was kindness in her voice. 'Don't you be getting jealous; you know there's plenty of room in my heart for you and the only man you've ever truly loved.'

She picked up her knife and fork and began to tuck into her lunch, 'And make sure you eat your salad, you always did try to shirk away from eating your veg, just remember no pudding unless it's all gone.'

Camilla was grateful that Auntie Edie had finished her admonishment with a little humour, this lady had been a constant in her life even before she had lost her mum and she found her advice invaluable. Auntie Edie spoke a great deal of sense and Camilla knew she would be a fool not to listen to her. She tucked into her salad until not one leaf was left.

After lunch they had a wander around the garden centre which was always a treat, they looked at candles and ornaments and unusual furnishings. The store had a fabulous team of creatives and it often felt like stepping into another world. The current theme was Alice in Wonderland and it was fun seeing the characters and other accessories peeking from the displays of garden furniture and other delights on sale. They each bought a scented candle labelled 'Mad-Hatter's tea party' and made their way out to the car park where a small group of children had gathered around the cupcake van.

Camilla still smiled broadly every time she saw it, to her it represented friendships and she knew she would be completely lost without hers. They had got her back on her feet again and the cupcake van had given her a new lease of life. Edie chuckled every time she saw it and Camilla knew how much it had played a part in her recovery. Something precious had been taken from her but she had been given something so wonderful in its place, and it showed her that she was loved. Having lost the woman who had given birth to her it was something Camilla needed to know.

The children were asking their parents for ice creams and although she couldn't help them out there she had a pretty delicious alternative to offer them in the form of cupcake kisses, which were the same as her normal cupcakes but tinier versions. She always tried to take a small supply around with her as people were sometimes disappointed that she wasn't a real ice cream seller, however they soon cheered up when she gave them a cupcake kiss in a cute paper bag and with a handmade label attached which had all of her details on.

Edie was delighted to help to serve everyone from the hatch and she chatted excitedly on the journey home. As she left the van and headed up her path she called to Camilla,

'You grab this opportunity with both hands and don't let that man slip away again.'

Camilla smiled at her and blew a kiss, she headed back to Cupcake Cottage to call the love of her life and invite him on that second first date.

Having Angela around had changed Camilla's life dramatically; just having time to stop and breathe had made a huge difference. Being able to leave the cupcake making and decorating to her had meant that Camilla could now take some time out to concentrate on where she was going next.

Camilla's vlog was gaining momentum in terms of hits and followers and so with the help of Jackson – who was quite the little expert – she had invested in a good quality camera and microphone which along with her phone allowed her to to film and edit from different angles.

After a few practice shots she pressed record. She always spoke a little self-consciously at first and could feel her cheeks burning but eventually would relax in front of the camera. She tried to channel Jackson and wished she had just a smidgeon of his confidence. The cake in the shape of the shop was coming along beautifully and she could feel the energy and imagination coming back to her bit by bit. Feeling the cool icing between her fingers brought back happy memories of being with her mum. They had often created weird and wonderful shapes of dogs and birds and people. Her skills had improved a great deal since turning professional. It felt good to be getting back in the game again. She paused the camera as she saw Tillie come into the orangery.

'Look, Auntie Milla, I've made a doggy.' she held up the mangled piece of icing, which had gone sticky in her hand.

'That's amazing, Tillie, well done. Now would you like to make a pussy cat?' Tillie nodded and Camilla lifted her up to sit on a stool and handed her some black icing, which she immediately began rolling in a ball with her chubby fingers. The smell of cupcakes was in the air along with puffs of icing sugar. Camilla smiled at the child. She saw herself through her mother's eyes, face shining with wonderment at creating even the simplest shapes out of icing. Once Tillie left the room Camilla started filming again. She spoke to camera.

'Now I've been given free rein over flavourings. This special couple wanted something a little bit different and fresh for their wedding renewal vows and a little birdie told me they were going on a Caribbean cruise so I thought this would fit the bill perfectly. The layers of the cake as you saw earlier are made up of sponge flavours, some of which I've never tried before but it's good to experiment. Here we have luscious lemon, orange, lime and pineapple sandwiched together with a white chocolate, coconut and tropical fruit ganache. The combination simply tantalises the taste buds.'

She covered the cake with icing and showed her decorating tools to the camera, explaining what each one was for. 'Now I need you to put all of the clear boiled sweets into a freezer bag, like so and give them a hefty whack with your rolling pin.' She began smashing the sweets with her wooden rolling pin. Thoughts of the dodgy house thief or he who shall not be named came into her mind and the rolling pin bashed the wooden chopping board until it bounced a good few millimetres off the table.

'If you don't feel you're hitting it hard enough then don't worry, just imagine it's someone you don't like, maybe a lousy fraudster,' she muttered, expletives escaping her mouth with every bash. She would need to edit the video anyway so she may as well have fun with it. In between bashes she heard a knock coming from the window behind her. She turned and jumped on seeing the window cleaner looking at her with concern etched on his face. She'd completely forgotten that she'd arranged with the landlord for him to come today.'

'Are you okay?' he mouthed.

'Yes, fine thank you. I'm filming right now,' she mouthed back, her hands doing the charades sign for a camera, her cheeks aflame after having been caught being very enthusiastic with the weapon she was yielding. The poor man looked terrified but nodded his understanding and moved to the kitchen window.

'Now we just put all the bashed-up sweets onto grease-proof paper and into the oven, and that is going to make the window for the shop. We can paint the leaded pattern on with one of our edible ink pens.' She continued until the cake was completed, despite a couple more interruptions from the window cleaner being back in shot again and the sound of his squeegee squeaking along the window, which made her cringe in the same way as fingernails scraping down the chalkboard.

'Oh seriously! What bit of "I'm filming" does he not understand?' she growled. 'If he's not careful I'll shove that squeegee where the friggin' sun don't shine.'

A sense of pride and contentment washed over her as she put the finishing touches to the cake. She checked the details on the email from Lucy and was able to tick off everything the customers had asked for apart from the crowning glory. 'Where's that?' asked Tillie who had wandered in to the orangery, wearing her coat ready to go home, quickly followed by an apologetic Angela who'd been trying to keep her out of the way. Luckily they were behind the camera and not in shot..

'Where's what?' asked Camilla deep in concentration as she placed an edible version of the happy couple in front of the cake.

The video ended with Camilla placing the perfect replica of the shop next to the photo that she'd been working from and with huge relief turned off the cameras. 'Where the friggin' sun don't shine? And what's a squeegee?'

'Tillie!' Angela yelped with laughter and Camilla wanted the ground to swallow her up.

'I'm so sorry, Angela, it was just the noise of the bloody window cleaner – squeeeek squeak – it was going through me.'

Angela nodded her head towards the camera. 'What about the filming?' she whispered.

'Oh, it's okay. I'm going to play some music over the sweary bits, so it'll be fine.

Angela smiled and blew a kiss goodbye.

'Wait, before you go, I need Tillie's opinion on the flavours I've used today,' said Camilla holding up three spoons.

The mixing bowls were soon scraped clean by two wooden spoons and one teaspoon. The only evidence that the delicious mixture existed in the first place was around Tillie's mouth as she was not as adept as her mum and Camilla at feeding herself. Camilla decided that tropical cakes had definitely scored ten out of ten on Tillie's Yummy Factor and would add a fresh citrusy tang to her cupcake repertoire.

'Oh, I nearly forgot,' said Angela. 'When you next see Blake can you give him this please.' She handed a card over.

'Yes of course.'

'It's a thank you card from all the mums at the shelter.'

'A thank you card?' Camilla looked puzzled.

'Yes, he bought us a new cooker – a really fancy one. 'He called the house phone the other day when you were out on deliveries. He introduced himself to me and asked

239

if we still needed a new cooker as you'd mentioned about our old one. He then asked me for the website address so he could make the donation. He was going to do it anonymously but had to tell me because naturally we're not allowed to give the actual address out. It's made such a difference to us; he's also bought some new play equipment for the garden.'

'Oh,' said Camilla.'

'He's obviously a good guy with a big heart.'

'A very big heart,' she replied, her own heart swelled, her voice full of pride. 'My mum always said he was one of the good guys, a real keeper.'

She carefully loaded the finished cake into the cupcake van and drove round to the venue, turning on the chimes as she approached. The Signal Box Café was decked out beautifully with red balloons and flowers. Mr Ives had come out to greet her and helped her into the building with the heavy box. Camilla held the box while Mr Ives gently lifted the cake out if it and placed it carefully on the stand, which was nestled amongst exotic flowers. His eyes opened wider in admiration after seeing his precious shop perfectly re-created in cake form and he called his wife over.

'Sandra, come and look at this.' Sandra joined him and tears sprung to her eyes. She was wearing a red shift dress and a red pillbox hat, just like the little icing version of herself.

Camilla gave her a hug. 'Congratulations on your fortieth wedding anniversary and on renewing your wedding vows.'

Mr and Mrs Ives looked at each other tenderly and thanked her. Their daughter Rosie joined them; her mouth opened wide when she saw the cake. 'It's perfect,' she announced, retrieving her phone from her bag to take some pictures of it. She turned to Camilla. 'It's going to be *Serendipity*'s tenth anniversary in a few months. I don't suppose you could create a replica of that for me, could you? It would be amazing.'

Camilla's first reaction was a sharp feeling of apprehension across her stomach but then she saw the looks on the guests' faces as they admired her work and the camera flashes going off all around. Seeing everybody trying to get a closer look at the edible masterpiece, she truly felt a tremor of excitement. Her mind started whirring into overdrive. She'd never made a cake in the shape of a narrow

boat before so that might be fun, and *Serendipity* was such a beautiful café boat. She mentally started working out how much and what colour icing she would need; Camilla always delivered a handful of business cards with every cake and so was able to hand one to Rosie.

'That's lovely – thank you so much. I'll give you a call and maybe you can come and have a cream tea at *Serendipity*, and we can discuss flavours and things.'

'That sounds wonderful,' Camilla replied, her heart filled with a warm and fuzzy feeling.

She wasn't alone, she had been broken and whilst she still wasn't fully mended, she felt the pieces of her were beginning to be put back together by those who loved her – not neatly with glue so you couldn't see the joins, more like with duct tape. The joins would always be visible and there was still a risk of darkness creeping through the cracks. She knew she would never be as good as new but to be just good, just okay, that would be enough for now.

She spent the evening editing the video of her making the cake and uploaded it.

Chapter 30

Spring was in the air and the charity night at the Signal Box Café was in full swing. As well as raising money for a good cause it was a chance for everyone to dress in their finery. The ladies wore elegant ball gowns in a variety of colours. They looked like tropical birds; a beautiful contrast to the staid and handsome tuxedos that the men were wearing. The walls of the venue had been draped in a pale pink silk with a backdrop of fairy lights that twinkled magically. The waiting staff stood behind silver serving vessels filled with delicious hot food, succulent roast beef, turkey and lamb with roast potatoes and plenty of fresh vegetables and all the trimmings.

Camilla was dressed in a beautiful deep pink gown, which had a sweetheart neckline; it gathered in at the waist hugging her figure and flared out in a fishtail at the bottom. The bodice was decorated all over with sequins that sparkled as she moved. She felt like a film star. It was one of the most beautiful dresses she'd ever seen and she'd bought it from a charity shop in Hummingbird Lane, just off the high street, for a fraction of its original cost. Thankfully she had been the first person to see it as they put it on display. She felt that luck was definitely on her side.

She was sitting on a table with her friends: Lucy, Dom, Gracie, Finn, Carrie and Jim. They were waiting for Edie to arrive with her plus-one. Camilla suspected it could have been a man called Richard from the widows and widowers' club she'd been attending lately, although Edie was giving nothing away. Catching a glimpse of Auntie Edie at the door, Camilla walked over to greet her when Ged, who'd been buzzing around, bumped into her as he headed for his table.

'You scrub up well,' he said in his Belfast twang and leaned in for a kiss.

'You're not looking too shabby yourself, Ged. How are you doing?' She placed her hands on his upper arms and kissed him on both cheeks. However, his answer dissolved into background noise when her eyes met Blake's. He was laughing with a giggling Auntie Edie as he pulled her into a bear hug. He smiled and winked at her, which made her heart flip.

He took her breath away; she had never seen him look so handsome; his thick black hair and dark beard were complemented by the tuxedo. He looked sexy and mysterious, like James Bond; she felt flutters in her heart and deep within. She hadn't seen him since they'd had their chat; but they'd spoken on the phone a lot. Both had heavy work schedules and the preparations for this event had kept Camilla busy. She thought their second first date should be fun with friends and the charity do was the perfect place for that.

She approached Edie. 'Auntie Edie, I'm so glad you made it. How are you?'

'I'm very well thank you. I'm afraid Richard couldn't make it tonight, so this handsome young Canadian man offered to escort me.'

'Hi, Blake,' she said, unsure whether to greet him with a kiss or not. He took the decision out of her hands by leaning in to her and brushing his lips against hers.

'You look stunning tonight,' he whispered into her ear. 'I'm looking forward to starting all over again with you.' His voice felt delicious as it tickled her ear. The words were exactly what she wanted to hear. He held out his arms to her and Edie, and both ladies slipped their arms through his as they made their way to their table. Blake ensured he was sitting between the two of them. Lucy, Carrie and Gracie exchanged knowing glances and seemed excited for their friend.

As the food arrived the conversation flowed easily. Blake was introduced to everybody and the chat involved the whole table so nobody felt left out. Blake and Finn exchanged business cards as Blake needed someone to help renovate a few properties he'd bought.

Camilla sat back and watched as her past became inter-twined with her present and would hopefully develop into a wonderful future. The butterflies in her tummy fluttered every time she looked at Blake and she hoped that feeling would never stop. Whenever their eyes met she would look away quickly, frightened to become too absorbed in his because she knew that she could get lost in them so easily.

Lucy leant over to talk to Camilla when Dom was at the bar.

'Jackson wanted me to tell you how funny he found your vlog and he showed me. Oh, Camilla, it's hilarious. It's had about ten thousand hits. He's well impressed.'

'What?' replied Camilla. 'Just on that one post? It's only been on a couple of days and it really wasn't that exciting. It was just me making a cake. I'd completely forgotten about it to be honest; I've been so wrapped up in organ-ising this.' She pointed around the room.

'I haven't seen it all but the part where you bash the sweets up was hysterical.' Lucy was rifling through her phone to show her how many hits it had had. Camilla suddenly felt very hot. She had uploaded the edited version, hadn't she?

'Here look,' said Lucy. 'It was up to fifteen thousand and she could see the window cleaner's face on the video.

'Oh shit, it's the wrong one,' she exclaimed.

'Is everything all right?' asked Blake who'd been talking to Auntie Edie.

'Yes, all good thank you,' Camilla replied nudging Lucy's phone out of the way. She'd have to swap it for the right one as soon as she got home. Blake winked at her and made her feel hot for a different reason. She smiled and was distracted by the noise of the microphone.

Ged was in charge of the fun auction and his humour stole the show. He had a gavel that they'd borrowed from the local mayor and he banged it comically during bids as he was heckled by the audience. The auction was held downstairs but was being filmed and played live on the TV screens upstairs so that all of the audience could see what was going on. The screens along the walls usually played videos of train journeys to add to the authenticity of the Signal Box Café looking like a train compartment inside.

So many kind business owners and individuals had offered up auction lots in the form of items and services, from three-course meals at Belvedere Manor, to photography sessions by Lucy's sister-in-law Abbie, to offers of babysitting, cleaning and DIY for the day. Pretty much everything was covered and the bids were very generous. Camilla put a few bids in for a long weekend stay in someone's holiday home in France but she was outbid by an elderly couple. She wasn't too disappointed because it meant that more money was being raised for the homeless charity.

'So that's £250 from Mr Brown for the hire of a narrow boat for the day to take in the joys of the river Bram and that's been donated by Finn and Gracie Calahan, so thank you very much for that.' The captive audience clapped and cheered. Ged took a swig of beer and continued.

'The next lot is from a very good friend of mine, Camilla Lockley. Where are you Camilla?' He put his hand over his eyes as though looking into the distance even though she was on the table nearest to him. Camilla waved shyly back at him. 'Ah there she is. Now Camilla was always destined to make cakes; in fact I heard that her mum asked for her to be called Vanilla when she was born but the midwife misheard and called her Camilla and like buttercream, the name just stuck.' The audience laughed. 'So as I was saying Vanill . . . sorry I mean Camilla has offered to make a celebration cake worth three hundred pounds in the shape of anything you want. And if you were wondering what her cakes taste like, it was she who made the cupcake towers for this evening. So as there are now none left, I can safely assume that you all thought they were delicious.'

One of the ladies from the homeless charity held up an A3-sized picture of one of Camilla's creations and walked up and down with it. Ged continued, 'So who will give me £50 to start?' Four hands shot up around the room and there was a shout from one of the volunteers who was checking the upstairs tables. He held three fingers up to let Ged know how many were interested there. The price shot up by fifty pounds each time until it got to six hundred pounds.

Camilla had kept her eyes closed the whole time as she felt nervous, and then heard a voice from the bar shout, 'One thousand pounds!' The room fell silent for about ten seconds and then erupted into huge cheers. Many of the guests were volunteers from the charity and they were so happy. Camilla's eyes opened wide. Her hands flew to cover her mouth. The voice was unmistakably his. The sexy Canadian twang did things to her body that nothing else could.

'One thousand pounds going once, going twice, sold to the very generous Canadian at the bar.' Blake raised his beer glass in acknowledgement.

Her eyes met his across the room and he smiled and winked at her. Her heart skipped a beat and she mouthed thank you at him. She was finding it unbelievably hard to tear her gaze away from him.

The clapping and cheering went on for some time, creating an atmosphere of laughter and happiness.

'He's an amazing compere and should do stand-up comedy,' said Auntie Edie clapping along with everybody else. 'And I wouldn't kick him out of bed either. You do well with your admirers – I'll give you that,' she added to Camilla who blushed instantly and choked on her wine. Thankfully Blake was still at the bar so didn't hear the compliment. Lucy did though and she had to stifle a giggle.

Ged was approaching the end of the bids when he was handed an envelope and a bag.

'Please can I have your attention, everyone. It's just been brought to my attention that one of our lots has had an unfortunate accident with a pair of skis and a very snowy mountain. So, I'm afraid that we will have to cancel this lot unless we have a tall dark handsome man who would like to step in. Do we have any takers?'

The sound of heckling followed, and people shouted various names out. Blake had just returned from the bar with drinks for the table and was still standing up when

Edie shouted at the top of her voice, 'Blake Daniels will do it. He's bloody gorgeous.' She turned to Blake who hadn't paid any attention to the announcement as he'd been chatting to someone at the bar. 'You were only just saying that you would have liked to have offered a service or something weren't you,' said Edie. Blake tried to disappear into his chair, but Ged wasn't going to let go.

'Not only has our Canadian friend put in the highest bid of the evening but he has now volunteered to stand in for the poor unfortunate Callum Thomson who is in hospital with two broken legs.' The audience clapped and cheered as Blake nodded, resigned to his fate. Ged called him over to where he was standing with the microphone and Blake put his drink on the table and joined him.

'This is a first for me so what I'm thinking is that this could benefit everybody tonight, so I'm going to auction this one as a mystery service.'

Blake frowned but Camilla knew he could pretty much turn his hand to anything so should be able to cope with the odd bit of DIY or gardening.

Ged continued, 'So for a bit of fun I'm going to let the audience see what it is and our friend here will be the only one who doesn't know what he's let himself in for. So, it seems poor Callum had offered to provide this particular service for the rest of this evening and then for a further two hours in the winner's home at a time of their choosing. So are we ready for this?'

'Yeeees,' the audience replied.

'Well that was pathetic. Now I mean are we really ready for this?'

The audience replied louder, banging spoons on the table and whooping loudly. Blake was smiling and shaking his head, obviously wondering whether he'd made the right decision.

'Okay here goes,' said Ged. 'Laura, can you please show our very generous audience here what Callum was offering.' Laura held up the picture behind Blake's back and the audience shrieked with laughter and some of them wolf whistled. They could hear the rumble of laughter following from those upstairs as they had a couple of seconds' delay on the screens. Camilla and Auntie Edie had tears streaming down their faces and Edie's arm shot up in the air. 'Fifty quid,' she shouted. Blake tried to turn around to see what he had in store but Laura was quick and turned it away from him.

'Hold on a minute, Edie, I haven't even started the bidding yet but go on then. Do I hear fifty quid?'

A middle-aged lady with ginormous boobs put her hand up. 'One hundred pounds,' she offered, licking her lips as she studied Blake.

Two more women shot their hands up. 'We'll club together and that's two hundred pounds,' one of them said.

Ged took a couple more offers and when it reached three hundred and fifty pounds, he struck down his gavel. 'Going once, going—'

Blake looked pleadingly at Camilla. The woman with the final offer looked scary. Camilla could imagine she was into bondage and very strong. She couldn't picture Blake having to think of a safe word with her.

Camilla surprised herself by jumping up. 'Four hundred pounds!' Blake raised his hands in mock prayer as the cheering went up again.

Ged turned to the other woman who looked like she'd chewed on a lemon her mouth was so tightly pursed. 'Five hundred,' she shouted.

Camilla shook her head and shrugged at Blake, mouthed 'I'm sorry,' and, laughed as she saw him facepalming.

'So that's five hundred pounds going once, going twice. Congratulations, Mrs Bainbridge. I hope you enjoy your hot naked waiter.' The room erupted into laughter again. Blake rolled his eyes and offered his hands up in mock surrender as if to say, 'Okay, you've got me, but I'll do it.' Ged handed him the bag, patted him on the back and pointed him in the direction of the toilets.

As Blake walked off Ged spoke into the microphone.

'Huge thanks to Blake for being such a good sport and an even bigger thanks to everyone for making this evening possible. Especially to Camilla Lockley for organising the whole wonderful event and to Lucy Cavendish for allowing us to use her fabulous venue free of charge for this evening. Special thanks to everybody who donated such fantastic lots and for the company who supplied the delicious food and those Signal Box staff who've cooked it so perfectly. You'll find the details of all of the donors in the special programme you should have received on the way in.

'Oh and one last thing: it seems we have raised fifteen thousand, four hundred and thirty pounds, which is an incredible amount to go towards our homeless shelter. So please give yourselves a huge round of applause. You've done brilliantly and now I'm going to shut up because the dancing is about to start. Have a great time everyone and thanks again.' He switched off the microphone and the music started playing whilst staff cleared tables away to create some dancing room.

Camilla's heart burst with pride at what they'd all achieved. She really felt as though she had given something back. Ged hugged her and thanked her again. They were promptly disturbed by loud wolf whistles and the Tom Jones song 'You Can Leave Your Hat On' blasting out of the speakers. Her insides flipped as Blake appeared carrying a tray of drinks. Dressed in nothing but black silk boxer shorts, white collar and cuffs and a dicky bow, his eyes were twinkling. The first thought that went through her head as she took in his tanned skin, hairy chest and muscly physique was voiced loudly by Auntie Edie who was standing by her side, eyes wide open and mouth agape.

'Bloody hell he's been working out!'

Camilla took the glass of champagne he was offering her and as her eyes met his she wondered what other surprises this night had in store for her.

Chapter 31

The next morning when she woke up with his arm around her, it took her a little while to adjust to what had happened. But as soon as she saw the cuff still round his wrist and discovered he still had the collar and dicky bow on too, the memories of their eventful night came flooding back. She giggled to herself and he shuffled round. Still asleep he pulled her in close to him. She kissed his forearm as it was the only part she could reach and then she drifted back off into the most contented sleep she had had for a long time.

Her mind felt completely free, no worries, no wondering about her mum's house. She realised that material things meant nothing and if her mum was here now she would be ecstatic knowing that she was back with her one true love.

Thank goodness for Auntie Edie. She was the greatest connection to her mum as they were always extremely close, and she had worked so hard in bringing her and Blake back together. She would be forever thankful to her and whilst Auntie Edie was around Camilla felt as though a piece of her mum was too. Her mum had always been so proud of her and not long after she died one of the first thoughts that went through her head was: "Who will be proud of me now?" And then one day she realised that Auntie Edie was always proud of everything she did and that made her feel so warm inside.

She'd also realised that her best friend Lucy was proud of her. They'd grown so close over the last couple of years and worked well together on their wedding packages: Lucy being the wedding planner and Camilla providing the cakes. Even when Camilla had the blip over the house and couldn't fulfil an important wedding cake order, she had felt that she'd let Lucy down, and again when she left the cake on the bus. Yet Lucy had never held anything against her and had been so supportive. She knew if it wasn't for Lucy she would not be where she was now. Lucy had held her hand and encouraged her at her own pace, just taking baby steps, first of all helping Jackson with his school cupcakes. That had been so scary for her, but Lucy hadn't put any pressure on her and now look at her: she was back on top of her game.

Her other close friends had helped too, of course. Carrie, who had given her a home when she didn't have one, and Ron giving her the cosy little cupcake van, which she loved so much. It was the perfect vehicle for her and everyone said it really suited her personality. Lucy and Gracie had done a wonderful job of helping her to decorate it. They had been amazing, and she couldn't have done any of it without them. Considering she had hit rock bottom, due to horrible greedy people being in this world, thanks to her precious friends Camilla now felt on top of the world. She was ready to conquer anything and she couldn't wait for this man of hers to wake up so she could conquer him again.

When she awoke later on, she could hear him clattering about in the kitchen so she put on her white cotton robe and followed him downstairs. The smell of bacon came wafting up the stairs and took her back to their time together when he would bring her a breakfast of bacon, pancakes and maple syrup up to bed on a Sunday morning.

She felt a little self-conscious as she entered the kitchen, very aware that this wasn't the skinny kid who'd left her behind all those years ago but a fully-fledged man and a very sexy man at that.

'Morning,' she said as she entered the kitchen. He had his back to her as he poured their coffees. He was wearing nothing but the silky black boxers and she had to strongly resist the urge to squeeze his firm bum cheeks. She giggled at the thought. He turned to face her, dropped the coffee spoon on the counter and swept her up in his arms, kissing her full on the lips. She blushed as it was so unexpected.

'I didn't hear you get up but I wanted to surprise you with breakfast in bed just like old times. Here, you take the coffees up and I'll just be a couple of minutes.' His hair flopped over his forehead as he mixed the eggs in a bowl. She could see he'd got all the utensils – pans and chopping boards – out which was something she used to tell him off for all those years ago. But when he'd gone she would have given anything to have him back and empty every cupboard and drawer in the house. She now knew what was important and it wasn't the contents of her kitchen cupboards.

She made her way back upstairs and opened the bedroom curtains; they could eat at the window seat as it was definitely made for lovers. She decided to have a quick shower before he came back upstairs and as she stood under the hot water she remembered last night and how special it was.

After he'd escaped from a few of the touchy-feely women at the charity event, he had asked her to dance and she had melted into his arms.

'I never thought I'd say this to you but my buttocks are killing me.' He laughed. 'There are a lot of ladies here with very long sharp nails.'

Camilla laughed too. 'You were such a good sport for joining in with that and thank you so much for your generous bid for my cake. I don't think Ged could believe it. You'll have to let me know what cake you'd like and when.'

'I was thinking maybe you could make one for the shelter where Angela and Tillie are.'

'Oh yes, that would be perfect, maybe we could let the children choose the shape of it.' A strand of hair had come loose from her barrette and fallen across her eyes. She blew it out of the way but it landed straight back in the same place. He gently swept it across her face and tucked it softly behind her ear.

'I've been dying to do that since we rescued Bertie.'

'Oh yes, the dragged through a tree backwards look.' She chuckled. 'I hope it's not as messy now as it was then?' Her hand instinctively swept across her hair, smoothing it down.

'Not at all. I mean I just wanted to touch it again. It's so soft and silky. I can't believe I'm holding you in my arms again after all this time. And although part of me would say you haven't changed, you most definitely have. You were a very beautiful girl when I left and now you have matured into a stunningly beautiful woman.' Camilla had to drop her gaze from the intensity of his eyes. He was doing things to her that made her want to rip off what was left of his clothes and they were still in a public place. Then he said the words that clinched the deal for her.

'I never stopped loving you, Camilla. I hope you'll allow me to prove that to you now.'

She reached forward. Their lips met; her tongue searched for his. She could feel his heart thudding as fast as hers was. The years apart just melted away. They were together again; the dream she had long since given up on had somehow come true. She'd always said he was her soulmate, her one true love, and now they could begin their future together. Camilla felt as though she'd never stop smiling when Lucy appeared in front of them and held her phone up. Blake pulled her in even closer as they posed for the photograph.

'Gorgeous,' said Lucy showing them the image before searching out Gracie and Finn.

They spent the rest of the evening in each other's arms, swaying to the music, and when it stopped she didn't want to let him go. Blake had already danced with Auntie Edie and she was enjoying the attention from the other men including Ged, Finn and Dom who had all taken turns to twirl her around the dance floor. But she was getting tired now so Blake and Camilla took her home in a taxi. As soon as he had seen her safely into the house and heard her lock the door he was back in the taxi with Camilla and for the ten-minute journey they kissed non-stop, so much so that when the taxi driver asked for directions Blake just used his hands to point in the direction they needed to go.

At home they headed straight for the bedroom. Blake stood behind Camilla to slowly pull the zip down on her dress, kissing her neck as he did so. As it fell to her waist his hands reached round to her breasts stroking them gently. Her sharp intake of breath let him know that she was longing for him as much as he was for her; he continued to pull the zip down and she stepped out of the dress as it slithered to the floor. The sequins felt sharp on the underside of her feet. She reached around to him. Her hand stroked the smoothness of his boxers and as her fingers slid into the waistband, she felt something unusual and crinkly.

'What's this?' she asked as she held what felt like a piece of paper in her hand. As they unfurled it Camilla threw her head back and laughed like a demented rabbit. 'It's a twenty-pound note,' she exclaimed.

'I'm going to kill Dom when I get my hands on him.' Blake laughed. 'I saw him whispering something to that handsy woman who kept pinching my butt. Quick, help me get them off so we can see if there's any more money in there.' As he slid them off he gently pushed Camilla back on the bed and the thought of money was soon forgotten.

Chapter 32

After breakfast they had returned to bed to rediscover each other all over again. She watched him whilst he slept, still not quite believing that he was back in her life. A delicious shiver ran through her body as she remembered how tightly he'd held on to her all night as if scared she might disappear as he had done all those years ago As much as she would have loved to have stayed in bed with him she very reluctantly peeled herself away and sneaked into the shower as she had a busy day of cupcake making today.

Even though they had shared such intimacy before she found that she felt very bashful around him now. Giggling like a silly schoolgirl if he so much as looked at her, and last night he had wanted to look at every inch of her as they rediscovered each other and reclaimed what they had both thought had been lost forever.

Whilst he had a sleep and a shower she made a start on cupcake making and the third batch had just gone in the oven. She made sandwiches and brought two mugs of coffee into the orangery as she placed them on the table, she felt his arms come round her waist and squeeze.

'You are amazing,' he whispered in her ear.

His hot breath sent shivers down her spine and she giggled as it tickled her ear.

'You're not so bad yourself actually, mister.'

He turned her round to face him, his skin still damp from the shower and his hair ruffled where he'd towel dried it. Her hands stroked down his smooth back stopping at the towel tied around his waist. He turned her face to him and his lips found hers, not as urgently as the night before, but more gentle, softer as if relishing every moment.

The smell of warm chocolate began to permeate through the essence of bacon and sausage in the air and mingled with the strong aroma from the coffee machine.

Blake took in a deep breath. 'I don't know what to devour first: coffee, lunch, cupcakes or you.' He kissed her neck as he said it and pulled her close to him; she nuzzled into his neck but was interrupted by the dinging of the oven timer.

'Why don't you start with lunch and then make your way through the rest, if you've still got an appetite that is.' She pulled out a seat for him and went into the kitchen, whipped the oven gloves from over her shoulder and took out the third batch of cupcakes before replacing them with the fourth lot. She twisted the timer on again for another twenty minutes and joined Blake at the table.

Tucking into his sandwiches he gestured to the rose bowl in the centre of the table. 'Nice flowers.'

'Thank you, they're from the garden. I'm not much of a gardener but the previous owner obviously knew what they were doing. It's still a bit over-run so when I find time I'll have to sort it out. It seems a shame to let all their hard work go to waste.' She cut into her sandwich but wasn't sure how she would manage to eat it as her tummy was flipping every which way. She could hardly believe he was physically here in her house after spending one of the wildest nights she'd ever had with someone. They had certainly made up for lost time. A shiver shook through her entire body at the memory of it.

He wiped his mouth with the napkin and screwed it up on his plate. 'I'll have a go of tidying it up for you and then get some of the guys round to finish it off sometime in the week if that's okay with you.'

Camilla just about managed to squeeze the tiny bit of bread down her dry throat and had to wash it down with copious amounts of water before she could answer him.

'Oh no, you really don't have to do that. I'm sure you're busy enough already.'

'It would be my pleasure, and after all I intend to make it my mission that you are completely satisfied.' He took her hand and gently pulled her to her feet. 'In every way.' He leaned down to find her lips and crushed them with his own. Her senses were overloaded. He smelt fresh like oranges, and tasted like coffee. His skin felt warm and smooth beneath her fingers. Hers was on fire from his touch; he began to undress her and dropped his towel to the floor.

'How long have we got before that bloody dinger on the oven goes?'

'At least fifteen minutes,' she replied as she led him up the stairs.

Half an hour later she took the burnt offerings out of the oven and threw them straight into the outside bin; the oven timer had long since given up trying to call her attention. Today it didn't matter about burnt cupcakes. They were replaceable and as she'd discovered since losing Blake and finding him again, he wasn't.

She'd tried to make it work with other men and they'd been very nice and decent people but it had never felt as right as it did now with him. She'd finally got all she'd ever wanted. She had Blake and he seemed just as deliriously happy to be back with her.

Blake arrived back in the kitchen wearing the trousers and shirt from the night before. He breathed in deeply. 'This house tastes amazing; God knows how many calories are in the air here.' He laughed. His phone rang and he answered it. 'Right, the taxi is here. I'm off home to get changed and to leave you in peace for a little while.' He drew her into him and kissed her firmly on the lips. She gently pushed him away.

'Oh no, look, you're covered in icing sugar now from my apron.'

'I really don't care.' He pulled her back into his arms and kissed her again. 'Now then what do you fancy doing tonight? We could go out for a meal or I could bring us back a takeaway, what do you think? Also as I have to leave early for Canada tomorrow I wondered whether you wanted me to stay over again? I don't want to be presumptuous.

'Yes of course I want you to stay, I really wish you didn't have to go so soon though.'

'I know but the good news is it should be the last time for a good while and I'll be back before you know it.'

Camilla thought that if they went out for a meal then she would have to share him with waiters and other customers and the rest of the world and she felt greedy tonight; she wanted him all to herself. She stroked her finger gently along his lip before kissing him gently. His beard tickled her face.

'There's a lovely new Thai restaurant just opened up in Bramblewood high street; maybe you could pick up a takeaway from there,' she said.

'Sounds perfect. What would you like?'

'The mixed starters are nice and they—' his lips touched hers softly '—do. a. lovely. lamb. massaman. curry. with.

coconut. rice.' As she spoke, he punctuated every one of her words with a kiss to her lips.

He squeezed her hand and laughed. 'I don't want to leave you even for a second, Cami; I love you so much.'

'I love you too,' she replied, breathing in his warm breath as though it were the only thing she needed to make her thrive. 'I simply can't believe you're really here. Let's forget the takeaway and live off nothing but cupcakes for the rest of our lives.' She giggled.

'I won't be long, I promise.' His hand held her cheek softly as he pulled himself away from the kiss he didn't seem to want to end. They were rudely interrupted by the taxi driver beeping his horn outside.

'See you soon.' She reluctantly closed the door after him. She felt like her insides turned to buttercream every time she was with him. She soon had to snap back into reality when the beeper on the oven called her back into the kitchen. Her phone pinged with a text from him.

She took the cupcakes out of the oven, replaced them with the next batch then replied to his text.

She began weighing for the next load. These ones were brownie cupcakes: brownie mix with chopped nuts and a succulent fondant centre with chocolate and vanilla swirls of buttercream on top, sprinkled with tiny cubes of fudge. As she made them she became lost in concentration. She was putting the final touches to them by drizzling choco-late sauce over the top of them when her phone pinged with another text.

She pressed the button on her phone with her knuckle, the only part of her hand that wasn't covered in something sweet, and a smile rose up from her heart as she read it.

Using the piping bag full of chocolate sauce, she piped straight onto the table, 'I love Blake,' which she then surrounded with a chocolate sauce heart. She took a photograph with her phone and sent it to him as a reply.

She spent the rest of the afternoon packing the cakes into the various boxes and loading up the cupcake van ready to make her deliveries.

Once parked outside the Signal Box Café she turned on the chimes to alert Lucy that she was there. Lucy came out of Railway Cottage with the keys, hugged her and brought a large trolley rack from the Signal Box, which they loaded the cupcakes onto and wheeled back into the kitchen. Lucy opened one of the boxes with the brownies in and inhaled deeply, a look of sheer pleasure on her face.

'I'm afraid I'm taking a box of these home for Dom and Jackson – and me, of course. They smell far too delicious though. I might have to start going to Cupcakes Anonymous if you keep coming up with these amazing flavours. Have you got time for a quick coffee?'

Camilla checked her watch. 'Just a quickie then as I'll burst if I don't tell you what happened with Blake.'

Lucy's eyes lit up in anticipation. 'Oh my God, you're blushing. What have you been up to?'

Camilla covered her cheeks with her hands and went to speak but Lucy stopped her.

'Hold on wait a minute I want to give you all my attention. You get comfortable in one of the booths and I'll bring the cappuccinos out.' She ushered her through the door and gestured to one of the comfy seats in the booth at the window. 'Do you want choccy sprinkles on yours?'

'Ooh I don't know. Are you having any?' She settled herself into the booth, which was exactly like sitting in a train carriage.

'Hell yeah,' Lucy replied as she burst through the swinging kitchen door, 'after all this is a celebration.' She placed the tray on the table and offloaded the drinks and a plate of assorted biscuits. 'I thought you might need a change from cupcakes.' She laughed.

Camilla smiled, picked up a pink wafer and took a bite. Lucy took a chocolate bourbon and dipped it deeply into her frothy cappuccino. 'Right then spill before one of us bursts. What happened?' She settled back and chomped on the soggy biscuit.

'Well, we kind of got together a little bit at the charity do,' she began.

'Yes I saw you dancing and you looked stunning together, especially as he was almost naked. What a good sport he was for joining in with the fun and I noticed he was very popular with the ladies.'

'You won't believe how popular. His bum cheeks are covered in bruises from all the pinching.'

Lucy shrieked with laughter. 'And how do you know this?'

Camilla's face was a deep shade of beetroot and she almost choked on her pink wafer. 'That's nothing, I also found a twenty-pound note down his boxers. Apparently Dom gave it to that woman who couldn't keep her hands off Blake. It was so funny.'

Lucy was holding on to her belly and laughing deeply. 'That's hilarious. Oh poor Blake. So how was it then? Are you in luuurve?' she teased.

Camilla had a faraway look in her eyes as she remembered his arms around her in this very room. She shivered.

'It was amazing, Lucy, and the truth is I never stopped loving him, not ever. Our sex life was always good but those years apart and I suppose the fact that we're both a lot older has added another dimension to it. I've never known anything like it before.'

Lucy smiled at her and sipped from her large cup as she relished the details. 'What – not even with Freddy?'

Camilla blew some froth from the top of her cappuccino and sipped from the warmth below it. 'Poor Freddy, to be honest I always felt like I was short-changing him. He was always second best in my heart, the runner-up to my affections. I feel really mean saying that but it's true. I can't help it. Blake was always on the winners' podium in my eyes but I never ever would have thought that I would see him again. It's like a crazy dream come true.'

'You know me; being a wedding planner I just love a happy ending – and look, you're giving me goose bumps.' She lifted her arm to provide the evidence.

Camilla smiled at her and checked her watch again. 'I'd better get back as he'll be on his way back round soon and then he's off to Canada for a week.' She drank another mouthful of coffee and wiped away her cappuccino moustache with a napkin.

'Oh no, that's bad timing. You'd better make the most of him tonight then.' She winked and collected the coffee cups onto the tray. 'I'll see you during the week anyway but call me if you're lonely and we can get together.'

'Will do but I'm so busy that I don't think I'll even have time to think this week. I've been getting so many orders in from far and wide. Luckily I have Angela to help out as she's been a godsend.'

She picked her keys up from the table and stood up to go.

'Thanks so much for the coffee and the chat. I really don't want to raise my hopes this time with Blake, as it seems like every time we get together something drags us apart again, but this time I'm not going to let him slip through my fingers. I can promise you that.' She hugged Lucy tightly.

Lucy gave her a squeeze. 'I'm so happy for you, darling, I really am. You deserve nothing but happiness.'

'Fingers crossed,' replied Camilla as she hopped into the little cupcake van and drove home, waving to Lucy with her fingers still crossed.

Chapter 33

Back at Cupcake Cottage, Camilla breathed in the sweet scent of vanilla, which delicately fragranced the air. It was such a welcoming place to be and so homely. She lit the fire in the living room as the air had a chill to it. She wiped down the work surfaces now that the icing sugar had had a chance to settle. After mopping the floor she was satisfied that everywhere smelt lemony fresh and ran up the stairs to have a quick shower before Blake arrived with the takeaway. Her heart flipped at the thought of him returning, especially as she had asked him to stay as he had an early flight the next day.

Her thoughts flashed back to how he'd made her feel the night before and she almost gasped as her breath was taken away by the memory of him touching her and taking her so passionately, as though they had never been apart. Yet there was something so much more grown up about them both, a maturity that she supposed should be expected after ten years apart. She tried not to think about the fact that they had both had experience of being with other people.

She wasn't a naturally jealous person but the thought of Blake being with anyone else cut into her deeply like a knife. The fear of losing him hadn't totally gone away if she was honest. Their relationship was still so new, and her heart still bore scars from the first time they split up. So, it wasn't going to be easy to put all of her trust in him and allow him access to her fragile heart once more. She could at least console herself that when they had split a decade ago it was through no fault of their own. Their stars were misaligned; maybe it just hadn't been their time right then, but now, there would be no stopping them. They were together at long last.

She changed into a soft lilac off-the-shoulder jumper and pale blue jeans. Her platinum blonde hair tickled the bare skin of her shoulders as she shook it out from her ponytail. Apart from lip balm with a slight shimmer to it, she wore no make-up and her freshly moisturised face glowed with anticipation of what was to come.

When she read the text message from Blake to say that he would be there in ten minutes her stomach felt as though someone was inside it sashaying around with a hula hoop. She padded into the kitchen in bare feet showing off freshly painted toenails and put the plates in the oven to warm up. She pulled two large wine glasses down from the cupboard and fumbled in the drawer for the corkscrew. Once she had retrieved it she uncorked the bottle of red she'd taken from her small wine rack on the kitchen counter. The plummy scent, desperate to escape the confines of its glass prison, filled the air around her as soon as the cork popped out. She filled the glasses and couldn't resist taking a sip of the purplish red liquid as she took them to the table in the orangery.

Even though she was expecting him it didn't stop her from jumping when she heard the doorbell ring. With her heart still pounding she ran to the door and opened it to see him beaming a white-toothed smile and holding up the paper bag from the Thai restaurant in one hand and a leather sports bag in the other. She threw her arms around his neck and planted a kiss firmly on his lips. He gathered her close to him dropped his bag to the floor and lifted her off her feet, walking into the cottage as their lips remained locked together. He reluctantly put her down in the living room and handed her the takeaway.

'Either you're pleased to see me or ravenously hungry,' he joked, grabbed his overnight bag from the front step and shut the door. He dumped the bag ungraciously in the living room and followed Camilla into the kitchen where she was already crunching on a prawn cracker. He took one from the bag.

'Ah that confirms it; you just wanted me for my dumplings and my prawn crackers.'

Camilla turned to him and giggled; she bent her head and took the prawn cracker from his hand with her mouth. He grabbed her to him and kissed her neck until she surrendered with laughter.

'Here, you take these in to the table.' She handed him some warm side plates and the box with the starters in it and put the main meal boxes in the oven with the dinner plates. He was sitting at the table when she entered the orangery and when he looked at her she had to stop just for a couple of seconds to close her eyes and breathe deeply.

He still had the same effect on her that he always had but now it was even stronger because she knew what it felt like not to have him in her life and she couldn't bear to let go of him again. His dark curls and beard made him look like a hero from a romantic movie. She half expected him to jump up and rip off his shirt to save her from some disastrous situation she'd found herself in. His brown eyes sparkled and reflected all the memories they'd shared together. The small crinkles at the sides of them intrigued her. She knew that she had helped some of those lines appear; they had laughed a lot for those years they had together.

'I was just thinking about all the wonderful laughs we've had over the years. Remember sliding down the snowy hills on a makeshift sledge where we both ended up in a heap at the bottom?'

'As if I could ever forget,' he replied. 'We couldn't move because our legs were tangled up together and we laughed so much we thought our ribs were broken.'

She laughed as his eyes sparkled at the memory. 'I remember you smiled, and so much snow came out of your mouth. I couldn't stop laughing.'

'That's because I landed face down in the snow to protect you.' He chuckled. 'What about the time I was taking a picture of you by that statue and I fell backwards very unceremoniously into the duckpond?'

Camilla threw her head back and shrieked with laughter. 'Yes, and you were completely submerged under the water apart from the arm that was carrying the camera, which somehow remained completely dry. It was even funnier that you carried on clicking the camera button to take the pictures anyway for dramatic effect before pulling yourself out.'

'You could hardly pull me out as you were bent over double laughing hysterically. I seem to remember the resulting pictures showed your face horrified at first when you obviously thought I'd died, then gradually smiling and eventually grinning like a maniac as you got closer and closer to the camera.'

'And then I got one of you taken when you emerged, soaking wet with that cheeky grin on your face; it's funny though because in my memories you didn't have a beard.'

He had framed that photo and for many years it never failed to make them laugh. They had shared so many happy times together and Camilla was honoured and proud to be part of the history of his face. Their happiness was etched into those lines and hopefully they had the rest of their lives to share many more moments of happiness; after all, this was just the beginning.

He pulled her onto his knee and they kissed between sips of red wine and feeding each other spring rolls, satay chicken dipped in peanut sauce and prawn toasts. The main meals weren't eaten until much later on after they had moved to the living room and made love leisurely on the fluffy rug in front of the roaring fire. Camilla felt herself float away on a cloud of pure pleasure that she had never felt before. Her hands had grasped his hair whilst he played her body as if it was the most exquisite instrument he had ever seen. His touch was electrifying, leaving blazing trails of fire in its wake. The waves that racked her body felt like they would never stop. Eventually they lay in each other's arms, covered with the velvet throw from the couch. He stroked her face, his finger trailing gently over her soft skin, and followed it with soft butterfly kisses.

'I never in my wildest dreams expected to be back here with you in my arms.' He kissed her nose. 'I truthfully expected you to be married with a couple of kids. You know, like we used to talk about.'

'I never even considered it with anybody else.' She clasped her hands over his chest and lifted her head to look into his eyes. Just looking at him sent bolts of desire shooting through her body. 'I'm never letting you go ever again,' she said. Her heart swelled with so much love for him, bursting through the remnants of imaginary plasters and duct tape she had tried to stick it back together with. It was strong again, beating to the rhythm of their love, this time invincible because he promised to look after it for her, now that he'd made it whole again.

He kissed her, his tongue just gently slipping into her mouth.

'You, young lady, have made me ravenous.' He pulled on his boxers and she retrieved her underwear, which was dangling from the living room lamp, and put them on.

As she pulled the jumper over her head Blake showered her bare shoulder with kisses, which sent tingles through her whole being. She giggled and shook him off. 'You're insatiable, Mr Daniels; now let me feed you first.'

'What do you expect?' He placed his arms around her from behind, kissing her neck as they walked into the kitchen. 'I've got ten years to make up for.'

Blake grabbed the wine and Camilla brought the main courses into the cosy living room where they sat on cushions on the floor and ate at the coffee table, remembering the past with great affection.

'That was one of the best meals I've ever had, especially the bit between the starters and the main; I can't wait to see what's for dessert.' He winked at her lasciviously then laughed a deep hearty laugh as she whipped him with a napkin. He sat up on the couch and pulled her towards him; she sat next to him with her legs across his lap.

'I've just had a memory flash into my mind of you and my mum singing carols together, do you remember?'

'Yes I do, she'd come round for dinner and you got held up at work. We cracked open the brandy and joined in with a carol concert on the telly.'

'You got on so well together. My mum would be so happy to know we were back together. She always felt so guilty—' She sighed her voice cracking with emotion, remembering how well her mum and Blake had got on. Then unable to finish her sentence a feeling of dread overwhelmed her. Her heart crashed through to her stomach, which suddenly felt as though she'd filled it with concrete and not the delicious Thai food they'd just enjoyed. The tears followed like an avalanche, streaming down her face as memories of her precious mum came flooding back.

For months she had painted a thin seal over her loss, happy to stay in the denial stage of mourning because then she didn't have to face up to the pain. She had fallen apart at the loss of her mum's house but thanks to the love of her friends and Blake coming back into her life she was coping with that. As Auntie Edie had said, 'It's only bricks and mortar, dear, no one can ever take away the love and those precious memories that you and your beautiful mum shared.'

Camilla had developed her own coping strategy. If she tried hard enough she could imagine that her mum had gone on holiday and was having an amazing time. She'd always wanted to go to Hawaii so she would picture her there, surrounded by exotic cocktails and palm trees, powder-white sand and crystal clear blue water. For her fiftieth birthday Camilla had taken her mum to Milan for a long weekend and they'd had such a happy time. Eating flatbreads in a café outside the Duomo and a day trip to Lake Como where they joked about looking for George Clooney.

One of the most breath-taking scenes they had ever seen had been on a boat trip, which they had thought was just a short trip around the lake. But it went further than they thought it would and as they sailed around the side of the mountain, the scene opened up and snow-capped mountains appeared before them. It was ethereal, almost like the backdrop of a movie set and certainly the most beautiful place they'd ever been to. When Camilla needed to think of her happy place during yoga or meditation, this was always the place she drifted off to. She was happy then; she had her mum.

'Cami, are you okay?' Blake interrupted her thoughts, kissed away her tears.

She grabbed a tissue from the box on the side table and dabbed at her eyes. She took his hand and squeezed.

'Sorry, it's just thinking about my mum. The only way I can cope on a day-to-day basis is by believing she's still here. The thought of facing up to the reality of her loss is too huge for me to process. I've seen that chasm of complete blackness and have teetered around the edge of it, so desperate not to fall into the oblivion within.'

Her throat felt constricted as she choked on her words.

'I have clung on so tightly to the edge to keep hold of it and so I'm having to drip-feed my grief little by little, if that makes sense. This is my coping strategy. I don't want to go on medication and I've tried therapy, which has been good for helping me learn to meditate and calm myself down. But with this grieving process, if I'm honest, I don't want to stop grieving. I will grieve for the rest of my life anyway and I know that I need to adjust to a new life without her in it. But I feel as though if I stop mourning it means I loved her slightly less than before.' Her voice trembled.

Blake gathered her up in his arms as though she weighed nothing; he kissed the top of her head and squeezed her tight.

'I really wish I could just wrap you up in cotton wool to protect you from the pain but I know that even that won't protect you from the agony you're feeling on the inside. I loved your mum too. She was an amazing woman. Your relationship was so very special and that's something to cherish.' He held her tighter. 'Just let it out, Cami – I'm

274

here for you. But just to be sure, your mum knew how much you loved her just as you know how much she loved you. You were like two peas in a pod.'

She gave in and her whole body shook with heavy sobs and an almost animalistic cry that she'd never heard before emanated from her.

When the crying had subsided, Blake carried her up the stairs to bed. She was physically and mentally exhausted. She snuggled into the foetal position and felt cocooned by his warmth as he spooned her.

Camilla woke to Blake's alarm going off. He grabbed his phone and bashed it with his finger, trying to switch it off. She rubbed her eyes, which were red and sore. The muscles around her throat ached from the crying but other than that she felt good. In fact, a sense of something being released washed over her. The grief built up inside her sometimes like Auntie Edie's pressure cooker until it reached a crescendo and then she would feel better for a few months before it happened again. But last night felt different; it was bigger, more powerful but felt less lonely as she was in Blake's arms and she knew he understood her pain.

As Blake had nodded off again she put on a robe and skipped downstairs to make coffee and bring him some orange juice up as she knew that's how he liked to start his day. When she arrived back in the bedroom she saw the bed was empty and could hear the shower going. She cheekily stripped off and slid into the shower cubicle with him.

'I thought as you're so tired you might need someone to soap you up.' She squirted the shower gel into her hands and started at his chest.'

The coffee was lukewarm by the time they sat in the window seat to enjoy it. The weather was dull outside, the sky grey and overcast but inside the room the sun was beaming. Electricity crackled whenever their eyes met over the tops of their cupcake-patterned coffee cups.

'Are you sure I can't get you anything to eat?' she asked.

'No I'm fine thanks. I'll have breakfast in the airport lounge to pass the time away.'

His Canadian twang was so sexy and she could feel her insides pull towards him as though he had them attached by string. There was no doubt about it: her heart was well and truly his now. In fact, she realised, it always had been. She leant over and kissed him.

'Right that does it,' he said, pulling his phone out of his pocket.

'What?' she asked.

He smiled wickedly and dialled a number.

Camilla's hands flew to her open mouth to stop an excited squeal from escaping as he told his secretary he was unable to make the trip and asked her to put everything back a week due to unforeseen circumstances.

The next seven days were complete bliss for Camilla, she introduced Blake to Angela the next morning and she made Camilla laugh by pulling an approving face, she normally only reserved for Jake Gyllenhall, behind Blake's back. She was happy to take up extra cupcake making so that Camilla and Blake could pop out for a few hours a day. They walked hand in hand along the river and stopped at Serendipity for coffee.

'You know that saying that you should take time to smell the coffee is so true. I mean I never even knew this place existed.'

'It's beautiful isn't it? There are so many special places to visit in Bramblewood, it's such a quaint little town, I'm so happy to be living here and it's really good to see you so relaxed. You're such a workaholic.'

'Well I never really had any reason to take a pause, until you.'

She blushed as his eyes held hers and he beamed at her.

'So where to next?' he asked as he drank the remains of his coffee.

'We can just carry on along the river if you like, it's so relaxing.' She finished her drink, they thanked Rosie and left.

Blake's phone pinged, he took it out of his pocket, laughed and showed Camilla a picture of Lottie on a sailboat with her boyfriend.

'She's grown into a beautiful woman,' replied Camilla.

'I'll tell her you said that but she won't believe you though. Say cheese,' replied Blake as he held his phone up to take a selfie of them with Serendipity in the background. Seeing the image of them together on the screen sent a cluster of butterflies loose in her stomach.

"*Call that a boat,*" he said out loud as he typed, "*This is a boat.*" He pressed send and a couple of seconds later received a reply which he held out to Camilla.

"*So that's why you're not back here. Say hi to Camilla for me. You look so cute together and the boat is adorable. Love you.*" She followed it up with a cross eyed selfie.

He laughed, typed a quick reply and put his phone away as they carried on walking along the towpath.

'She'll miss you if you do move back here for good, won't she?'

'Yes she will but I'd still be visiting there quite a bit with work and she can come over to England again. She's still in touch with a few friends from over here and she's got lots of friends there too. She'll probably be glad to see the back of me for a bit because she says I'm very "parenty."'

Camilla laughed and he put his arm around her, pulling her in close to him.

'This feels so good,' he said. 'For the last ten years I've tried to get on with my life but losing my dad left a void where my heart used to be. I thought I'd lost it forever but now I've realised that you had it all along for safekeeping. It's always belonged to you and I'm just sorry that I never took such good care of yours.'

Camilla looked up to him and he bent his head to kiss her softly on the lips.

'That's all in the past now but thank you.' She squeezed his hand.

'Ahoy there.' A familiar voice shouted from a narrow boat along the river.

'Finn how are you,' Camilla shouted back, 'Is Gracie on board?'

Her question was answered when Gracie and a giggling Matty appeared in the window waving.

'We thought we'd pop over to the pub for drinks and a bite to eat, fancy joining us?'

Camilla looked at Blake and he nodded and smiled.

'We'd love to, thanks.'

'Okay great, stay there and I'll pick you up.'

Finn manoeuvred the boat toward the bank, lassoed the rope and Blake pulled them closer. They climbed on board and Camilla joined Matty and Gracie in the living room area whilst Finn let Blake have a go of steering.

'Camilla's heart swelled as she heard the two men laughing, it was so important for her that her friends liked Blake too.

'I'll text Lucy and Dom and see if they're free too.' Said Gracie as Mattie bounced up and down on Camilla's knee.'

Lucy and Dom joined them later on and as Camilla watched the friendships build and grow she felt it was one of the best days she'd had in a long time.

The week flew by and Camilla had new treasured memories of Blake helping her out in the cupcake van at the farmer's market. He'd bantered with the customers and with Ged and had become a dab hand at swirling the topping on the cupcakes. They'd even had a cheeky snog in it at the end of the night in the Unicorn carpark.

The morning of departure arrived far too soon,

'I can't believe it's time for you to go, I'm going to miss you so much. When will you be back?'

He stroked her hair. 'Saturday morning, bright and early, and I already can't wait. Let's go out for a nice meal to a fancy restaurant on Saturday night, or better still a boozy lunch somewhere beautiful where we can explore in the afternoon and then have dinner later on. How about Cambridge? We used to have such good times there.'

'That sounds absolutely perfect, I can't wait. Can we go punting again? But this time try not to lose the pole.' She teased.

'I'll try but to be fair a bee did fly into my face.' He laughed.

'It wasn't a bee it was a willow branch.'

'I got the pole back didn't I?'

'Yes but we had to go round for the rest of the day with a wet arm each after trying to frantically paddle back to it.' She giggled.

'If my lady wants to punt then we shall punt, but you'd better bring some waterproofs just incase.' He swigged the last of his coffee and stood to leave. He took her hand as they went downstairs. She opened the front door for him, ran her fingers through his damp curls as he stroked away a strand of her wet hair from her face.

'I love you, Cami. I'm so thankful to have you back in my life again.' He crushed her lips with his own, his beard gently scratched her face and they held each other tightly, neither wanting to be the first to let go. He eventually forced himself to tear away from her, checking his watch.

'Don't worry, I'll be back before you know it.'

'I'll have baked over two thousand cupcakes by the time you get back,' she said, trying to lighten the mood and to stop herself from being a wuss and crying.

'In that case I'll see you in two thousand cupcakes.' He laughed, winked at her and got into his car.

Camilla went into the kitchen to make her first batch. 'I'll see you in two thousand cupcakes,' she whispered to herself and smiled.

Chapter 34

The week started off with business as usual at Cupcake Cottage. Angela's daughter was now at nursery a couple of days a week, which gave her more freedom to bake. Thanks to Camilla giving her a job, Angela was ready to move out of the shelter and had found a small flat to rent. She had been so excited to tell Camilla.

'I feel as though I've got my dignity back,' she'd said with a gush of pride. Camilla had hugged her; she couldn't have chosen a better employee. Angela was loyal, reliable and was now a fantastic baker. She'd come such a long way from those burnt offerings she had brought to her interview and her daughter was thriving too. Sometimes people just needed a leg-up to be given a chance to prove themselves.

'Angela, I've been thinking, I'd really love to do something for the other mums at the shelter. I'm hoping to expand the business, maybe look for premises locally and offer employment to the others. What do you think?' She was interrupted as the doorbell rang and Camilla opened it to Ged. He wore his usual cheeky grin as he kissed her on both cheeks.

'Come in, Ged, the kettle's on, and we're just putting the final touches to your order.'

Ged followed her to the kitchen and greeted Angela in the same way.

'You know I swear this whole cottage is made out of cake. From the outside it looks like one of those chocolate box gaffs and even the air tastes good in here.' He swiped his finger round the bowl in the sink and licked it, clearly enjoying the tantalising zest of lemon buttercream fizzing on his tongue.

'Oi,' said Angela, 'here's one for you.' She added an extra swirl to one of the cakes she was decorating and placed it in his hand at the same time as Camilla put a mug of coffee down on the worktop in front of him.

'This is my favourite place in the whole world to be. Do you know that?' he said before biting into his ginger and lemon cupcake, half of it remaining stuck to his face.

'And yours is our favourite job to do,' said Camilla with a laugh, handing him a couple of squares of paper towel.

'Everyone at the shelter is so grateful to you for your contribution; it makes our visitors feel so special to have something so beautiful and hand-made especially for them instead of leftovers or foods past their sell-by date. I tell you I see their eyes light up like kids at Christmas when they're about to tuck into one of your creations. It's magical. And I hear your cake-making sessions are going down a treat at the local shelter. The kids love it.'

'It's our pleasure. I know it's nothing life-changing but it gives us a nice feeling being able to bring even a small amount of joy to people,' Camilla said as she put a coffee in front of Angela too. She filled him in on her idea of expanding the business.

'That's a great idea,' he mumbled with a mouth full of cake.'

'I wanted to thank you, actually, for introducing me to so many new places with the cupcake van. My orders have gone through the roof; in fact I've got a double celebration at the weekend from someone who picked up a leaflet at that huge market you took me to when we first met. Oh that reminds me, Angela, is there any chance you could do a double delivery for me on Saturday? It's about time I got you insured for the van.'

Angela beamed. 'Of course, I'd be delighted to. I'd need a little practice drive in the week, just to get used to the cupcake van, if that's okay.'

'That's fine; you'll be doing me a huge favour.' Camilla could hardly contain her grin at the thought of seeing Blake again.

Ged smiled. 'Oh that's great news. I'm really pleased for you. I knew you'd be a huge success.'

'It's been amazing. So tell me. How're the plans for your round-the-world trip coming on?'

He nodded as he chewed the last of the cake and wiped the buttercream from around his mouth. He took a swig of coffee to wash it down. 'Ah they're going great. In almost two weeks I'll be gone and then it'll be, hey world, here I come. I can't wait, and the offer is still open to you if you want to come with me. I promise it will be great fun.' He tossed her a cheeky wink.

Angela looked up from her piping and smiled at Camilla. 'I don't think Blake will be too happy about that.'

Camilla flushed. She shouldn't feel awkward about it but for some reason she did. She felt she had to explain.

'Yes, Blake and I are back together, and I don't think he'd be too pleased with me gallivanting around the world with an Irish charmer such as yourself.'

Ged held his hands up in mock surrender. 'Who me? Sure I'm as good as gold and apart from looking like he wants to kill me some of the time, that Blake seems like a good bloke. He was a real good sport at the auction, but you tell him from me that if he ever hurts you I will find him and I will kill him. And by the way, don't forget that my offer is always open to you. I could show you the world. I mean what's he got to offer apart from a fit body, a handsome face and—' he stopped to stroke his own chin '—a beard to die for.'

Camilla laughed and slapped his arm. 'I really do appreciate the offer, Ged, thank you; but you know as well as I do that I would only cramp your style and what about all the lovely girls from all those exotic countries who will fall at your feet? I would surely be doing them a disservice if I came with you.'

Ged pretended to be giving it some thought. 'Sure you know I hadn't quite thought of it like that but you're quite right about that bit: it just wouldn't be fair on them.' He chuckled as he helped Angela load the rest of their donated cupcakes into the box.

'Thanks, Angela.' He had the boxes piled up in his arms, so Camilla opened the front door for him and walked him to his coffee van. He loaded the cakes into the back of his van and slammed the door shut, Camilla was waiting to wave him off and he placed a gentle kiss on each of her cheeks and gently touched her on the arm.

'Seriously I am so pleased for you and I hope you'll both be very happy, but if you ever need me for anything you know where I am.'

'Well I do for another week or so but after that you could be anywhere in the world.' She laughed. 'But seriously thanks, Ged.' She squeezed his hand. 'That means such a lot, and yes thank you we are really happy.' As she spoke, she remembered the holiday voucher she'd won from Jackson's role model award; maybe she would suggest to Blake that she accompany him on his next trip to Canada.

Ged climbed into the van, beeped his horn as he drove off and doffed an imaginary cap at her. She went back into the house with a beaming smile and began to prepare another batch of cupcakes. The taste of vanilla in the air welcomed her back into her comfort zone and her heart sang as she and Angela enjoyed the rest of the day chatting and baking cupcakes.

Whilst catching up on some admin, Camilla noticed emails from a local radio station. It seemed that her inadvertently posting the wrong video had caught the attention of numerous media outlets.

'Oh my God I don't believe it!' she gasped.

'What is it?' Angela paused holding the icing bag over a cupcake.

'I've been invited to appear on a radio show since my video went viral. They saw the video before I took it down and replaced it with the correct one and they loved it. They've checked out my website too and have fallen in love with the pictures of the cupcake van. I'm just going to ring them. I've had so much publicity that business is booming so it might mean more hours for you, Angela, if that's okay.'

'That's brilliant for me. Congratulations. I can't wait to listen to it.'

'You know my mum always said I should have a book out with all my fantastic cakes in it -her words not mine- but then she was my number-one fan, so she was bound to say that really. Maybe that's something I could look at doing in the future.'

'I think it's a great idea but it's notoriously hard to get a publishing deal. I had a friend once who tried for years to get a book deal but eventually self-published. It was about babies and did amazingly well. Maybe you could do that?' said Angela. 'Your cakes are incredible and really everybody should know about them. I'm so proud of you and grateful for your help in getting me back on my feet.'

'Thank you so much, lovely. You've been such a star. That's a brilliant idea and I'd say the logical next step to my cake-baking empire. I'm going to do it. That's my new mission. I'm going to have to go through all my pictures now for the best ones. Oh and I'll be donating a percentage of the profits to the shelter,' she said.

As she left the room Camilla couldn't help but feel as though her mum had taken her by the hand and led her to this moment. Things were finally going right for her and each time someone told her they were proud of her she took it as a little message from her because she was unable to say it anymore. Her heart glowed at the thought of it.

Chapter 35

The little peppermint green van with cupcakes painted all over it attracted lots of attention as it drove around Bramblewood and surrounding villages, mainly because it was such an unusual sight. But even more so today because it was bouncing along like a kangaroo with the old ice cream music jingle playing loudly and the windscreen wipers on full when there wasn't a cloud in the sky. Camilla could see a thin film of sweat on Angela's flushed face.

'I'm so sorry,' said a flustered Angela as the van came to an abrupt halt when it eventually stalled. 'Maybe this was a bad idea; I haven't driven for such a long time.' She switched off the engine and went to open the door to swap places with Camilla.

'Nonsense, you were doing fine. I was exactly the same when I first started driving her. She's a bit of a temperamental old thing but once you gel with her she goes like a dream. So come on, just start her up again and we'll go somewhere quiet where you can practise in peace.'

'Are you sure? I don't want to break her.'

'I'm positive.'

Angela started the engine and after the third attempt and despite sounding like an old lady who smokes a hundred fags a day, the engine roared into life, this time without the music and the incessant throb of the wipers. Camilla cheered and Angela drove away much smoother this time but still a little nervously. They drove round for half an hour along country roads before Angela felt she could manage a few local cake deliveries. She tentatively opened the large box of cupcakes to check they hadn't been smashed up due to her erratic driving.

'Hurray, they're all fine,' she said and replaced the lid. Camilla was about to help her when her phone started ringing. Angela gestured to her that she could manage and walked into the sports centre to deliver them to the children's party.

Camilla had just finished her conversation when a smiling Angela joined her in the van. She waved a piece of paper. 'I've picked up three more orders in there just from that party. Isn't that great?'

'Wow that's brilliant, well done, and I've just taken a booking for the cupcake van for a really posh wedding in the grounds of Belvedere Manor. Maybe we'll need those extra staff sooner rather than later.'

Her phone beeped and her heart leapt when she saw it was from Blake but then sank as she read it.

Angela started the car, again on the third attempt, and again it bounced along making embarrassing noises as though it were dragging tin cans along behind it.

'Oh damn, I really don't want to let you down but I think I might need a lot more practice before I can drive to that place on Saturday.'

Camilla winced at the grating noise. 'Really, Angela, don't worry. I promise you will get used to it after some more practice but there's no rush now, as it turns out I can do Saturday's deliveries after all.'

Camilla could sense Angela looking at her in concern and tried not to let her see the disappointment in her eyes, which was nothing compared to the sinking feeling in her stomach.

'But, I thought you had plans. What about your day out with Blake? You've been so looking forward to that.'

'That was him on the phone. Something urgent has come up, and he needs to help out an old friend. He said he'll explain properly when he's back. But it's all fine and we're still going out in the evening and doing all the lovely things we planned for Saturday on Sunday instead.' She smiled and tried to lighten her tone, more to convince herself that she wasn't upset than Angela.

'And this means that you get much more practice driving our cosy little cupcake van before we let you beyond the realms of Bramblewood.'

Angela beamed. 'I'm not going to lie but my whole body has just relaxed with relief and I think that calls for a celebration.' She flicked the chimes on intermittently for the ten-minute journey back to Cupcake Cottage, bringing smiles to the faces of those they passed on the way.

'Don't forget the chimes can only be on for twelve seconds every two minutes,' said Camilla.

'Oops, sorry, boss,' Angela replied.

Having Angela do the local deliveries gave Camilla the luxury of some time to herself so she tried to shake off the disappointment and look forward to her hair and nail appointments on Friday, but she couldn't ease the sinking feeling in her stomach. The thought of Blake letting her down again was too much to bear.

Chapter 36

Despite the week being exceptionally busy, as far as Camilla was concerned it had dragged and Saturday had seemed like it was unreachable but here it was. She sprung out of bed and enjoyed coffee and honey on toast in her bedroom window seat. The sunshine warmed her face as she looked out to a clear blue sky; the framed pictures on the windowsill caught her eye. Two silver frames were hinged together. The first one was of her and Blake at a friend's wedding, taken twelve years ago, their faces beaming with the joyfulness of youth. The other a picture of them dancing at the auction that Lucy had taken. They were laughing. Apart from shorter hair, a beard and a couple of extra laugh lines at the sides of his eyes, Blake had hardly changed at all. Her heart danced at the thought of seeing him in less than twelve hours.

She showered quickly and sang loudly. She fizzed with nervous energy and felt she had to keep herself busy today. She gave the house a quick once-over. The icing sugar seemed to get everywhere but she chased every last bit away with some furniture polish and a duster.

It would take her an hour to get to the nursing home where she had a double delivery for a ninetieth birthday cake in the shape of a large Singer sewing machine for a lady who had been a seamstress in her younger days. It had been one of the hardest cakes she'd ever made, along with ninety cupcakes, each with a tiny version of the sewing machine made out of icing, which she and Angela had been making for days. The other delivery was for a gender-reveal cake. The customer had confided in Camilla that the inside of the cake should be pink as she was expecting a girl. The pink sponge was iced in white with pastel-coloured baby toys made out of fondant placed around the outside with a little teddy made of marzipan sitting on the top.

Camilla had loved baking the gender-reveal cake and decided to add that idea to her leaflet before the next print run. She would also add them to the website. Gender-reveal cupcakes would also be a huge hit for baby showers. She packed them into their boxes and carefully loaded them into the back of the cupcake van. She locked her front door and began typing the address into the sat nav on her phone. Long journeys to deliver cakes were always a tad traumatic because there was more time for something to go wrong with her masterpieces so she drove extra cautiously.

Eventually she pulled up in the car park of the nursing home. The building was pretty and modern with flowering hanging baskets at either side of the front door. She rang the bell and saw a lady in a white overall smile at her through the glass and wave. Camilla heard a buzz and the door clicked open; she could smell a hearty beef stew just like the one Auntie Edie made, which caused her stomach to rumble.

'Hi can I help you?' asked the friendly staff member.

'Oh yes please, I'm Camilla from Camilla's Cupcakes and I have a cake delivery for a Mrs Bradley. I wondered if you had a trolley I could borrow as the cakes are quite large.' She gestured behind herself to where the cupcake van sat with the door open.

'Of course – just give me a minute and I'll go and get one from the kitchen.' She disappeared through a door and the lady behind the reception desk smiled at Camilla and gestured for her to sit down. Camilla sat in one of the comfortable leather armchairs for a couple of minutes, making small talk with the receptionist until she could hear the rattling of the trolley as the other lady reappeared.

'Here you are. I've brought some tablecloths so we can pretty it up.' Camilla glanced at the name badge and grabbed the front handle of the trolley to help steer it out of the building towards the van.

'Thanks, Jan, at least there's a slope here so that makes it easier.'

'Yes we have to be accessible, you see, for wheelchairs,' said Jan as she shook out the folded crisp white tablecloth and smoothed it down on the top of the trolley then did the same for the second shelf. The bottom shelf was filled with plates and napkins and cups and saucers.

Camilla carefully unboxed the large cake and placed it on the trolley to plenty of oohs and aahs from Jan.

'Carol, come out here and see this – it's amazing,' she shouted. The receptionist was out there in a flash.

'That looks so real. Mrs Bradley will love that won't she, Jan! She used to be a seamstress back in the day. She even said she made costumes for the West End once upon a time.'

'Ah that's lovely,' Camilla replied. 'Sounds like she's had an interesting life.' The phone rang and Carol ran back in to answer it.

Jan helped to arrange the cupcakes on the lower shelf, whilst Camilla placed the smaller cake next to the other one and arranged cupcakes around those too. She slammed the van doors shut and locked them. Camilla pushed the trolley from the back whilst Jan steered from the front.

'What an achievement to get to ninety,' said Camilla as they walked down a long corridor, passing doors that opened into glimpses of people's lives that they'd had to pack up for one reason or another.

'Ah yes, though she's very poorly now and hasn't got long left at all, but her granddaughter has made today so special for her. This morning a string quartet turned up to play her favourite music that she and her husband used to dance to and she's had these beautiful cakes made with enough for all of the staff and residents to have some.

'They lived abroad for many years, but the granddaughter came back to England about six years ago and brought her grandma back with her. Unfortunately, she's now got dementia so we're all hoping that she will still be around long enough for the baby to be born. Although I think that's one of the reasons why her granddaughter wanted the gender-reveal cake so that at least her gran will know whether it's a boy or a girl. They're very close, oops, hold on.' She stopped talking to pull the trolley into the day room.

'Oh no, dementia is such a cruel disease isn't it.' Camilla's thoughts flashed to Auntie Edie and the small bouts of forgetfulness she had at times.

'Yes, it really is. She's having a good day today, I think. We've had to move her bed into the day room so that all of her family can be with her. Right, now let's light these candles and I'll dim the lights, then as you push the trolley I'll start off the singing.'

Jan bent down to the bottom of the trolley and revealed the candles in the shape of a nine and a zero. She reached into her overall pocket and pulled out a lighter. After a couple of flicks it eventually shot out a flame that nearly singed her eyebrows, and then she lit the candles.

About twenty family members were standing around the bed with disposable plastic flutes half filled with champagne. The old lady in the bed was frail-looking with wispy white hair and liver spots on her hands and face. She was wearing a pretty pink bedjacket over a white cotton nightie. She sipped at a glass of champagne and held hands with a heavily pregnant woman next to her bed. There was a twinkle in the old lady's eye as she laughed with the younger woman and the dark-haired man who had his arm around her; they were obviously a close family.

Jan dipped the lights and began to sing happy birthday as Camilla pushed the trolley towards them. Jan steered from the front as the cake was so high that Camilla could hardly see where she was going and didn't want to smack the trolley into the old lady's bed. When everybody stopped singing, a little boy asked if he could blow the candles out and when it was done everybody cheered and Jan turned the lights back on.

'And now for another surprise, Gran,' said the pregnant woman. 'It's time for the gender reveal! Let's find out if you're going to have a fifth great-grandson or a first great-granddaughter.' Mrs Bradley clapped her hands in anticipation as her granddaughter picked up the knife to cut the cake. The man she was with, turned towards the trolley and that's when Camilla's world collapsed.

The man's face had frozen as his eyes locked with hers. Acid rose up in her throat and blood raced through her body, burning as though it were volcanic lava. When it reached her newly mended heart it shattered it over again into irreparable pieces. Her legs felt wobbly and there was an awful ringing sound in her ears. She watched as Blake's eyes seemed to plead with her before he shook his head and looked down.

Camilla felt as though she and Blake were taking part in a mannequin challenge, stationary like statues whilst everyone else was cheering after seeing the inside of the cake. Mrs Bradley and her granddaughter were crying tears of joy mingled with sadness that this older lady would not be a part of this precious little girl's life. Everyone else was moving but they were frozen solid, like ghosts watching other people go about their everyday lives whilst their lives were stuck in limbo for eternity.

It took a few seconds before Camilla realised the pregnant lady was thanking her and telling her what a wonderful job she had done with the cakes. Then to Camilla's horror she put her arms around her and hugged her. Camilla could feel the swollen belly touching her, Blake's baby. She disentangled herself from the woman, who must have felt like she was hugging an ironing board as she had been so rigid.

'I'm sorry, I have to go. I need to be somewhere.' She stuttered and walked out of the room. She couldn't wait to be out of that place, but her legs wouldn't allow her to run. She felt as though she was wading through treacle. Each step drained her of her life force. She noticed a door marked 'ladies' and only just made it to the sink where she threw up bile and acid. She pulled a paper towel from the container above the sink and ran it under the cold tap then held it on her forehead to try and ease the burning sensation. Her eyes felt on fire from unshed tears that threatened to flow and her throat ached with the golf-ball-sized lump that appeared to be stuck in it.

Her need to escape overruled any need to stick around for one more minute in this place and so on shaky legs she made her way back to her cupcake van where she could feel safe again.

She pulled out of the car park and drove until she could find a motorway services to stop and take stock of what was going on. She knew it was unsafe to drive in the state she was in so she bought a camomile tea and a bar of chocolate and sat in the cupcake van until she had calmed down. As the chocolate melted soothingly in her mouth, she picked up her phone and turned it on again as she'd turned it off to make the delivery. It immediately buzzed into life; she had several missed calls and texts from Blake. She could see the first line of one of his texts without having to open it and she laughed in disgust.

'It's not what you think.'

Surely you can think of a better one than that, she was tempted to text back, but she stood her ground. She deleted all of his texts and answerphone messages and then blocked his number. She had a flashback to him standing there with his arm around that woman, then the look of abject horror that was frozen on his face and at the same time of that woman pressing her belly against her when she hugged her. She had heard him call her name as she stumbled down the corridor. The secrecy and lies from this man were disgusting. Whatever happened to the Blake she knew of old? Where had he gone? A pang of hurt ripped through her heart at the loss of what might have been for the two of them.

Anger began to flood her veins as she thought about his betrayal. Was he one of those weird men who lived a double life? Thank God she found out now before she had invested any more time in him. She had seen her future in that man and now it had all come crashing down; it was all a façade. She held on to the anger and used it to power herself home. She didn't know what she was going to do yet but she knew she needed to get away from all of this.

When she arrived home to the comfort of Cupcake Cottage, the heavy heart had disappeared and had been replaced by a hollow feeling. Even her limbs felt empty. She opened a bottle of red wine, poured herself a large glass and put some music on. Feeling peckish she rummaged in the large kitchen cupboard for some crisps and nibbles and accidentally knocked a bag of flour off the shelf.

'Oh damn,' she muttered to herself as everything looked like it had been caught in a snowdrift. She pulled out everything from the bottom of the cupboard and dusted off the boxes, one of which was from her room in her mum's house. She swept up using a dustpan and brush, then vacuumed and mopped. Once the floor was dry she slid the freshly wiped storage boxes back into the cupboard but took the one from her mum's house into the living room.

There was no time like the present to go through it. After all, she didn't think she could possibly be any more miserable. She topped up her wine glass and filled a bowl with crisps, this time being careful not to cause any more mess. She had found it quite cathartic to clean up; now if only she could clean up the mess that her life had become.

She rifled through the box and pulled out a scrapbook that had belonged to her mother. She ran her fingers along the soft brown cover and breathed in the warm smell of leather. It was a common sight when she was growing up, to see her mum with magazine cuttings all over the table. Camilla would help glue them into the scrapbook for her. Anything to do with Hawaii, the place her mum had always wanted to go, had gone in the scrapbook. She cuddled it to her chest and warmth spread through her body like a linctus soothing a sore throat.

Camilla knew what she wanted to do and called Auntie Edie. She answered eventually and Camilla could visualise her wandering around the house wondering where she'd put the phone.

'Auntie Edie, can I pop round and see you tomorrow? I've got something to tell you,' she spluttered in one breath.

'Yes of course you can, my darling; come at a quarter to four as there's something I'd like you to see.'

Camilla filled her glass and took a sip, just as her phone rang. She jumped, and her wine sloshed all over her face. *Unknown number* flashed up on the screen. Could it be Blake calling from someone else's phone? She really didn't want to speak to him, as much as it hurt her heart to say it. It was over between them. She cut the call but a couple of seconds later it rang again so she answered it.

'Hello, Cami, it's me. Please don't hang up.' The sound of his voice almost melted her heart. She so wanted him to have an explanation that made all of this go away but that was an impossible task. She knew what she'd seen: a happy little family unit.

'What do you want?' she whispered.

'I want you. Please let me come round and explain.'

'You lied to me.' Her voice was stronger.

'Yes, well no . . . not really. Please let me come and explain.' He sounded desperate.

'Answer me one question? That's all I need to know.' Her voice was stronger and she felt more in control.

'Anything,' he replied.

'Who was that woman?' She willed him to say it was his sister or a cousin. Any of those would do and would stop this nightmare situation. Her heart was pounding in anticipation of the answer. He paused; she could hear him breathe a heavy sigh.

'Who was she?' she shouted. She couldn't help herself.

'She's my ex-wife.' She could hear the suppression in his tone as though he knew he wouldn't stand a chance in convincing her that she should listen to him now. 'But please let me explain . . .'

Her stomach was filled with rocks; her heart became stone. His ex-wife was pregnant – he'd forgotten to mention that little nugget of information – and they'd all looked so happy together: he with his arm around her, both laughing. Happy families!

She gripped the phone so tightly that her knuckles were going white; her voice became so deep it was almost a growl.

'Don't you ever contact me again. You're nothing but a liar and I hate you.'

'Oh, come on, don't you think you're over-reacting just a little.'

'Over-reacting? Look, I don't want to hear from you again. So why don't you just piss off back to Canada and leave me alone.' She had a burning urge to slam the phone down but instead she switched it off and threw it on the rug. She would need to block that number now. Her heart was beating rapidly so she took a few deep breaths and decided to meditate for a little while, until she felt calmer.

She wasn't going to wallow in self-pity. A few months ago she would have crumbled because of what happened with Blake but now she was able to cope with anything that life could throw at her. She saw the voucher she'd won and realised it was time to cash it in. She deserved a holiday and she knew just the person to call to accompany her.

Chapter 37

A couple of weeks later Camilla was sitting on a plane sipping champagne and laughing with her companion, the one person who she knew would never let her down. Her business was left in capable hands with Angela, who had drafted in a friend to help. Lindsey had also been living at the shelter and had two school-age children. She was an accomplished baker and had also just needed someone to give her a chance to get back on her feet. Camilla decided that she could deal with everything else, including her exciting novelty cake book, when she got back from her holiday of a lifetime.

She rummaged through her bag and pulled out the scrapbook she had found in the box from her mum's house, alongside some of Camilla's first pictures and Christmas decorations she had made at primary school. Sitting in the middle of the box had been the Christmas angel that her mum had bought in a charity shop; the dress had once been lacy but had been tattered when she bought it. However, every year her mum would make a new dress for the angel using scraps of material. Camilla had stroked it lovingly when she found it.

The memories of a happy childhood with just the two of them fell from her eyes and rolled down her cheeks. She remembered one year they had so little money that her mum made the dress out of tinfoil and Camilla had gazed in wonderment as the angel sparkled on top of the tree. That had been her favourite dress and her mum had made her one too. Those were such simple times when some tinfoil fashioned into a crown, a dress and jewellery had made her feel like a real princess.

The book was battered and dog-eared but as Camilla stroked the pages she could sense the depth of longing and hopes and dreams that her mum had poured into it as a teenager and had continued to add to as she had gone through her life. The pages were bursting with magazine cut-outs and newspaper articles, along with a complete written itinerary of everywhere her mum had wanted to visit and everything she wanted to do in Hawaii.

Camilla was going to make sure that she could fulfil her mum's lifelong wish by scattering her ashes in every place mentioned in the book. She offered her glass up for a toast with her travel companion.

'To my mum,' she said, her heart bursting with pride for the woman who had raised her.

'To Iris,' said Auntie Edie as she clinked the glasses together.

'I'm so glad you could come. It means so much to me. You've always been such a wonderful friend to Mum and I.' She dabbed her eyes with a tissue.

Auntie Edie hugged her. 'I'm surprised you didn't take Ged up on his offer to travel round the world. But I'm so glad I could join you; you mean the world to me and you know I loved your mum like a daughter. If I'm honest I loved her more than my own daughter.' She giggled naughtily. She took her knitting out of her bag and was soon zoned into the relaxing click-clack of the needles.

'No, he has definitely gone alone. He's sent me a couple of pictures of Thai beaches so I'm sure he's having a ball,' said Camilla.

'Any more news on Blake?' asked Edie without looking up from her knitting.

Camilla was relieved that Auntie Edie couldn't see her face as it was burning up at the sound of his name. 'Erm, no, not really apart from flowers arriving! Although, I did have a call from his bloody ex-wife.'

'Really? What did she want?' Edie had stopped mid stitch.

Camilla took a sip of champagne, allowing the ice-cold bubbles to fizz in her mouth for a while before tickling her throat; she wasn't sure whether she liked it as it seemed to have a funny aftertaste.

'She wanted to explain; she said it was all her fault. Apparently, with her dementia her grandma had forgotten they were divorced, and she loved Blake a lot and wanted him to be at her ninetieth birthday party. Blake had loved her too and that's why he agreed to go along with it all.'

'Why do people have such complicated lives?' asked Edie, shaking her head as she commenced her knitting again.

'I really don't know, but his ex is actually married to someone else and that's who the baby belongs to. Why Blake had to get involved is beyond me. And why couldn't he have just told me beforehand?' She folded her arms and looked out of the window but couldn't see much except clouds.

'What would you have said if he'd told you?' Edie rolled her eyes, knowing full well what her answer would be.

Camilla was flummoxed. She knew she wouldn't have been happy about it but she couldn't really stop him. She took another sip of champagne and shrugged her shoulders. 'I really don't know.'

'You know what Blake's problem is, don't you?'

Camilla's heart fluttered and sent ripples through her body at the mere mention of his name. 'I could probably think of a few.'

'He's a sucker for an old lady and his heart is far too big. I'm sure he would have done the same for me if I was confused and dying. Rightly or wrongly with what this ex-wife has done, I'm sure his intentions were to make an old lady a little bit happier on her deathbed. How self-centred of him. He is such a villain; I'm not surprised you never want to see him again.'

'I suppose if you put it like that then he's not all bad. In fact his ex-wife told me that her gran did sadly die two days after her birthday.'

'So if he rang you then you would talk to him?'

'He can't because I've blocked his number.'

'Then why not unblock it and stop wasting precious time,' she said, accidentally dropping the white ball of wool onto the floor.

Camilla laughed. 'Okay maybe I will once we get there.' She bent between the seats to retrieve the wool. 'Anyway, what is it you're knitting? It looks tiny.'

'It's a baby's cardigan; I've already made the bobble hat and bootees to match. Here look,' said Edie, her voice filled with pride as she pulled them out of her bag.

'They're adorable.' Camilla took them from her and admired the intricate stitching of little hearts in the pattern. 'Who are they for?'

'A very good friend of mine – you might know her actually. Hold on, I have a picture of her somewhere.' She rifled through her heavy Mary Poppins bag and pulled out a circular disc with a faded picture of Venice on it. She handed it to Camilla who frowned at it and looked back at Edie whilst chewing on the inside of her cheek as she tried to work out what to do with it.

'Here, give it to me; it's the wrong way round.' She flipped the disc over and Camilla realised on seeing her reflection that it was a mirror. She looked back at Edie and then back into the mirror, searching it as though she expected a photograph to magically appear on it. Edie tapped her knitting needle on the mirror.

'There, look – there's my special friend.'

'But why are you knitting these for me?' She waved the bootees, which were now on her fingers.

'Because, my darling girl, I recognise the signs – those dark shadows under your eyes, you couldn't drink the tea in my house the other day and just in general I have a sixth sense about these things. You mark my words.'

Camilla pulled her phone out of her pocket to check her notes. She scrolled through endless shopping lists and cupcake recipes until she found what she was looking for.

'Ah, here it is now, let me see: monthly schedule.' She took a loud and sharp intake of breath and her hand clasped over her mouth. 'Edie, I'm actually two weeks late but that doesn't mean—'

'Told you,' said Edie with unwavering confidence. 'I'm never wrong.'

She wrapped the wool around the needles to store safely in her bag until they'd eaten their food that had just been placed in front of them.

'Would you like a nice glass of champagne with dinner, ladies?' asked the steward.

Camilla was ashen-faced and still staring into space.

'Yes please for me and a glass of water too for my friend,' Edie replied. When the steward had moved on, she clicked her fingers in front of Camilla's face. 'Earth to Camilla, is there anyone in there?'

Camilla turned to her, eyes brimming. 'I wish my mum could be here for this moment. I didn't expect to have to live my life without her.' She clutched Edie's hand and cried without making a sound.

'Now you listen to me, young lady, life is dreadfully cruel sometimes and your mum was taken far too soon but don't think she has ever left you for one minute. She is around you all the time and if you ever want to feel close to her then just look in the mirror because you are the image of her.'

Edie held the mirror to Camilla's face and gently stroked the tears away from her cheek with her other hand.

'Your mum is the sunlight glinting in your eyes, the curve of your mouth when you smile, the sound of your laugh when you feel joy and the beating of your heart as you live the life that she gave you. And now that you have another heart beating inside you, you will be able to pass on all of the love that your mum gave to you.' Edie squeezed Camilla's hand as she sniffed and sobbed quietly. 'And one more thing: if you need any more proof that your mum lives on, you wait until this little one looks at you in a certain way, or yawns or smiles and you see your mum in him or her. That is the most wondrous feeling ever.'

Camilla hugged the old lady who always knew the right thing to say. 'Thank you so much, Edie, I love you.'

'I love you too, darling girl.' She kissed her gently on her damp cheek, then took her tray from the air hostess who was standing patiently waiting. 'Why don't we tuck in to this delicious food. Don't forget you're eating for two now.'

Camilla smiled. She loved the confidence with which Edie spoke but the smell of food turned her stomach. The only thing she managed to swallow were a few chunks of the dry bread roll that she tore apart with her fingers. It helped to calm the nausea and settle her stomach but didn't help to sort out her unsettled mind. Whilst Edie drifted off to sleep Camilla decided that the first thing she would do when she got to the hotel was find a chemist and buy a pregnancy test.

She closed her own eyes for a minute or two and her thoughts turned to the day she had visited Edie to invite her on holiday. The anger had built up inside her like she'd swallowed a volcano and she imagined if her temperature rose any more she would be blowing steam out of her nostrils like a cartoon bull. She'd put the scrapbook in her shoulder bag and was about to pull it out and present it to Edie like a magician pulling a white dove out of thin air when Edie called her to the window.

'Here quickly.' She gestured with her fingers for Camilla to hurry and join her. Edie put her arm around her young friend's shoulders as they waited. Bella and Bertie squawked excitedly.. 'Any minute now, just you watch.'

Camilla was feeling more than a little on edge. She couldn't imagine what she was supposed to be looking at and was eager to surprise Edie with her amazing idea.

'Quick, quick look, they're coming.'

Camilla saw a young woman walking along past her little cupcake van and heading towards her mum's house. Holding on to her hand was a little girl of about four or five with plaits in her hair. She skipped along in her red and grey uniform, her mouth constantly in motion as she chatted happily to her mummy. They began to walk up the path and Camilla's hand flew to her mouth in shock as she saw the woman reach into her bag for a key and push it into the lock of her mum's house. A sob escaped her lips.

'They're such a lovely little family,' said Edie with affection. 'She's a single mum just like yours was and you were the same age as that little one when you first moved in. I thought I'd lost my marbles when I first saw them. It was as if I'd gone back in time.' Edie moved into the hall and headed to the kitchen. 'I spoke to her and she said she would never have been able to afford it at the normal price.' She shouted down the hall to Camilla. 'So, I suppose some good has come out of it all, as that awful man reduced the price to get a quick sale. I'll just put the kettle on and . . .'

She was interrupted mid flow by the sound of the front door opening and Camilla shouting, 'Excuse me,' as she ran across the road.

'Oh no, I thought you were ready for this,' she heard Edie calling after her.

Camilla could feel her heart pounding in her ears as she raced up the path to the surprised-looking lady who still had her key in the lock. The little girl peered up at her through big round eyes.

'I'm sorry,' said Camilla. 'This is, I mean this used to be my house.'

'Did it really? When?' asked the little girl.

Camilla glanced at Auntie Edie. 'Oh it was a long time ago now.' Auntie Edie blinked and gave a gentle nod.

'Mummy said I can have a kitten if I keep my new room tidy. It's pink. Would you like to see it?'

Camilla felt a pull on her heartstrings but didn't answer the question. 'Do you see that little van over there?' she asked instead.

The little girl nodded. 'It's an ice cream van.'

'If you look really carefully you can see that it's actually got cupcakes on it and if Mummy says it's okay you can have some cupcakes.'

'Oh yes, look, Mummy it's a cupcake van. I've never seen one of those before. Can I have a cupcake, pleeeeeease?'

The lady looked at her daughter and laughed.

'Come on then.' Camilla's smile was bigger than the little girl's as they crossed the road to the van. 'My name is Jilly and this is my daughter Emily, by the way.'

'I'm Camilla and it's lovely to meet you both.' She climbed into the van and put the chimes on much to the delight of Emily and her mum. Camilla slid open the serving window and picked up a cupcake. 'Right, will that be chocolate or vanilla topping for you?'

'Chocolate, chocolate,' shouted Emily.

'Please,' her mum reminded her.

'Please,' she said sweetly.'

Camilla decorated and put six of them into a box. Jilly pulled her purse out from her bag and opened it.

'Oh no, this is my treat; it can be a little housewarming present.'

'If you're sure, that's lovely, thank you,' said Jilly. 'Okay, Emily, hold this box very carefully and say thank you to Camilla.'

'Thank you, Camilla.' Emily concentrated really hard.

Jilly placed her hand on her shoulder and steered her back to the house. 'Would you like to come in for a cuppa?' she shouted over her shoulder.

The gesture was so unexpected that Camilla felt bile rise up from her stomach at the thought of being in there again. Her face blanched and she felt a warm hand at the small of her back. She looked down into Auntie Edie's face, full of wrinkles and kindness.

'Maybe not today, but thank you, Jilly.'

Jilly waved and entered the house with her daughter. Then popped her head out of the door again. 'By the way, did you hear about what happened to the man I bought the house from?'

'Only that he did a moonlight flit?' Camilla answered.

'Well it seems he got scammed on the house he was buying in Scotland and lost every penny. The scammers hacked into his estate agents' email, they're so sophisticated these days aren't they? It's awful isn't it?'

'Terrible,' said Camilla. She didn't feel happy about what had happened but she felt a hell of a lot lighter, she liked to think it was her mum having the last laugh.

'Flat on his arse – what did I tell you,' muttered Edie under her breath.

'Are you okay?' She gave Camilla a squeeze, and led her back into her house.

'Yes, thanks, I'm fine – just a bit of a shock, that's all.'

'I'm sorry. I probably should have warned you that somebody had moved in, they've been there a little while.'

'No really, it's fine. I'm fine honestly.'

'Okay, lovely. In that case what was it you wanted to see me about?'

Camilla's eyes darted to the envelope that she'd placed on the counter in her haste to decorate the cupcakes for Emily. 'How do you fancy a little trip to Hawaii? I've got a £1000 voucher we can share.'

'Are you serious? That sounds amazing, love. Do you know what? Your mum would be so proud of the woman you've become.'

A ripple of warmth spread through Camilla. 'I know,' she replied with complete certainty that she'd made the right decision. There were some nasty people in this world and sometimes horrible things happened to nice people but guess what? She was fine.

Lost in the memory she had drifted off to sleep until the air hostess woke her to put her seatbelt on ready for landing.

Chapter 38

It hardly seemed like five minutes ago when they'd arrived and were greeted with kisses, and leis made of kika and Jasmine blossoms had been placed around their necks. They had drunk virgin cocktails on the beach, tasted delicious fresh foods bursting with colour at luau buffets and laughed whilst being pulled up to join in the hula dancing by the hotel entertainers. The week had flown by in a blur and now it was time for Edie to go home.

Camilla, her skin kissed by the Polynesian sun, held Edie close to her and squeezed her tight.

'Thank you so much, Auntie Edie. I never could have gone through all this without you.' The old lady, who had been pleasantly plump for most of her life, felt like skin and bone beneath Camilla's arms, which reminded her of how fragile she was.

Edie squeezed back just as tight. 'Thank you for a lovely holiday, my darling girl, and it was a pleasure sharing in your special moments. I'm sorry I couldn't stay for the second week but Bella and Bertie would miss me too much and be swearing at the neighbours even more.'

Camilla sniffed. She thought back to a couple of days ago when they had taken a cruise on a glass-bottomed boat. A whole new world had opened up to them in the form of live tropical reefs, sea turtles, which were known as *honu*, and schools of tropical fish, which darted this way and that in a blaze of colour. They had watched the sunset from the rippling water and neither had ever seen a more beautiful sight. Camilla noticed Edie's eyes had taken on a glassy look, her face wistful. She had smiled at Camilla.

'Are you ready?'

Camilla answered with a nod and her own eyes filled up as she took the urn out of her beach bag. They each held it and shook the ashes out into the welcoming water. Fireworks from another boat caught their attention. They held each other tightly as colours exploded into the sky with bangs that made their ears ring.

'I got you here, Mum,' whispered Camilla, 'and I have to say that's a pretty impressive send-off.' As the fireworks subsided leaving a gunpowder smell in the air, they could hear music, which had been drowned out by the loud bangs. 'Listen,' said Camilla. Her hand flew to her mouth as it opened in surprise.

'This was the song we had at Mum's funeral, remember? She'd chosen it herself.'

'I remember, darling girl,' replied Edie as she wiped her own tears away and held her precious young friend whilst her body shook with sobs as they listened to the haunting sound of 'Time to Say Goodbye', sung by the powerful voice of Sarah Brightman.

'Now I don't want you to get mad, but someone asked me to give you something from them at this moment,' said Edie.

Camilla had no idea what it could be and watched as she rummaged in her bag and pulled out a small gift box. She held it in her hands before turning it this way and that. Eventually she pulled the ribbon and opened it to find a heart-shaped pink stone in a silver setting. From the inscription inside the box she could see that the stone had a sprinkling of her mum's ashes in it. Her breath caught in her throat, she gently untangled the chain from the box and kissed the stone, before fastening it around her neck and then holding the pendant in her hand. 'I love it so much.

'So, you'll forgive me for stealing some when they were at my house?'

'Of course I will. I love it. I must admit once I'd scattered the ashes, I felt quite bereft. This is the most wonderful and thoughtful present I've ever had. Was it Blake?'

Auntie Edie nodded. 'Yes, it was. He had the idea a little while ago.'

'Thank you from the bottom of my heart for aiding and abetting him.'

'He loves you so much darling.'

'I know and I've never stopped loving him. But I feel sad that my mum never got to experience true love in her life.'

'Oh she did, she told me so . . .'

'Really?' asked Camilla.

'Yes really. It was when she had you.'

Camilla's eyes opened wide and she clasped her hands to her chest.

At the airport Camilla held Edie for one last squeeze before she joined the new friends that she'd met, who were on the same flight back.

'Thank you for being with me at two of the most important times of my life, saying the most painful but beautiful goodbye but also saying hello to someone special too.' Her hand instinctively touched her stomach. 'I love you.'

Edie smiled an 'I told you so' smile. 'I'm never wrong. Now you enjoy this next week without me and I'll see you when I get back. I love you too.'

Edie let go of Camilla and headed through the security gates where she soon began a conversation with her new friends.

Camilla waited until she couldn't see her anymore. She rifled through her bag for a tissue. She had a whole other week of total relaxation to look forward to, but she would miss having Auntie Edie around. They got on so well. Her lips curled into a smile as she remembered Edie flirting with the waiters and wrapping them around her little finger.

She slung her bag back over her shoulder and looked around for the signs to see which direction she should go in and that's when she saw him. Standing there leaning against a pillar; his eyes pleading, his mouth not daring to smile. Her heart froze in shock before jumping around as if it was on burning hot coals. Those brown eyes knew how to stare into her soul. She blinked a couple of times and looked away before looking back at him just to make sure he was really there and not just a figment of her imagination.

It was definitely him. No one else had ever come close to making her heart race the way it was now. He was on the move, making his way through the hustle and bustle of the crowds and heading in her direction. Their eyes had locked and she was frightened to blink in case she lost the intensity of that look, a look that was affecting her deep within and setting her on fire. She had promised Edie she would talk to him when she got home and let him explain properly about what had happened.

She knew they had a lot to talk about and even more so now with the news she had discovered on holiday. The thought of that sent a shock wave through her body. She was having this beautiful man's baby. He had one more hurdle to get past before he could reach her as a large family reunion was taking place between them, the family members all hugging each other. Her phone buzzed in her hand, making her jump but she didn't break eye contact with him and finally he was there, his solid body standing right in front of her, his strong arms held open waiting for her to fill them. His eyes were filled with pain, searching hers for forgiveness. Hers broke contact first but only to focus on his lips before she kissed him with an urgency she had never felt before.

'I'm so sorry for everything,' he murmured into her mouth. He pulled away from her holding her at arm's length to look at her.

'I know,' she replied.

'Can we start again, please. I promise I'll never hurt you again. I should never have put anyone else before you. It was really last minute, the thing is . . . it wasn't just for her birthday. I needed to say goodbye. She meant such a lot to me – just like Edie does. She was the lady I was telling you about, the one who saved my life. She later introduced me to my ex and well you know the rest.'

She put her finger to his lips to stop him.

'It took an old lady who happens to be a very good friend of mine to appreciate why you did what you did. She made me realise what a good guy you are and I don't want to change that. You have such a huge heart and not many men are as thoughtful as you are. I really don't want you to stop being who you are because that's the man I fell in love with all those years ago and the man I never stopped loving.'

'I love you so much,' he replied as relief shone in his eyes.

'But, how did you know where I was?' she said as she stroked her hand in his hair, feeling the silkiness between her fingers. He pulled her to him again and felt a vibration in his pocket at the same time as Camilla received a text. They laughed and Camilla glanced at her phone to read it as Blake retrieved his and did the same.

'Aloha lovebirds! Enjoy your Happy Ever After. Love Edie Xx'

'Does that answer your question?' Blake pressed his lips against hers and wound his arms protectively around her. She felt loved, safe and finally she felt proud of herself for her achievements. To top it off she was also deliriously happy. 'Come on, let's go. We have a lot of catching up to do and I don't want to waste a single moment with you.'

Camilla hugged her secret to herself. There would be plenty of time to tell him later over a romantic meal at a beachside table for two. She clasped her hand in his and as they walked out of the airport she looked up to the bluest sky and allowed her thoughts to catch on the faint Hawaiian breeze and carry a special message to the most important woman in her life.

Mum, it breaks my heart to think that you will never get to meet your precious grandchild because I know that you would have been the best nan that he or she could ever have wished for. I consider myself so lucky to have had you as my mum and I know that if I could be half as good as you then this little one will be just fine. Life without you here is hard and I'll never stop missing you, but with you watching over us and this man by my side, I think I'm going to be okay. I'm looking forward to making future memories that I can look back on and be proud of, just like the ones I have of you. I love you forever and always.

Blake turned to look at her, his eyes filled with love.

'Oh, you have something in your hair.' He gently untangled it and handed her the fluffiest white feather she had ever seen. She put it in her bag for safekeeping and blew a kiss up to heaven.

Acknowledgements

This book was written straight from my heart. After the sudden loss of my beautiful Mum, I came across this quote by Jamie Anderson, 'grief is just love with nowhere to go', which I thought was lovely and so apt. When I confided in fabulous author and friend Milly Johnson about my loss, she encouraged me to channel my feelings and pour them onto the page. So, thank you Milly for that advice and for your support on my writing journey.

The Cosy Little Cupcake Van is based on friendship and love and the unbreakable bond between mothers and daughters. It also focuses heavily on the precious relationship between aunties and nieces. My Auntie Margie is a very special person in my life and as I've grown up, our relationship has grown with love into a wonderful friendship. The cheeky parts of Auntie Edie's character are inspired by a combination of her and my Great Auntie Edie who is sadly no longer with us but who was always the life and soul of the party. Great Auntie Edie also had a parrot whose name was Ringo, I remember him squawking when I was younger and he inspired the 'Liver Birds' Bella and Bertie in the book.

Thank you to my gorgeous niece Camilla Kutschker whose name I borrowed for my leading lady, I love you and Darcy so much and wish you lived nearer and that you had a real cupcake van.

I would like to thank my early readers who are also my fabulous friends, Margaret Morris, Kay Davies, Sandra

Woods, Katie Nash, Barbara Stone, Carolyn Mead, Jennifer Edwards and Lynda Good, your feedback was invaluable so thank you from the bottom of my heart.

Thanks also to my wonderful book blogger and author friends for all their love and support and friendship. Special thanks to Kim Nash, Linda Hill, Debbie Johnston, Anne Williams, Vicki Bowles, Dawn Crooks, Claire Knight, Lynne Shelby, Lara Marsh, Julie Boon, Kirsty Clifton and Karen Cocking for all their hard work on my cover reveals and blog tours.

Thank you to my lovely London Chapter friends the Muses, for all your amazing support and for keeping me sane with rose wine.

Thank you so much to the hard-working team at Orion Dash, I couldn't have asked for more beautiful covers for my books and Victoria, Olivia and Rhea have all been wonderful to work with.

A huge thank you to my beautiful family Johnna, Jake, Damon and Lydia (my fab little editor at the other end of the dining table.) I love you all and Toby the dog who always wants cuddles when I'm trying to write. I would also like to thank each and every one of you for reading my books and reviewing them. I hope you enjoy *The Cosy Little Cupcake Van* but just a word of warning, you may want to get some baking ingredients in first.

Lightning Source UK Ltd.
Milton Keynes UK
UKHW041918160821
388971UK00002B/498

9 781398 708112